Giants Want Ragnarok

Books by Jack Hillman

There Are Giants in This Valley
Giants Want the Lost River
Giants Want Ragnarok

Giants Want Ragnarok

Jack Hillman

SPEAKING VOLUMES, LLC
NAPLES, FLORIDA
2021

Giants Want Ragnarok

Cover design by Hannah Linder

ISBN 978-1-64540-597-9

For Bonnie
Always

Acknowledgments

No one writes in a vacuum. There have been many people whose efforts have aided in the making of this missive. To anyone I miss, I apologize profusely.

Multiple thanks to my Pennwriters critique partners for keeping me on track and motivated (negative reinforcement does work!): Aaron Peters, Scott Toonder and Ed Weir. And thanks to sister Judi Leinhauser for editing assistance, since I'm a writer, not a speller.

Incalculable thanks to my agent, Cherry Weiner. And to her spouse, Jack, for permitting me to borrow her for a while.

And to Bonnie, my long-enduring spouse, who had put up with more than even I can write about in this space.

Thanks to Raven, Thorin Oakenshield, Grey Mouser and Merlin for occasional inspiration.

Thanks to grandson Pierce Zechman for helping "Grumpa" through the technical quirks.

Thanks, folks.

Chapter One

Eric Johnson liked flying.

He looked down at the ground far below and saw the shadow passing across the ground as he and Fornir moved high over the fields of the Lehigh Valley. The wind whipped his hair back from his face and he felt the change in temperature as Fornir breathed out with each flap of his mighty wings.

"Too heavy for you?" Eric called out to his friend.

"The air of your world is too thin for proper flying, young warrior," the dragon replied. "Little wonder your people have seldom seen a wyrm in flight. My ancestors must have all crashed to the ground as soon as they leaped into the air."

Eric laughed. "Well, you're giving people nightmares already with all the sightings since you came to Midgard," he said, using the name for Earth that Fornir would recognize. "It's a good thing Vili and the other Norns made that stealth shield for you."

Fornir snorted and Eric got a whiff of methane from the dragon's flame reservoir.

"If your people knew how to fly properly, they would not be afraid of a simple creature like myself. Then we could fly together and not hide like thieves in the night."

Eric laughed again. "Let's take a pass toward Dwarvenheim," he suggested. "Odin was supposed to come watch the game today and I wanted to talk to him about the connection to Mimir at the village. Tommy was saying something about a full sensor array to protect the dwarves."

Fornir dipped his wings in response and they dropped away from the Blue Ridge they had been following toward New Jersey and swung back over the Lehigh Valley. From up here, Eric could see the network of roads that wove across the cities, leading through the farmland on the western side of the valley. Things seemed peaceful, but Eric was one of the few people who knew what was going on beneath the surface.

In the three years he had lived here since moving from Philadelphia, Eric had met Norse Gods, rock dwarves, talking computers, blonde Valkyr on white stallions and, of course, his current partner in flight, Fornir, a dragon created by the Frost Giants as one way to frighten humans into working for them. Then there were the Frost Giants, the Vanir of legend, who were trying to take over the world, or possibly destroy it. On any given day, Eric would not have been willing to bet on either outcome from the Giants. Odin, the leader of the Aesir, probably would not have made a bet either way himself.

Eric had learned a lot these past three years, not only about himself, but about the world around him. Odin, Thor, Loki and the Valkyr weren't just myths or fairy tales read in books. They were real people, aliens from another dimension who had been forced here by a weapon of the Vanir during a great war that was probably still going on back in their home dimension. But just as the good guys, as Eric thought of his new friends, were real, so were the bad guys. Frost Giants really existed. And even if they weren't fifteen feet tall, they were taller than humans, and they really did want to control everything they touched. The only thing that had stopped the Giants from taking over the earth was the Aesir. And now Eric was part of that fight, the fight to save his world.

As they reached the far west end of the Lehigh Valley, Dwarvenheim appeared below. What had once been a compound for training Giants long left asleep in their transport ship was now the home of several hundred rock dwarves Eric had rescued from Jotunheim.

Eric was expected at the game, and he wouldn't let his team down, but he smiled as he looked down on Dwarvenheim for just another second. The rock dwarves were good people. *Just keep them away from chocolate chip cookies if you want any for yourself.*

* * *

A shout from the middle of the field drew everyone's attention. From the sidelines, the judge held the ball aloft, then threw it up into the air over centerfield. A rough circle at midfield comprised of all four Valkyr and six Aesir, including Thor and Loki, waited for the powerful throw of the judge to come back to Earth.

Thor looked up at the ball, still rising in the light gravity of Earth, then over at the judge, who shrugged and called out, "Wait for it!"

Finally, after almost a full minute, the ball fell back and the players shifted to watch where it would land. As the ball came close, Loki and another Aesir both leaped into the air to intercept the ball. Their jump in the light gravity gave them time for some swift interplay with their respective paddles—an aerial fencing match. Then the ball popped out to one side and Svala had it firmly in hand. She stood her mount, Sword Breaker, on his hind legs and spun toward the far goal. At the same time Stephanie spun Mist Walker and matched the Valkyr from the other side of the field. The two Valkyr mounts outraced the rest of the players and drove down the field like twin arrows. Again Svala stopped at the line and rose in her stirrups to hammer the ball toward Stephanie. Stephanie timed her own stop perfectly and rose in her stirrups as the ball raced toward her. With a double arm swing she slammed the ball toward the goal like a bullet, right at the buckler Eric held across his chest. The ball drove the boy off his feet and onto the ground, then bounced through the goal posts for a score for Stephanie's team.

"Heylah!" Svala cried. "Good hit, young warrior." She trotted across the field, stuck her paddle under her left leg, and gripped forearms with Stephanie as she pounded the young girl on the back with her other hand. "We will make a Valkyr of you in truth, and in not too long a time at this rate."

Her team gathered around Stephanie, except for the goal tenders who jumped and hollered from their end of the field. The three Aesir members of the team, recruited from those on Asgard who wanted to spend time on Earth, all slapped the girl's leg or shoulder in appreciation. The judge's whistle called them back to the center of the field for the next play and Stephanie took a moment to look at Eric, now back on his feet. He was smiling at her in appreciation of her accomplishment.

"Good shot," he called. "But the game's not over yet!"

"Soon," Stephanie called back. With a wave of her paddle she trotted to centerfield to await the next toss.

* * *

At the side of the field, other Aesir and dwarves watched the game to cheer on their friends from both teams. With some creative financing arranged between Odin and Uncle Al, the property was now owned by many of the dwarves who had been rescued from Jotunheim. The buildings used as dormitories by the Giants were now homes for the dwarves as they built their own separate structures on the huge farm, and the fields surrounding the compound were tended by dwarves and modern machines. The huge field once used as a parade ground was now a playing field for a variety of sports, including this game imported from Asgard.

"The children are growing into formidable warriors," Odin said to Uncle Al. The dark Aesir sat in a folding chair along the sidelines with many of the other Aesir and dwarves. He might not be jumping and shouting with the rest of the spectators, but the smile on Odin's face showed he was just as pleased at Stephanie's goal as the others.

"I just hope they don't have to be real warriors any time soon," Uncle Al answered. He looked across the field at his nephew, Eric, and smiled as the young man—no longer really a boy after all he had been through—straightened his helmet and prepared for the next toss of the ball. "Fighting Giants isn't really something children should have to do as often as these three have done. They need time to be children and grow up properly."

"They are indeed proper," Odin said. "But I understand your concern. It is our hope that the few Giants remaining will hide and regroup for a time. That should permit the children to reach an age more appropriate for the final battle."

Uncle Al looked over at Odin. "Final battle? You think the Giants are going to push for some conclusion in all this, some sort of last ditch effort?"

Odin nodded. "Those Vanir we have captured have stated their leaders have prepared for one last push to take over at least a part of Midgard. Once they control enough of this world, they will take what they need to repair their ship and either try to return home without the proper coordinates, or else find a way to force the Aesir to give them that information in Mimir's memory banks. In either case, the battle will be the last between the Aesir and the Vanir for this world. Either the Aesir triumph and halt the Vanir's plans, or the Vanir will destroy everything on this planet in their lust for power."

"There's a happy thought," Uncle Al said sarcastically. "So they want to bring Ragnarok to life, the final battle from all those old legends." He shook his head. "Twilight of the Gods. I never thought I'd have a front row seat."

Odin smiled. "Do not worry so much. That is my job as commander of the Aesir forces. And we have our secret weapon after all, one well suited to foil Vanir plans as it has in the past. Seven times if my accounting is correct."

"Oh?" Uncle Al looked at Odin with raised eyebrows. "And what weapon is that?"

Odin pointed out at the field and the goal where a boy with red hair blocked an incoming ball and slammed it back up the field. "There. Eric John's Son, the newest Aesir warrior."

* * *

Eric stripped off the Valkyr chain mail and dropped it into his bag on top of the buckler and wooden paddle. He picked up his towel and rubbed his head to get the sweat out of his hair and off his face and neck. He was almost knocked over when a large hand slapped him on the back.

"Eric good ball player. Soon will be fit to play goal guard on true Aesir team." The rock dwarf standing behind Eric smiled wide enough to look like the top of his head could come off if he tipped back. "Eric still need to grow a bit to stop balls hit by true warriors."

"Cut me a break, Sudri," Eric answered. He hung the towel around his shoulders and tossed the helmet into the bag on top of the other gear. "Steph just caught me off balance. I could have stopped the ball if I'd been ready for it."

Sudri waved a finger the size of a cucumber in front of Eric's face. "Aesir warrior must always be ready, must always know what happening around him. Otherwise Vanir have too easy time with their plans." He tapped Eric on the nose with his finger. "Eric need more training. Maybe Uncle Al should ask dwarves to be in charge of feeding Eric so he grow bigger, stronger."

"No thanks, Sudri," Eric said. "If I eat the way you guys do all the time I'd weigh three hundred pounds in a month and not be able to move at all."

"Not worry." Sudri smiled. "We work it off you just as fast. Build muscle, grow bigger soon."

"Sounds like a good idea, Eric," Uncle Al said as he came up behind the pair. "Maybe I need to bring you down here to the dwarf village after school for training rather than just training you and Tommy in the back yard. Another style of training might make you pay more attention."

"I'll pay attention, really I will, Uncle Al. Just don't make me come down here and dig tunnels and lift rocks all night." Eric wiped some sweat off his forehead. "Besides, you still have three katas to teach Tommy and me this week."

"Teach Tommy what?"

The point goalie from the other team walked up and slapped Eric on the shoulder. "We got you that time, Eric. Maybe I need to teach you some stuff about playing goalie." Tommy smiled almost as wide as Sudri.

Tommy was no longer the small, skinny kid Eric met a bit over a year ago, but the young boy was still smaller than Eric. In addition, his large glasses gave him an owlish expression in keeping with his preference for reading books and studying Aesir technology. Odin had been arranging for Mimir to teach Tommy the basics of Aesir science, on top of the training all three children received in swordplay from Thor and riding lessons from the Valkyr. Tommy might not be the biggest of the three children adopted as part of the Aesir team, but he wasn't the weakest link either. All three children were well on their way to becoming formidable warriors, according to the reports Thor and the Valkyr had been passing to Odin.

"Yeah? And who was it tried to stop a ball with his head?" Eric shot back at his friend.

"Bring Tommy to dwarf village as well. We make you both true Aesir warriors," Sudri suggested.

"Not me, guys," Tommy said with one hand raised to hold off any more suggestions. "Between learning karate with Mr. Johnson and all the training I'm doing with Mimir, and trying to keep up with my home-work, I don't have enough hours in the day as it is."

"Maybe you need to ask Mimir for some of the variable time stuff between here and Jotunheim," Eric suggested.

Tommy shook his head. "With my luck I'd either get turned into a baby or wind up ninety years old and hard of hearing."

"You're already hard of hearing, Tommy Kuhns," Stephanie said as she walked up to the group. "I've been calling you for the past five minutes. The team wants to go out together and have some pizza and ice cream and you're invited." She turned to Eric and poked him in the chest with a finger and smiled at him. "You, however, are decidedly not in-vited. You lost the game." She spun on her heel, grabbing Tommy by the arm as she started back toward her team. She waved a hand casually over one shoulder. "Later, all," she said.

Eric watched his two friends walk away and smiled.

"Tommy and Stephanie good friends, yes?" Sudri asked with a smile of his own.

"I have a feeling Tommy doesn't really know how good a friend Stephanie really is. And I think she likes it that way." Eric shook his head. "Girls!"

"Some things the same, no matter how different," Sudri stated. "Dwarf women the same with dwarf men. Let men chase until woman catches the one she want. Then he spend rest of life not sure how he got where he is, but liking it."

"Yep," Eric agreed. He dropped the towel back into his bag and zipped it up. "So, Sudri, you up for some cookies? I think Aunt Cindy has a batch fresh out of the oven at home right now."

"Cookies? You bet want cookies!" Sudri agreed. "Get rest of team and meet at your house soon." He trotted off to collect the others on their team.

Uncle Al looked at the retreating dwarf, then down at Eric. "I just hope your aunt made a double batch this time."

"Me, too. I want more than one cookie this time," Eric agreed. "Let's get going or Sudri, Thor and Loki will eat them all between them."

Chapter Two

Eric's house was closer to the end of Bifrost than Enigma Caverns, so it naturally became the meeting place for folks coming to visit Midgard from Asgard. The fact that Aunt Cindy usually had chocolate chip cookies on hand also helped in that selection of meeting places. The tree house in the back yard was full this afternoon, two days after the games. Sudri and Dwalin joined Eric, Tommy and Stephanie to help with a project planned for the cave. Freawin and Svala had also joined the group. Stephanie needed additional training with Mist Walker and the plan was for her to go riding with the two Valkyr once they were done with the planning session.

That many people in a tree house usually meant the tree started to tilt. But Sudri and the dwarves who helped Eric build this particular room had done a good job. The unusually brisk wind was kept outside, while energy crystals from Asgard kept the inside warm.

"Not understand this," Sudri said to Stephanie. "Are going to put fake flying mice in cave to make people think real flying mice in cave, but flying mice not really scare people because people know they are not real?"

"Yep, that's right," Stephanie answered.

Sudri looked over at his cousin. "You understand this?"

Dwalin smiled and shook his head. "Not make sense to me either. Also not make sense to use fake spiders and little pieces of cloth that pretend to be ancestors' spirits."

"Ghosts, Dwalin. They're called ghosts." Stephanie looked at the two rock dwarves. "So can you do this?"

Dwalin shrugged. "No problemo, dudette," he said in a copy of Sudri's sayings. "Can put stuff wherever you want it to be. Just don't understand why you need to put it there. If you want to scare people, dwarves can make other stuff that really will scare them. Do job properly if going to do job at all."

"Sorry, Dwalin. We can't really scare them," Stephanie said. "If somebody slipped and got hurt in the cave, they could file a lawsuit and take everything my father has, including the cave."

"This lawsuit stuff like what Giants tried to do with the bad chemicals in water last year?" Sudri asked.

"Sort of," Eric answered. "In this country you can file lawsuits against people for almost anything. And the courts are so weird a lot of times people like Mr. Fuller have to pay for other people doing dumb things, even if it wasn't Mr. Fuller's fault. So Stephanie just wants people to think they're scared, not really scare them."

Sudri looked over at Freawin as she sat smiling in the corner.

"You more like these people than dwarves. You understand this stuff?"

Freawin shook her head and smiled wider. "No, my friend, I do not. But if Stephanie Mist Walker's Rider states this is what we must do, I would not argue with her. This is her home and she knows the customs of this world better than we."

"Hmmph," Sudri snorted. "Okay, we do it. Don't understand it, but we do it."

"Thanks, guys," Stephanie beamed. "We really appreciate it. With your help, we'll be able to put up decorations that are just so cool."

"Need to be not scary and not warm," Sudri said to his cousin. "Make sure not to use crystals so not heat fake flying mice before putting on ceiling of cave."

Eric laughed. "No, Sudri. Stephanie means the decorations will be very much appreciated by everyone. To say something is 'cool' just means that it's done well and well done."

Dwalin nodded. "Had this discussion with Stephanie last week. Cool is good. Hot is good. Way cool is both good and interesting. Way hot is very good but probably not appreciated by Stephanie's parents so must not make way hot. Okay for Freawin and Svala to be way hot, but not Stephanie."

Sudri looked from Dwalin to Stephanie, to Eric and Tommy, who were trying to hide smiles. Then he shook his head. "Much to learn on Midgard. But think it best for dwarves to stick to digging in cave and stay away from trying to be hot or cool." He slapped his chest with a resounding crack. "Dwarves not feel hot or cool, so let Stephanie figure out what works for her."

Stephanie laughed. "Sudri, with you and Dwalin helping, this will be the best Halloween Enigma Cavern has ever put on. We should make enough money to get back what we lost last year with the Giants talking the government into shutting us down and all the stuff with the dogs attacking the cave. People are still talking about that. I just wish there was more we could do to pay you back for all your help."

Dwalin smiled. "Stephanie and her people give dwarves a place to live on Midgard. All those who came with Suori very comfortable at old Giants' camp. Not have to live underground anymore. This is a good thing for dwarves. We do well underground, but sometimes, sun is much nicer."

Stephanie threw her arms around Dwalin, even if they only went halfway due to his size. "But you still want to come back to the cave, don't you?"

Dwalin patted Stephanie with his huge hand. "Always come back to first friend on Midgard. Stephanie very special person to Dwalin and his family."

Freawin cleared her throat as Stephanie held onto Dwalin. "Are you done with these plans yet, sword-sister? We still have much work to do and Mist Walker waits for you below."

"Yes, of course, sword-leader," Stephanie said. "I'll be ready in a minute." She gathered her papers and placed them in a folder, then in her backpack. "Ready, Freawin."

The tall Valkyr nodded and turned to the others in the tree house. "Ride swift, warriors," she said to the two boys and the two dwarves. "We will return Stephanie to her home when we are done with her lesson."

Freawin, Svala and Stephanie skinned down the rope from the front of the tree house and Tommy stepped to the door to watch as the three blondes, two Valkyr and one young girl from Earth, mounted their white stallions and rode off toward Enigma Caverns. Tommy turned back and saw Eric, Sudri and Dwalin. The three looked at Tommy and smiled.

"What?" Tommy asked the three. "I like looking at the horses."

"Work for me," Sudri said.

"If you say so," Eric said to Tommy. "Not like you'd like to go riding with her or anything."

"Of course I'd like to go riding with her. But she's training." Tommy snorted and sat down. "Let's finish the plans for the cave."

As Tommy looked down at the chart on the table, Eric, Sudri and Dwalin smiled at each other over the young boy's head.

* * *

Loki Odinsson stood on Market Street in Philadelphia and looked up at the buildings surrounding him. He was in the city today, far outside his normal home of Asgard, for a special purpose. Today he was hunting Giants.

The sensor in Loki's hand vibrated as it locked on to some Vanir energy field. Hiding the sensor in his hand, Loki swung around to try and get a direction, then followed the guiding buzz of the unit further down the street toward a tall building. As Loki approached the building, the vibration grew stronger, then dropped off as Loki kept walking. Loki stopped and looked up at the address on the building next to him, as if he was checking to see where he was, then turned and walked back the way he had come. He stopped at the point where the vibration from the sensor was strongest and stepped out of the flow of foot traffic. He looked up at the building and debated going inside.

"Interesting architecture, isn't it?" a voice said to his left.

Loki looked down at the old man on the bench next to him. Two coats and at least as many sweaters poked through various holes in the man's layers of clothing and the edges of newspaper folded up from inside his shoes, insulating his feet. He had his hands clasped around a steaming cup of coffee and an open book in his lap.

"Know anything about this place, when it was built or what it was used for before it became apartments?" Loki asked the man. The sensor in his hand stayed focused on the building, suggesting to Loki the man was exactly what he appeared to be.

The old man shook his head. "Nope. I just like looking at it. I get the feeling there's something more to that building that the bricks I can see here in front." He tilted his head to the side as he looked up at the gargoyles at the corners of the roof. "I kind of wonder if this is the first sign I'm slipping away."

"What do you mean?" Loki asked.

The old man pointed to the building. "Two weeks ago, that building wasn't there, and now it is. And do you think anyone noticed that one of their alleyways just up and disappeared? Nope. Just keep on walking by as if it's always been there." He took a sip of his coffee.

"Interesting," Loki said, more to himself than to the man as he looked up at the building again. He looked down at the old man. "So why don't you think anyone noticed the change, or why you know something has changed?"

The man shrugged. "Probably because I'm so drugged up my brain isn't listening to that song that keeps coming out of that place. It's telling everyone to ignore the changes, and just keep walking on by." He shrugged again. "I got nowhere to go until my next appointment at the shelter. So I just stay here and watch the edges of the building melt a bit." He tilted his head the other way and looked at the windows. "Kind of an interesting effect, don't you think?"

Loki took a twenty dollar bill out of his pocket and dropped in the man's lap. "I think I'll find out just how interesting it really is. Thanks for your help."

"No problem."

Loki crossed through the passing people to the side of the building. He leaned against the wall of the building and adjusted the sensor in his hand. Then he brought a second unit out of another pocket, fed in the information from the sensor, and pushed a button. The wall he leaned against softened and he walked through into the building and out of sight of the people on the street. Nobody paid any attention to his disappearance.

The alleyway Loki found himself in was one of many in the city that ran for a block or so then hit a dead end. In this case Loki saw the alley lead down a single block, then dead end into the back of another structure. Parked in the alley, one on the ground and the second on a ramp way overhead, were a small van and a sporty sedan. The Giants were using this alley as their own dedicated parking space. Given the high cost of parking, and the limited availability of spaces in the city, the Giants must want easy access and a fast getaway if they needed one.

Loki moved carefully down the alley, watching for movement and checking his sensor for any traps.

Loki looked up as a door opened.. At the end of the alley, in the building on the right, a young boy stepped out into the alley for a moment. When he saw Loki, he darted back inside the building, leaving the door closing slowly. Loki raced for the door and caught it before it closed completely. He stepped inside the building, one hand pulling a small rod from his belt. If Vanir were inside, Loki was ready to fight. Down the hallway, the boy stepped out of an alcove and raced away from the dark Aesir.

"Wait!" Loki called out. He followed the boy at a run.

The boy was faster than the Aesir in this enclosed space. Four turns later, Loki was little closer to the boy than when he started. The child darted through a door at the end of the hallway. Loki followed him through and stopped. At the far side of the room, a Frost Giant sat behind a large wooden desk.

"Bor," Loki said. "I should have known."

The young boy Loki had followed stood at Bor's left side, smiling at the Aesir. Loki looked down at the sensor in his hand and frowned. Then he raised the rod in his hand and pushed a button on the side. Nothing happened.

"This room is shielded, of course," the Giant said. "Which is also why your sensor did not detect our presence." He reached out and caressed the child's head. "You have done well, my son. Now go and prepare for your next class."

The boy wriggled in pleasure at the Giant's touch and darted to the side of the room, opening a disguised panel and slipping inside.

Loki growled and started across the room toward the Giant. But before the Aesir took more than a step, there were three soft puffs of air and three darts entered his body, one in each leg and a third in his chest.

Loki dropped to the floor and his legs twitched as the muscles lost the ability to function properly. The Giant behind the desk smiled down at Loki, a slim air pistol in his hand.

"These humans are so inventive sometimes," Bor said. "A simple weapon, filled with the proper mixture to subdue an Aesir, and your sensors could never detect it, even without the shielding. It took only a minimum of effort to make this a multiple shot weapon, to deal with someone like you."

"I'll kill you," Loki said through clenched teeth.

The Giant raised the gun and shot Loki in the chest again. The Aesir dropped limp to the floor, all signs of resistance gone.

"Not today," the Giant murmured.

The door to the hallway opened and a human helper of the Vanir entered. The man had changed out of the dirty closes he had worn on the bench outside and was wiping the last of the dirt from his face as he entered, leaving a much younger man.

"Good work, Keyes," Bor said approvingly. "The fool of an Aesir took the bait easily."

Keyes bowed to his master. "I live to serve."

"And you do it so well." He gestured toward the still body of Loki. "Take him to the van and then to the laboratory. We need to get through the new barriers Odin put in place and he will be our way in." He gave Loki a light kick. "You will work for us again, my friend. Oh, yes. And you will make good toys for us again, like your wolf, and your wyrm. I'm sure there is something more hiding in that skull of yours."

"And the children?" Keyes asked. "They are ready for the meeting, but we have only a small time window with the viral implants. Unless we plan carefully we will miss the best time to infect the Johnson boy and the Fuller girl."

"Yes, the children. It is time for the next step. With that John's Son child and the whelp of the cave owner out of the way, their parents and the Aesir they are working with will be too busy to stop us from taking control of Mimir. And with Mimir we will have our way home." He looked up at the man and smiled. "But I think I will be staying here after the rest of you return to the war at home."

"Why is that?" Keyes looked confused. "You have always said you preferred to return home?"

. "Your kind have a perfectly good world here, with many subjects to work with, and experiment on, if we desire. Why should I give it up before we are done playing with it?"

"We, Master?" Keyes asked.

Bor looked at the human. "You have served me well for many years. Surely there is some place on this planet you would want to call your own, some small reward I can give you? Consider it an incentive to make sure the children do their job properly." Bor laid a hand on Keyes' shoulder. "With you guiding the boy and the girl to their targets, the Aesir will never suspect what we are doing. No Vanir technology, no disguises, just three humans moving among their fellows. Something as a small as a virus will never be found until they scan very carefully." He smiled at Keyes. "You will take the first step in turning this planet into a new home for the Vanir!"

"I think I can imagine a place or two I'd like to have as retirement homes," Keyes said. "Hot and cold running servants at my beck and call sounds pretty good to me.".

"Oh, definitely cold, my friend," Bor replied. "Definitely cold."

Both beings laughed.

Chapter Three

Eric and Tommy followed Uncle Al into the gymnasium, moving with the flow of people coming to the karate tournament. Uncle Al walked up to the registration table and leaned down to list Eric and Tommy on a clipboard next to the section designated by the first letters of their last names.

"Well, there's a sight I hadn't thought to see again," a voice said from the other side of the table.

Uncle Al stood up and smiled. He held out a hand to a man slightly older than himself across the table. "Good to see you again, George," he said. "If you're running the show today we should be seeing a good turnout."

George looked down at Eric and Tommy. "I think I remember something about never teaching again?" George asked. "Something change your mind?"

Uncle Al nodded to his friend, and put a hand on Eric's shoulder. "This is my nephew, Eric Johnson, Raymond's boy that I talked about. He's living with us now."

"Ah," George said as a flash of pain crossed his face. He looked down at Eric. "I knew your father years ago, when we were kids in school together. I was very sorry to hear what happened to him."

"Thank you, sir," Eric answered.

"And this is his friend, Tommy Kuhns," Uncle Al added.

George nodded to Tommy in greeting. "You two boys have one of the best teachers in the Valley. I expect to see some good technique from both of you today."

"Yes, sir," Eric and Tommy answered in unison.

"I have to get back to the tournament," George said to Uncle Al. He looked at his friend and tilted his head. "Any chance we can get you to sit on the judging table?"

Uncle Al shook his head. "Not with two of my students in the tournament. It wouldn't be fair and I seem to recall a lot of the schools still have a problem with conflict of interest."

George sighed. "I see you do remember how things work." He bowed slightly in good-bye. "I'll see you after the tournament, I hope."

"Count on it," Uncle Al answered.

As George left the table, Uncle Al finished registering Eric and Tommy then led the two boys into the gym.

"Was he one of your teachers, Uncle Al?" Eric asked.

Uncle Al shook his head. "He was one of my students, one of my best students. I'm pleased to see he has continued with his studies."

"What did he mean about not teaching again, Mr. Johnson?" Tommy asked.

Uncle Al was silent for a moment, as if he had not heard the question. He looked out across the groups of students in their gis as if he was looking for someone in particular. Finally he spoke. "Something happened about eight years ago that made me decide to stop teaching. George was one of the people who tried to talk me out of it, but my mind was made up."

"But you're teaching us?" Eric said, as much a question as a statement.

Uncle Al smiled and looked down at his students. "Which just goes to prove you should never say never. Life has a way of changing things and pushing you to do things you don't want to do, or don't think you can do. I'm sure both of you understand how that can happen."

"Oh, yeah," Tommy said. "Big time changes, and a lot of things I never thought I'd be doing."

Eric laughed and punched his friend lightly on the shoulder. "What, you don't like being kidnapped Frost Giants and running from giant dogs? I'm shocked."

Tommy punched back. "This from the kid who falls into rivers and comes back riding a dragon."

"All right, you two," Uncle Al said as he laid a hand on a shoulder of each boy. "Head for the showers and get suited up. I'll meet you by Section H." He pointed to one of the bleacher sections in the middle of the floor. "Make sure you pick up all your stuff and don't leave anything in a locker. There are too many people here today for anyone to have a private locker."

"Yes, Sensei," the two answered as they trotted off to the boy's shower room.

* * *

Eric stood in the middle of the hard rubber mat, facing the table of judges. His white gi was tugged into proper position and he had spend fifteen minutes tying and re-tying the knot of his green obi to make sure the dangling lengths were the same. The judge in the middle of the table nodded to Eric and he took a breath, then let it out slowly. He bowed to the group of sensei at the table and bent his legs slightly with his hands in front of him, palms flat, left on top of right.

"Kata Naihanchi," Eric said in a loud, firm tone.

His head snapped to his right to look at the imaginary opponent in that direction. He stepped, left foot behind right ankle, then right foot out to shoulder width. His right hand flashed out, palm flat and facing forward as his left hand snapped to his left hip in a chambered fist. Eric moved back and forth across an invisible line on the floor, his knees stayed bent and his head stayed at the same level while he went through the punches, kicks, sweeps and grabs that made up the kata. He ended the kata, straightened his legs, feet together, and bowed again to the table of judges. He paused for a moment until the center judge nodded to him, then walked off the floor toward Uncle Al and Tommy.

Uncle Al stood at the edge of the mat, arms crossed over his chest, a frown on his face. Eric bowed to him when he reached the edge of the mat.

"You still need to keep your cross chest punches level," Uncle Al said.

Eric hung his head and looked down at the floor.

"But for a green belt you did very well," Uncle Al continued. "I am pleased with your performance."

Eric's head snapped up and he looked at the smile on his uncle's face.

"You still have much to learn," Uncle Al said, "but you are doing as well as any of my students, and better than most."

Eric bowed to his uncle. "*Domo arigato gozai imashta*," he said, thanking him for his praise.

Uncle Al returned the bow, then reached out and slapped him on the shoulder. "Go get a drink. You and Tommy are up for *kobudo kata* in a few minutes."

"Okay, Uncle Al," Eric answered. He ran over to Tommy and they both grinned.

"Think we'll get a prize?" Tommy asked. "Your uncle seems to think we did pretty good."

"Pretty well," Eric corrected. "And I don't really care if we get a prize." At Tommy's look of confusion he said, "I think I just like the idea that Uncle Al is teaching again and that these people think his students are well trained."

"But a trophy wouldn't hurt, right?" Tommy pushed.

Eric smiled. "No, a trophy wouldn't hurt," he agreed with a laugh. "I'm going for some water. Uncle Al said we're up for kobudo in a few minutes and you're first. Better get ready."

Tommy nodded and reached over to take his bo, a wooden staff slightly taller than himself, out of its carry bag.

Eric walked over to the water fountain at the side of the gym, watching the competitors on the floor as he went. At the fountain he took a short drink, since he didn't want to be too full or have some other embarrassing reaction in the middle of his kata. He turned back to the floor and almost bumped into a young girl standing behind him.

"Oh, sorry." He started to move around her, but she moved to match him, blocking his path.

"You're pretty good out there," she said to him. "You must have a good teacher."

He stopped and took another look at the girl. She was tall, slightly taller than Eric. Her long blonde hair was pulled back in a braid down the center of her back. And around the waist of her white gi was a green belt just like Eric's.

She has green eyes, Eric thought.

"Uh, yeah. Well, my uncle is my teacher. He's teaching me and my friend some of the stuff he's learned over the years." Eric stammered a bit, not sure where this was headed and very uncomfortable talking to a girl he didn't know.

She stepped in closer, almost nose to nose with Eric. "Do you think your uncle might be willing to teach me, too?" she asked softly, almost breathing the words into Eric's ear.

"Um, well, I can ask him. I don't know. Um, maybe." Eric was flustered as she reached up and ran a soft hand across his cheek and neck. He felt a wash of heat from her touch and his knees grew weak. He started to reach up and touch his cheek when she leaned in and gave him a quick kiss on that same cheek.

"You're cute," she said. Then she turned and started to walk away. She looked back over her shoulder at him and winked. "See you later, tiger."

"Um. Um." Eric tried to say something but she disappeared into the crowd and he lost sight of her. He turned and walked back over to Uncle Al and Tommy.

Tommy was practicing some of the moves of the bo kata he would do for his part of the weapons demonstration. Uncle Al was watching Eric and smiling.

"New member of your fan club?" he asked Eric.

"Um, I don't know. Um, maybe." He looked up at Uncle Al. "That was weird."

"How so?" Uncle Al asked.

"Um, a girl never told me I was cute before," Eric said. He laid a hand on his cheek and felt the heat of her touch still moving across his face.

"Indeed," Uncle Al answered. He turned back to watch Tommy, still smiling.

Eric sat down on the nearby bleacher.

* * *

Across the floor, the young girl walked up to a man and bowed.

"You did well," the man said to the girl. "Both the touch and the kiss should have transferred the chemical compound to him. Together, he will not be able to avoid the effects. But he will react to the added amount of the compound. We should leave now and contact him again later." The man looked over at Uncle Al and the two boys. "Besides, the added time for the compound to move through his system will make him even more anxious to see you the next time." He looked down at the girl and smiled. "Come."

The two walked quickly to the exit and out into the parking lot. A chill wind whipped across the area but neither of them noticed the cold. They got into a black SUV parked among the other vehicles.

"Let's go home," Keyes said.

"Can we get pizza?" the girl asked.

Keyes considered her question for a moment, then nodded. "Yes, you have earned pizza. A small one."

The girl clapped her hands and leaned back in her seat.

"Only a small one, though," he said. "You still have much to do to get what we need from the boy."

"Piece of cake," the girl said. "He's all mine now."

"Ours," Keyes reminded her in a chill tone. "Not yours."

"Oh, yes, ours," she answered as she shrank back in the seat in fear. "I'll get him for us. I promise."

"I know you will," he said, caressing her head with one hand and driving with the other. "I know you will."

* * *

The ride home that evening for Eric, Tommy and Uncle Al was quiet. Uncle Al looked up in the rear view mirror at Eric as he sprawled in the back seat.

"You feeling any better?" he asked his nephew.

"Some," Eric answered. "My stomach still feels like it wants to bring everything I've eaten for three days back for review."

"Are you sure you didn't have anything for lunch other than what we brought with us?" Uncle Al asked again.

Eric shook his head and almost lost what was in his stomach again. "All I had that we didn't bring with us was some water from the fountain. I wanted something that wasn't sweet before I did the kobudo kata."

"Well, that didn't work," Tommy said. "Barfing on the floor before you go up to do your kata is not designed to make the judges lenient."

"Tommy," Uncle Al said in a warning tone.

"I'm just saying if Eric was that upset to do his kata in front of judges, why didn't he barf on the open hand stuff too?" Tommy looked at his friend. "You never did get to go up and do the sai kata you practiced."

"Well, I'm just glad one of us got something out of today," Eric answered.

On the seat next to Tommy was a second place trophy. He had done well in the open hand kata, and his bo kata was one of the best Eric had ever seen. But he had only come in second in the light sparring permitted at the tournament today. Still, second place for your first tournament was a good achievement for a kid who had been pretty much afraid of everything less than a year ago, Eric thought.

"If your stomach hasn't settled down by the time we drop Tommy off at home, I'm taking you to the emergency center for some testing," Uncle Al stated. "The fact that you are as sick as you are, with neither Tommy nor I feeling anything out of the ordinary, is more than just strange. I have to wonder if you didn't get into something toxic."

"What!" Eric exclaimed. "Where? I've been with you and Tommy all day. I haven't touched anything either of you haven't touched."

"Except the girl," Tommy joked. "Maybe she poisoned you with her touch."

"Yeah, right. Like that's going to happen." Eric slumped down in his seat. "You're just jealous she came up to me and not you."

"Me, jealous? You've got to be kidding." Tommy snorted. "Girls are nothing but trouble."

"I'll be sure to tell Stephanie you said that," Eric said from some-where inside the folds of his jacket. "I probably just have some sort of twenty-four-hour virus I picked up at school. I'll get over it by tonight."

"Stretch it to forty-eight hours and you might get off school on Mon-day," Tommy suggested.

"If he's that sick, he'll be under a doctor's care by then," Uncle Al said.

"Besides, you wouldn't want to miss Mr. Jarvis' quiz on Monday, would you?" Tommy asked with a smile.

Eric groaned. "Don't remind me."

"Yeah, well don't forget we're supposed to go down and help Steph-anie set up the cave for Halloween after school on Wednesday. I need you to help carry all that stuff around as she puts it in those nooks and crannies."

Eric groaned again. "Yeah, okay. I won't forget."

"And next weekend we'll go through those kata you did today and fix all the problems," Uncle Al said. "I want both of you up on the win-ner's stand next time."

"Yes, Sensei," the boys chorused, though somewhat muffled from the back seat.

The rest of the ride to Tommy's house was quiet. Eric and Uncle Al got out of the van long enough to stand with Tommy for some pictures when his parents saw the trophy. Mr. Kuhns was very pleased with his son's achievement and took Uncle Al aside for a moment when he thought the boys weren't listening. Eric heard him tell Uncle Al he had been considering sending Tommy to military school to "toughen him up," as he put it, before he met Eric and started this karate training. Now Mr. Kuhns wanted to know if Uncle Al would continue his training until he graduated from high school. Uncle Al said as long as the boys were friends, continuing to train them together was much to their joint benefit and Eric was gaining just as much as Tommy.

Back in the car on the way home, Uncle Al looked over at Eric.

"How are you feeling?" he asked.

"Okay, mostly," Eric answered. "I think I need some tea or something to settle my stomach, and then get some sleep."

Uncle Al nodded. "Okay, we'll keep an eye on you tonight. If you're okay in the morning, you just take it easy tomorrow."

"Okay, Uncle Al. Whatever you say." Eric slumped in the seat and was almost asleep by the time they got home.

And by the time the boy was inside and up in bed, all Eric could think about was blonde hair and green eyes.

Chapter Four

Enigma Caverns was busy the month before Halloween. Even without bats in the cave, people wanted to come into someplace dark and spooky . . . and safe. The mid-morning tour on Saturday was a school group from just north of Philadelphia and Stephanie Fuller growled to herself as she realized she was in charge of herding twenty kids through the caves. She had done enough tours to know what kinds of problems her own age group could cause, and she had a feeling this group of thirteen-year-olds was going to be one of the worst.

"Stephanie practicing to scare customers?" Dwalin asked.

She turned to look at the rock dwarf and had to smile herself when she saw the huge grin on his face. "Sorry, Dwalin. I just don't think today's tour is going to be fun, even if they are all my own age. *Especially* if they are all my own age."

"No problem," the rock dwarf said. "Let them feel how cold the water is and threaten to throw them in river and they be good students." He tapped the wall of the cave with a rock hard finger. "Or could threaten to put them in new room made special for them and close the door."

Stephanie laughed. "A good idea. But I have a feeling this crowd would prefer something like that to going home. They're from a pretty rough neighborhood, I hear."

Dwalin shrugged and, just like his cousin Sudri, he resembled a pile of gravel shifting with the movement. "I stay with the group. Any trouble, we give flying lessons."

"Oh, good," Stephanie said and clapped her hands. "Do you think you could light up the main chamber when we get there? With your crystals, I mean?"

"Sure. Have full charge in crystals. Use them to power link to Mimir and sensors for Giant hunting." He waved a huge hand in the air. "Piece of cake."

"Good. At least we can try to impress them a bit," Stephanie said. "Maybe that will keep them quiet."

Dwalin nodded. "Can impress them real good. You just watch."

Stephanie shook a finger at her flinty friend. "Don't you go showing off. We wouldn't want anyone to think this is something other than just special effects."

"Good special effects, Stephanie," Dwalin answered with a smile. "Real good special effects."

The crash of the door and a massive increase in the volume level signaled the arrival of the school tour.

"Well, time to get to work," Stephanie said. "Make sure the grating over the river is tight or I might be tempted to throw a few in before I'm done."

"No problem," Dwalin answered. "I hold it open for you."

Stephanie laughed and made her way to the main shop, where students were racing through the aisles of merchandise: an array of cave and rock related gifts and jewelry for all occasions. The students had never seen some of the things Enigma Caverns collected to sell to the public, mostly because these students seldom had a chance to get out of their own neighborhoods. When the school contacted Bob Fuller to arrange for the tours, he was pleased to offer a special rate for the school. Anything that got kids out of the harsh neighborhoods and into the country was a good thing, in Bob's way of thinking. Stephanie was a bit less enthusiastic than her father, but that was due to being one of the people that actually led the students through the tours. Her father hadn't done any regular tours for years, since he was more concerned with running the overall business and working with the jewelry shop. But special people still got the tour by the cave owner along with all the schmoozing they required to bring tour groups to the cave and pick up business. Running a cave was a difficult operation and more business was good business, Stephanie knew.

Stephanie had set herself up with the first tour of the group, before the students had a chance to get bored with the shop and start looking for things to do that would get them in trouble. Once her father had completed the initial arrangements with the teachers, and each of the students had received his or her pass for the tour, she clicked on the loudspeaker in the shop.

"All students holding a blue tour pass please move to the doorway at the south side of the shop. Your tour will begin in ten minutes."

Stephanie turned off the speakers and moved through the back door to the opening of the tunnel into the cave. Dwalin was waiting for her with a big smile on his face.

"And what do you have planned for the tour?" she asked her friend.

Dwalin's smile got even bigger. "Good special effects," was all he said as he laid a finger alongside his nose.

Stephanie shook her head and smiled in return. She moved to the door and opened it, then skipped back fast as the crowd of students moved into the tunnel opening. They stopped at the chain across the tunnel as she ducked underneath. One of the boys started to follow her under but Dwalin stood next to the chain, effectively blocking the way. The boy backed up and looked at the dwarf with an expression that suggested he wanted to start something, but then moved back into the group when one of the teachers tapped him on the shoulder and suggested he let the girls take the front row.

"Okay, everybody please hold up your tour ticket," Stephanie called out. Hands went up in the air and she saw a wave of blue tickets, with one orange ticket in the back. "Orange tour leaves next after this one.

Please go back in the store and wait for the call," she told the student with the wrong ticket. "We have these planned for just enough people so everybody can get through and hear what is being said. Thank you." Stephanie watched the student leave, followed by rude comments from his fellow students.

Stephanie smiled and faced the group. "Welcome to Enigma Caverns. The caverns were first discovered in the late eighteen hundreds by a group of stone cutters who were operating a quarry on this site. When they cut through the section of wall in what is now part of the parking lot, they opened the cave to the outside for the first time. Since then, we have explored about ten chambers, but only six are open to the public, since the others are very difficult to get into. Also, one of the chambers is only open if we have a really dry year, since there is a river that runs through the cave and fills the tunnel that leads to that chamber." She looked around at the students and was amazed that she still had their attention. "We call the river the Lost River, because it comes up from someplace deep underground and goes back underground to someplace we don't know."

Stephanie said that last part with a grin. Since Eric fell into the river last spring, they knew exactly where the river went: to Jotunheim, the home of the Frost Giants. But that wasn't something she could tell these students.

Stephanie moved over and laid a hand on Dwalin's shoulder. "This is my friend Dwalin. He works here in the cave and is very good at finding lost things, so none of you need to worry about getting back from the tour.

"Hey, nothing like hiring the handicapped," said the boy who had tried to duck under the chain.

Stephanie turned and was ready to say something to the boy when the student next to him jabbed him in the ribs with an elbow.

"He's probably forgotten more than you'll ever know about caves and he looks like he could crush rocks with those fingers, so you might want to be careful about making him mad at you." The student who spoke, a boy with blonde hair, turned and smiled at Stephanie.

She smiled in return, then glared at the smart-mouthed student.

"Students want to learn about caves, I teach," Dwalin stated as he looked at the smart-mouthed boy. "Students want to make trouble, we have good place for you to stay while other students learn. Maybe if you be good we let you out again, in one or two rock years."

"How long is a rock year?" one of the other students asked.

Stephanie smiled. "About a century," she said. "And Dwalin has the only key to that door."

"So be nice to him," the student who had defended Dwalin said to his companion. "We'd hate to lose you in the rocks."

The other students laughed, which Stephanie took to mean the student who had insulted Dwalin was not very well liked by his classmates.

"Okay, if you will all follow Dwalin, we will go to the entrance chamber of the cave." Stephanie stepped aside and let the students follow Dwalin into the cave. As the blond-haired student who had defended Dwalin walked past her, he turned and smiled at her. He looked like he wanted to stop for a moment and say something but the rest of the students behind him pushed him forward. He glanced back over his shoulder at Stephanie and shrugged.

With Dwalin at one end of the group and Stephanie at the other, the tour went as smooth as any tour can go. A few students slipped on the wet rocks, as the moisture dripping from the ground above left a layer of chemicals and algae over almost every surface. Many of the students leaned against a rock only to have a wet stain mark their jacket or sweatshirt. Stephanie stopped the group at each of the chambers and delivered the speech prepared by her father. The students asked the same questions visitors had been asking for decades: Where does the water come from? Where does the water go if it doesn't flow into the river? Is the river really lost?

Dwalin and Stephanie smiled as she delivered the part of the lecture about the river, explaining all the tests and trials the Fuller family had made over the years to try and find the outflow of the river after it dropped back underground at the end of the River Chamber. Until about a year ago, Stephanie's father had been certain the river went back underground and dispersed through the rocks into the series of aquifers under this part of the valley in such a way that the dye used to try and track the flow never reached any place in sufficient concentration to be seen. And the radio tracers were thought to have been locked deep in the rocks, too deep for their signals to reach any receiver. But since Eric had made his journey to Jotunheim, the Fullers now knew the real secret of the river: it traveled to another dimension, one reached only with great difficulty or an amazing amount of luck, as Eric had proved.

When they reached the Crystal Chamber, Stephanie warned the students to guard their eyes and turned off the lights. At a signal to Dwalin, the rock dwarf set off a series of flashes in the crystals that grew in intensity until suddenly the entire chamber was full of what looked like exploding flashbulbs in an amazing array of colors. The students "Oohed!" and "Ahhed!" for a moment then exploded in applause for the dwarf's efforts. Stephanie explained about the piezoelectric properties of the crystals, how the charge built up inside under the pressure of the rock and ground above, but she knew the energy came from the crystal's contact with Asgard, Dwalin's true home.

The tour ended back at the cave entrance and Stephanie collected the tickets from each student. The blond-haired boy was at the end of the line going through. He handed his ticket to Stephanie, then took her hand in both of his.

"I really liked the tour," he said as he looked into her eyes. "You really know your way around down here." He held onto her hand and caressed the back of it with his fingers.

Stephanie blushed and looked down for a moment, the looked back up into his green eyes. "I've lived here all my life. That makes it easy to know everything about the cave. I've played in places down here that the tours don't go to."

"I'd like to see some of those places," the boy said. He leaned down and put his lips next to Stephanie's ear. "Maybe you can show them to me some time," he whispered. Then he brushed her cheek with his lips and stood up. He let go of her hand with a last squeeze, then turned and joined the rest of the students leaving the cave. As he walked thought the door into the gift shop, he turned and smiled at her.

Stephanie stood as if in a trance, one hand touching her cheek where he had kissed her. Dwalin walked up to her and smiled as he saw the look on her face.

"Stephanie have new friend?" the dwarf asked.

"Huh? What did you say?" she said as her attention snapped back to reality. "What? No, I don't have a new friend. I just met him."

"Maybe wants to be new friend?" Dwalin suggested as his smile grew wider.

Stephanie looked down at her rock friend and slammed her fists on her hips. "I don't have time for this boy-girl stuff. He was just a nice kid. And he defended you too, so don't forget that," she said as she waved a finger at Dwalin's nose.

Dwalin continued to smile as he turned away and moved back down the tunnel to set up the Crystal Chamber for the next tour.

"Yep. Is new friend," Stephanie heard echo back through the rock.

"Is not!" she shouted to Dwalin.

The only response she got was the deep rumble of Dwalin's laughter.

Stephanie sighed and shook her head as she moved into the shop. She stepped out of the way of the tour guide for the orange tour and laid the pile of blue tickets on the desk in the small office next to the shop. Then she went looking through the shop for the blond-haired boy. She decided she wanted to talk to him again. In fact, she had a feeling she needed to talk to him again, which was strange because Stephanie couldn't think if a single reason why she really needed to see him. She just knew she had to. But she searched through the entire shop, even walking out into the parking lot to see if he had gone back to the bus that brought him to the cave. But the buses were empty, and the students walking around the picnic grove all said they had not seen the blonde-haired boy when she asked them. In fact, none of the other students seemed to know his name or who he was. They all just said he must have been in another class, even though Stephanie asked students from all the classes who came to the cave today if they knew him.

As Stephanie turned to go back into the shop, a hand on her shoulder stopped her.

"What do you search for that you ignore our call for so long, little sister?" the tall woman said as she took her hand from Stephanie's shoulder. "We have been trying to gain your attention for some few minutes, now."

Stephanie looked up at Freawin and Svala, two Valkyr from Asgard who were her good friends and trainers in the ways of the Valkyr scouts. In fact, Svala had been one of the Valkyr who helped rescue her from the Giants when she had first met Eric and Tommy, and the Valkyr had been wounded in the fight. That was when Stephanie had been "adopted" by the Valkyr and began her training. She even had her own mount—Mist Walker—who she rode when she visited Asgard or when the Valkyr came to Midgard—to Earth—to train her. For a moment Stephanie looked at the two scouts as if she didn't recognize them. Then she shook her head.

"I'm sorry. I really didn't hear you," Stephanie apologized. "I was just looking for someone . . ." She turned away from the Valkyr and started to walk away again, as if she was in a trance.

Freawin reached down and took a shoulder in each hand, looking deep into Stephanie's eyes. "Are you well, little sister? You see determined to find this person, whoever it might be. Do you require our aid?"

Stephanie stood for a moment, looking up at Freawin without really seeing her. Then she ripped herself out of the Valkyr's grasp, ran to the bushes alongside the building and leaned over the railing at the edge of the parking lot. By the time the two scouts reached the child, Stephanie had brought up her lunch, her breakfast and was working on the prior night's dinner. She shuddered with spasms as the two Valkyr held her carefully until she quit. Then, with a glance to each other over the top of Stephanie's head, the scouts led the girl up the driveway to her home, to place her in her mother's care.

* * *

None of the three noticed the black van at the far side of the picnic grove. The two people inside—a tall man and the blond-haired boy who had spoken to Stephanie watched the three move toward the house, then drove off down the road.

"Now we have both of them," Keyes said to the young boy as they drove away. "Soon we will have what they have, and can finally defeat the Aesir scum and make our way home."

"And I get the girl?" the boy asked.

The man smiled. "If you wish. When we are done with her."

"Good," the boy said with a cold smile. His green eyes were chips of ice as his thoughts turned to his own plans for the future.

Chapter Five

Tommy got off the school bus at Leather Corner Post Road and waved to the other students as the bus drove off in a cloud of dust. The cool October weather was just enough to keep him from sweating as he walked up the road and turned off at the Johnson house. He shifted the book bag on his shoulders and rang the bell to Eric's house. A minute later the door opened.

"Hello, Tommy," Aunt Cindy said. "How was school today?"

"All right, I guess, Mrs. Johnson. It was school, you know. I've got some stuff for Eric, from our teachers." He looked around her and into the house. "Is he still sick from Saturday?"

Aunt Cindy nodded. "I don't know what bug he caught but you better be careful you don't get it too." She opened the screen door and motioned Tommy inside. "He's upstairs in his room. The last time I checked he was sitting there almost reading a book. He could barely keep his eyes open. Go ahead up, if you want."

"Thanks. I'll just give him the stuff. He won't want to get behind, you know." Tommy headed for the stairs.

"More like a couple of new comic books, if I know you two," Aunt Cindy answered.

Tommy turned, his mouth open to deny the accusation, but Aunt Cindy smiled and waved him up the stairs.

"Don't worry about it, Tommy. Everyone's allowed a couple of sick days in their life. Go ahead up and see if you can cheer him up." She frowned for a moment. "He's been . . . different these past couple of days. Maybe you can snap him out of it."

"Okay, Mrs. Johnson. I'll see what I can do," Tommy promised. He bounced up the stairs two at a time and stepped down the hall to Eric's room. He knocked on the open door.

"Hey, how you feelin'?" Tommy asked Eric.

Eric looked up from the book in his lap with a blank expression on his face. "Huh?" was his first response. Then he slowly seemed to focus on Tommy and gave a half-smile. "Oh. Hi." He looked back down at the book.

Tommy stepped into the room and set his bag down next to the bed as he sat on the end. "You still look out of it, Eric. Did the doctor say anything about what you caught at the tournament?"

Eric still looked down at the book, not reacting to Tommy's comment.

Tommy reached over and lightly punched Eric in the shoulder. "Hey, dude. You in there?"

Eric reacted to the punch. He rolled off the far side of the bed and stood glaring at Tommy. "What do you want? Why are you here?" Eric demanded.

Tommy stood and raised his open hands in an "I'm not fighting" motion. "Easy, Eric. I just came to see how you were doing. I figured you were still sick when you didn't come to school today, so I brought along some of the work from our classes and a couple of new Manga books as a present to cheer you up. That's all." He pulled the books out of his bag and dropped them on the bed, along with several sheets of papers with the school lessons.

"You want something," Eric spat. "You always want something from me." He glared at Tommy. "Get out. I don't want your stuff. I don't need your help for school." He picked up the books and papers and threw them back at Tommy. "Get out. Get out of my house. I don't want to ever see you here again."

Tommy looked at Eric for a moment, the picked up his bag and turned to go out the door, the books and papers still on the floor. At the doorways he stopped and looked back at Eric. The other boy was still on the far side of the bed, his hands ready to attack.

"I hope you get better," Tommy said, then turned and walked down the hall to the stairs.

"I hope you die," he heard from the room behind him.

At the bottom of the stairs, Aunt Cindy stood, her eyes full of tears.

"He's really sick," Tommy said softly. "I hope the doctors can help him."

Aunt Cindy gave Tommy a hug. "You're a good friend, Tommy. Just remember, he doesn't mean what he said. I think it's the fever."

Tommy looked back up the empty stairs. "I hope you're right," he said as he slipped his bag on his shoulders. "I have to get home. Let me know if there's anything I can do to help."

"Of course," Aunt Cindy said. "And Tommy . . ."

He stopped at the doorway and looked back at her.

"Yes?" he said.

"You're always welcome in this house, you know that, don't you?" she asked.

He looked up the stairs again, then at Aunt Cindy. "Yeah. Well, we'll see." He turned and walked through the doorway, pulling the main door closed behind him.

* * *

After school on Wednesday, Tommy asked his father to give him a ride down to Enigma Caverns. Since the Johnsons usually provided the transportation down to the cave, Mr. Kuhns was a bit surprised, but when Tommy said Eric was still sick after the weekend, and had missed every day of school this week, he wavered for a moment before answering. When Tommy finished his argument with the statement, "I promised Stephanie I'd help!" his father gave him a look, raised both eyebrows, then smiled and said he take him down.

"Time I got the meet Mr. Fuller, anyway," Mr. Kuhns said. "I might need to know him better before things get too much further."

Tommy looked at his father. "Huh? What does that mean?" he asked.

When Mr. Kuhns just smiled at his son, Tommy blushed.

"She's just a friend," he said as he put on his jacket.

"You just keep thinking that for a while, son" Mr. Kuhns stated. "It might even be true." He nudged Tommy in the ribs. "But I doubt it." He laughed and walked out to the car with Tommy shaking his head as he followed his father.

The cave was quiet when they arrived after dark. The shop was closed to the public after five-thirty in the evening, which normally gave Eric, Tommy and Stephanie a good couple of hours to work without distractions. At least that was the plan.

Tommy introduced his father to Stephanie's father then headed down into the cave to find Stephanie at Mr. Fuller's suggestion.

"See if you can get her to pay attention," Mr. Fuller said to Tommy. "She seems to have some sort of bug and is just moping around these last couple of days."

"Must be going around," Tommy said. "Eric has the same thing, it sounds like. I'll see what I can do to cheer her up." He waved at the two men and went through the door to the tunnel.

"Steph," he called out. He waited for an answer, but no voices echoed up the tunnel. "Stephanie!" he called louder.

"Tommy! We in tunnel over river," the deep voice of Dwalin resonated through the rocks. "Come down."

Tommy headed down the tunnel as fast as the slippery floor permitted. He could see where Stephanie and Dwalin had already placed a number of appropriate decorations along the tunnel, both on the walls and attached to specific sections of the tunnel that would not damage the natural formations. He quickly reached the tunnel over the river and found Dwalin hard at work attaching a rubber bat to the hard limestone roof.

"Hey, Dwalin. How's it going?" he asked his rock dwarf friend.

"Go good, Tommy. But go better if understood why Midgard people attach fake animals to cave roof when so much easier to bring in real flying mouses. Can train them easy to stay away from visitors. Not be any problem." Dwalin picked up another fake bat and shook it, the wings waggling with the movement. "Not even fly like real flying mouse. How this scare people?"

"It's not supposed to scare people," Tommy answered. "The idea is to make people think that there might be bats in here, then they scare themselves, just a little. They really don't want to be scared for real."

"Midgard people very strange." Dwalin shook his head.

"Tell me about it," Tommy agreed. He looked around. "Where's Stephanie?"

"Down tunnel a bit." Dwalin stopped what he was doing and looked at Tommy. "Be nice to her. She not feel well. Miss school today."

"Yeah. Eric's got the same thing, I think. He's been out of school all week." Tommy looked down at the dwarf. "You guys don't catch colds and stuff, do you? I wouldn't want you to catch something from us and take it back to Asgard."

Dwalin shook his head and slapped his chest with the sound of two rocks colliding. "Dwarf body strong. Midgard illness not affect us. Aesir people also very strong. Not have any illness like this on Asgard." He smiled. "Aesir and dwarf get hurt, but not get sick. So try hard not to get hurt and we be fine."

"Lucky you," Tommy answered. "Let me go say hello to Stephanie."

But just as he turned to walk down the tunnel, Stephanie appeared. She kept her eyes on the floor and seemed to be in a sort of trance, not really paying attention. She almost ran into Tommy before she stopped.

"Um. Hi, Stephanie," Tommy said. "How are you feeling?"

Stephanie looked at Tommy for almost a minute without speaking. Then she said, "Why are you here?"

He looked over at Dwalin, then back at the young girl. "Um. It's Wednesday. Eric and I promised to come and help decorate the cave. He's sick, but I came to help."

She looked at him more closely, almost nose to nose. "So what do you want? A medal? You're here. Big deal. So do something."

"Ah. Sure, Steph. What would you like done first?" Tommy looked around to see what still needed to be decorated.

"What? You need me to tell you what to do, just like a little momma's boy. That's what you are, a momma's boy, aren't you?" She glared at Tommy and he took a step back away from her.

"Are you feeling okay?" he asked. "Do you want me to call your father?"

"That's it, go running to the parents, just like a momma's boy," Stephanie spat. "Just leave me alone." She spun on one heel and marched off down the tunnel, muttering to herself.

Tommy looked over at Dwalin.

The dwarf just shrugged. "Stephanie must be very sick. She should not talk to you like that. Tommy good friend to Stephanie. And to Dwalin." He laid one huge hand on the boy's shoulder.

Tommy's eyes were bright with tears at Stephanie's comments. It wasn't all that long ago that Stephanie's description of "momma's boy" would have been pretty much correct where Tommy was concerned. Only since he met Eric, the rock dwarves and the Aesir, had he changed. He was more self-reliant, and better able to take care of himself, as his accomplishments at the tournament proved. But he was still on the young side of thirteen years old. And Stephanie was a special friend to him, even though he had told his father otherwise.

"Let's get this tunnel decorated," he said to Dwalin. "At least we can do that much for her."

Dwalin nodded in agreement. "But we tell Stephanie's father she need to see doctor again. She not act like Stephanie."

Tommy stared down the tunnel after his friend. "There's a lot of that going around these days, I think." he agreed. "Must be an epidemic." He bent down and picked up a rubber bat. "Where do you want to hang this one?"

* * *

Bor looked down at the two children facing him across the wide desk.

"The Johnson boy and the Fuller girl should be ready for the next step by now," Bor said to the two. "I want you both to be sure the second contact takes place without any other people around and at a time when you will have at least an hour to work with them. We need to be sure the initial programming is well in control before they are in contact with the Aesir again. Our control will not be noted at first, but the change in behavior will be obvious. We can take no chances the Aesir will stop the two before they complete their missions."

"And once you have those two kids in your control, we get the money and a ride to wherever we want to go, right?" the boy asked Bor. "We'll be paid off, just like you said. Right?"

The girl nodded her head and smiled, also awaiting the answer. "I'm planning on someplace warm. I'm tired of Pennsylvania winters."

"That sound like a good idea," the boy agreed.

Bor waved a hand at the two. "You will both be paid in full when your job is done. What you want is a pittance against the wealth we have amassed on this world," he said more to himself than to the children. "And when we have control of MMR and the wyrm, we will have complete control of this world as well. A horde of flying creatures will patrol the skies, and all the computers on the planet will be under our control." He slammed a fist down on his desk. "And the Aesir will be locked away in their pitiful world of Asgard. We will control the planet, as we should have done from the first."

"Yeah, right. As long as we get paid," the boy stated.

Bor glared at him from across the desk. "Do not forget, child. We rescued you from that building you were living in. Another night in the cold and you would have died from both the exposure and the diseases you acquired from your companions." He pointed at the girl. "And you could have easily been the victim of one of those street predators that took your friend. One more day on the street and you would have disappeared just as completely as she has done."

The two children cringed under the glare of the Giant.

"We just want what you promised," the girl whispered.

Bor smiled. "And haven't we kept our promises to you?" he asked. "We have given you a place to stay, warm clothes, good food, whatever entertainment you have desired. And all we ask in return in this one small task. Admittedly you have done well so far, but the next step is the most dangerous. I would not have you believe this is—how do you say it on this world—a piece of cake. If the Aesir capture you, they will strip your mind from you and leave you back where we found you, for however long you might last."

"We'll do it. We'll do it right," the boy said. "We know what the payoff is for us and it's too important to us to mess it up."

The girl nodded in agreement.

Bor smiled again. "Excellent. Now go and prepare. We have been monitoring the two Aesir pawns and the time is right to make the next contact. Prepare yourselves well." He pushed a button on his desk and the door behind the children slid open with a hiss of air.

"We'll be ready," the girl said.

"Good." Bor kept the smile as the children left the room. Before the door closed again, Keyes entered and looked at Bor.

"The two we watch are home from school again, as you planned. They are in their rooms and the contact devices have been placed outside the buildings as directed. The nanites will react to the call easily at this range and draw the children outside." The human looked at Bor and waited.

Bor nodded. "Good. Be ready to transport our two messengers to both the cave and the John's Son house within the hour."

The man nodded and started to turn to leave the room. He stopped when Bor raised his hand.

"And prepare the treatment room for the two we seek and our two messengers." Bor's smile returned, this time as cold as ice. "Once we have the two Aesir-lovers, we will no longer need our two messengers in their present form. They will be a minor problem. And we will need to deal with them."

Keyes nodded and left the room. The door closed with another hiss and Bor turned in his chair to look out the window.

"Subtlety has not worked with the Aesir," Bor said to himself. "We have tried to avoid direct contact since the days of the Vikings. But now it is time for direct action."

"We will only have one chance to capture both MMR and the boy," a voice said from behind the Giant. "If we fail at this, there are no more Vanir left to carry our cause further. We will die on this speck of dust and will have accomplished nothing."

Bor turned. On the other side of the desk was an image of a Giant, projected in the air in the middle of the room.

"You and I remain of all those with power who came to this place, except for some few worker drones we have retained," the image said to Bor. "We must succeed."

"There are still those Vanir captured by the Aesir," Bor said. "If we succeed in this plan, we can rescue them and bring them back to our cause."

The image waved a hand in dismissal. "They were fools and weaklings to permit themselves to be captured. They show weakness we cannot permit to continue in the Vanir race. When we succeed, we will take them back, but only as workers to be used and discarded as needed."

Bor nodded. "True. They have lost much of what makes them truly Vanir, and the Aesir have had time to condition them against what we know to be true about the world and how it should function."

He looked at the image floating in front of his desk. "Yes, we will use them as needed, but they shall remain behind when we return to our home and conquer the Aesir. By word, I pledge this, Father."

The image smiled and nodded.

Chapter Six

Eric tossed back and forth in the bed, the light sheet his aunt had laid across his body now twisted around his legs. With a final lurch that almost threw him to the floor he kicked his legs free and lay on the bed in his pajamas, staring up at the ceiling. He wasn't awake, but not really asleep. His fever-heated dreams were a jumble of barely-remembered memories. The only things that stuck in his mind were a set of green eyes and wavy blonde hair.

As he lay in bed, he heard the music. He got up from the bed and went to the window to look out into the back yard. On the far side of the yard was a white figure, too far back into the trees for Eric to quite make out who it was. But a part of him knew who it was, and the music told him the rest. This was who he needed to be with to stop the fever. He needed to go out to the back yard right now or the fever would only get worse.

Eric quickly pulled a pair of jeans on over his pajamas, slipped out of the pajama top before a sweatshirt went over his head, and stepped into a pair of sneakers without stopping to put on socks. He crept down the hallway, past his aunt and uncle's bedroom and down the stairs. At the back door he disabled the alarm system Uncle Al had put in to protect the information he had in the house about Eric's new friends, and went out into the back yard.

At the edge of the yard, the figure in white beckoned to him, calling him out of the house and across the lawn. Eric never noticed the cold dew that soaked his sneakers. All his attention was the figure in white, with wavy blonde hair, and the music that called him toward her. At the edge of the yard, he stopped for a moment, but a hand reached out of the darkness and called him closer. Eric walked into the field that bordered his uncle's property. As he crossed the property line and stepped into the field, he saw her. In a white robe that reached to her knees, she stood, smiling and waiting.

"Hello, Eric."

Her voice rang in his ears like a bell and he could do nothing but stare at her.

"I've been waiting for you," she said.

Eric felt a cold needle stick him in the neck and he dropped into blackness.

* * *

"Tommy, come answer the phone. It's Mr. Johnson," his mother called to him.

Any excuse to delay cleaning his room on a Saturday morning was as good as any other and Tommy dashed down the stairs and took the phone from his mother. "Konichiwa, Sensei," Tommy said, bowing to the phone even though he knew Mr. Johnson couldn't see him. "How may I help you?"

"Tommy, I know you and Eric are friends and cover for each other sometimes, but I need you to tell me the truth. Is Eric at your place or do you know where he is?"

Uncle Al sounded worried, and there weren't a lot of things that worried Eric's uncle.

"I swear, Mr. Johnson. I haven't seen Eric since Wednesday when I stopped over your house," Tommy answered. "What happened?"

Uncle Al sighed. "I was afraid of that," he said more to himself than to Tommy. "When we got up this morning, Eric wasn't in his bed and the back door was wide open. We've looked all around the house and in the field nearby, but we haven't been able to find him."

"Do you think he ran away?" Tommy asked.

"I don't think so," Uncle Al answered. "His fever has been pretty steady all week and the only reason he wasn't in the hospital was the doctor told us he couldn't do any more for him that we were already doing. But if his fever went up another degree we were supposed to bring him right in to the emergency room." There was a pause before Uncle Al spoke again. "Are you parents nearby?"

"Yes, my mom's right here," Tommy said. "Do you need to talk to her?"

"No, but ask her if you can come to our house and help us look for Eric. Some of his special friends are here to help and we thought you might have some ideas where he could have gone."

Uncle Al put emphasis on "special" and Tommy realized some of the Aesir and the dwarves were probably there to help, and Tommy was to keep that information from his parents. He turned to his mother, who had been following his end of the conversation.

"Eric walked out of the house last night," Tommy said to her. "That fever of his must be pretty bad. Mr. Johnson wants to know if I can come over and help look for Eric, that maybe I know some of the places he and I go to play and stuff. Is that okay?"

"Of course you can help," his mother said. "Do they need some more people? I can call your father on his cell phone. He's doing a job for Mr. Hunsicker this morning, I think."

"No, I think he's got enough people there already," Tommy said. He wasn't too sure how his father would react to meeting Odin or Thor, or even Sudri and Dwalin. "I'll be there as soon as I can," Tommy said into the phone.

"See you soon," Uncle Al answered.

"Thanks, Mom," Tommy said, pulling his jacket off the rack by the door.

"You let me know if they need some more help," she said.

"I will," he answered as he dashed out the door.

The Johnson house was about three quarters of a mile down the road from Tommy's, and he made the entire distance at a run, thanks to his training with Eric and Mr. Johnson. As he ran up the driveway, he saw a white horse in the back yard and ran around the house rather than going up to the front door. The Johnson back yard was beginning to resemble a circus. In the yard were eight white stallions, mounts for the tall, blonde women standing at the back porch in a group as they waited for directions from their leader, Freawin. For a change, the Valkyr were dressed in blue jeans and sweatshirts or jackets, rather than chain mail and swords. In addition to the rock dwarves Sudri and Dwalin, Tommy also saw Sudri's brother, Suori, and about a dozen of the dwarves that had come through from Jotunheim a few months ago. They recognized Tommy and waved as he walked over to the porch where Uncle Al and Thor were leaning over the table. A map of the area covered the table, and the two men were dividing the area for the search teams.

"Ah, good, you're here," Uncle Al said. He held out a hand for Tommy to shake. "Thank you for coming."

"Well, of course I'd come," Tommy said. "Eric is my friend and you have all given me a lot of help this past year. Even if Eric has been a pain lately, I'd still help try and find him."

"You are indeed a proper young warrior," Thor stated, grasping wrists with the young boy. "Eric chose well in naming you friend."

The tall Aesir had his hair pulled back in a pony tail and tucked under a baseball cap, like a trucker. But Tommy didn't think Thor would ever be mistaken for a trucker. A football player maybe. Or a one-man furniture moving team. But the only way he would handle trucks would be to pick them up and carry them where they needed to go.

Uncle Al nodded in agreement to Thor and waved a hand at the map. "Any suggestions about where Eric might go?"

Tommy leaned over the map and oriented himself with the Johnson house, marked with a red dot. "There's that place up on the ridge where you can see the end of Bifrost," Tommy suggested. "But that would be tough to get to in the dark. And the observatory where we anchored the connection with Mimir, but that would take even longer to get there from here."

"Not for Valkyr," Freawin said as she looked over his shoulder.

"Did Eric have one of your mounts?" Tommy asked. "If he's on foot and delirious, I don't think he would have walked there." He thought for a minute. "Has anybody checked with Stephanie? Did he go to the cave, maybe?"

"No, he didn't," Aunt Cindy said, closing the back door of the house. She was holding the wireless phone from the kitchen out to her husband. "It's Bob Fuller. Stephanie's missing too."

Uncle Al took the phone. "Bob? What happened?"

He listened for a minute as everyone on the porch stood silent and waited while Bob Fuller reported.

"Sounds like the same sort of thing that happened to Eric." He listened again. "No, just wait there. I have a lot of the Asgard team at my house. I'll send some of them over to help you search. Knowing this bunch they'll almost be there as soon as you hang up the phone." He listened again. "Yeah. Me too. Hang in there." He turned off the phone and handed it to Aunt Cindy.

"What happened to our sister?" Freawin asked.

"Pretty much the same thing that's been happening to Eric, it sounds like," Uncle Al said. "She's been down with a fever all week and wasn't getting better. When Bob went in to check on her this morning, she wasn't in her room, wasn't down in the cave and he can't find her around the immediate house area. He was calling to see if maybe she went somewhere with Eric and Tommy." He looked down at the boy. "Your friends are pretty sick right now, it looks like."

"We will go and aid her father in the search," Freawin stated. "We can get there faster than your motor vehicles." She turned back to the other Valkyr and ran for Sky Stepper, her mount. "Come, sisters. We ride to find the young Valkyr!"

Dwalin ran across the lawn after Freawin and she leaned down from the saddle to speak with the dwarf. She reached down a hand and pulled the dwarf onto Sky Stepper's rump, where he grasped her waist with his strong arms. Uncle Al watched the rest of the Valkyr leap on their mounts and take off across the field like white ghosts after Freawin and Dwalin.

"I would hope that was what you had in mind for them to do," Thor stated with a smile as he watched his scouts depart.

"I certainly wasn't going to tell them not to go," Uncle Al answered. "But they do have the advantage of being able to search off-road. That will be a help to Bob." He looked around at who he had left for search teams to look for Eric. The rest of the dwarves, Thor and Tommy could cover a lot of ground, but not as much as the Valkyr.

"Ah, good. My father sends additional help."

Uncle Al looked where Thor pointed. At the edge of the lawn and headed toward the house were another dozen or so Aesir. Several of them carried boxes, which they brought up and set on the back porch. The leader of the group set down his box and turned to Thor.

"We have come to aid the search," said Vili, Odin's brother and Thor's uncle. "Odin also sends these sensors which we may be able to tune to aid in finding the young warrior."

Thor and Vili grasped arms in the Aesir manner, then Vili turned to Uncle Al. "I owe your nephew a debt. By his efforts was I rescued from the Vanir. I will do what I can to aid the search." The Aesir grasped wrists with Uncle Al as well.

"We're glad to have all the help we can get," Uncle Al said. "Especially since the hunt just grew to two lost children"

"Two?" Vili answered. He looked from Uncle Al to Thor and then down at Tommy. "What other youngling is missing?"

"Stephanie, Eric's friend and a Valkyr in training," Uncle Al answered. "Freawin and her team just headed down to the cave to help Stephanie's father look for her."

"Then we need set these sensors to work immediately," Vili answered. "Is there a place we can work, out of the weather and away from this home? The power used by your tools inside will interfere with the sensors' search."

"What about the tree house?" Tommy suggested. "It doesn't have any electrical stuff. Just some Aesir crystals."

"Good idea, Tommy," Uncle Al agreed. "Take Vili over and show him around inside."

"Okay, Mr. Johnson," Tommy said. He looked at the tall Aesir. "Can you come with me, sir? I'll show you where the ladder is."

Vili picked up his box again. "Lead on, young Norn."

Tommy looked up with surprise at the smiling Aesir.

"Odin has spoken of the young Midgard lad who seeks to learn the secrets of the Aesir. We were to meet soon, in any case, as Odin has asked me to be your teacher while I regain my strength." Vili bowed. "Lead on. We have friends to find."

Tommy headed for the tree house, Vili and two Aesir with their load of sensors close behind.

"Vili will be teaching Tommy?" Uncle Al asked Thor. "Is he back to normal after all those years with the Giants?"

Thor gazed after his uncle with a strange expression on his face. "Normal? No, I think not." He looked at Uncle Al. "I doubt any of us, other than perhaps my brother Loki, truly knows what Vili went through at the hands of the Vanir for all those centuries. Perhaps Loki might know since he has been through a small part of that same torture. I wish he was not off hunting Vanir at this time. But Odin's plan has its own safeguards. Vili will be teaching young Tommy with the aid of Mimir. Should some problem arise with Vili, or he begin to fall again under the control of the Vanir, Mimir will protect the boy, as well as all the Aesir."

"By the way, I expected to see Loki with all this running around. Where is he?" Uncle Al asked.

Thor shrugged. "Off chasing Vanir. Something he does whenever he feels he has time. He may be gone quite a while." He looked again at the tree house, as the four searchers disappeared inside. Then Thor shook his head and looked back at Uncle Al. "Enough of this. We have a warrior to find. Where would you have us search for Eric?"

Uncle Al and Thor leaned over the table again and quickly laid out a pattern for the rest of the searchers. In less than five minutes, the Aesir and dwarves were running across the field or down the road in all directions to look for Eric.

Uncle Al had wanted to go as well, but Thor laid a hand on his shoulder. "In this matter you must be the commander, to stay and coordinate all the rest," the Aesir said. "We all have communication devices to aid in that coordination and we will need you to tell us when Eric is found or we will stay in the search till the end of time."

Uncle Al nodded and watched Thor race across the lawn and out into the fields for his part of the search. Aunt Cindy came up and put her arms around his waist from the back, her chin resting on his shoulder as she watched the searchers depart.

"They'll find him," she said to her husband.

"I know. That's not what's bothering me." Uncle Al continued to stare out into the field.

"Then what?" Aunt Cindy countered.

Uncle Al turned and looked at his wife. "Maybe I'm getting paranoid, with all the things that have happened with Eric and to Eric. But I just can't help thinking. Maybe if it was just Eric that went missing, I might believe it was the fever and nothing else. But with Stephanie gone as well, I have to wonder if the Giants are up to something and have the two of them someplace. I can't think what they might want to ransom them for, but I can't just rule out that the Giants are being vindictive."

Aunt Cindy gasped. "You think they might torture the children?"

Uncle Al nodded. "From all that Odin and the others have said about the Vanir, and from all we've seen since we got involved in this war, I wouldn't rule it out."

"Isn't there anything more you can do? Call Lieutenant Harris or some other police force? The FBI? Somebody?" Tears rolled down Aunt Cindy's face. "There has to be something!"

Uncle Al shook his head. "I've already called John Harris and he's keeping a watch on the missing person reports as well as any lost children found that might not remember who they are. But as for anyone else . . . " He shrugged. "How long do you think it would take for me to explain about the Aesir and the Vanir to some cop who wasn't already part of this deal?"

"But they're just children," Aunt Cindy said in a whisper.

Uncle Al nodded. "And the Vanir don't care about that." He kissed his wife on the forehead. "I'm going out to the tree house and see if there's anything I can do to help. Hang onto the phone and let me know if anything comes up. I'll let you know if Thor or any of the others find anything and report on the Aesir communicators." He looked out across the field again. "I'd go out myself if I had any idea where to look. But we already have enough people in the field. We just have to trust them."

"Do you, Al? Do you trust them?" Aunt Cindy asked.

Uncle Al smiled at her. "Yes. With my life. And now I'm trusting them with Eric's life. They'll find him."

"Soon, I hope. Soon." She hugged her husband close, then pushed him toward the tree house. "Go. Let me know what happens."

"I promise," he said.

And just then a cheer went up from the tree house. Tommy's head popped out of the window on this side of the structure.

"They found Stephanie," he called out to them. "The Valkyr have her."

Chapter Seven

young girl lay still, barely breathing as the dwarf, her parents and the six Valkyr crowded around the bed and looked down at her.

"Is there any special medicine you have from Asgard that might help her?" Bob Fuller asked Freawin.

The tall Valkyr shook her head. "We do not get sick as our young sister is. We may be injured, or have some infection from wounds, but the small creatures that cause illness on this world have no means of affecting our bodies. So we have never developed the same means of treating our people as you have done. It has been many of our years since our bodies were prey to such problems."

"I was afraid of that," Bob said.

The doorbell rang and he left the room to answer it, returning less than a minute later with a man and a woman in black slacks and dark blue jackets proclaiming them Emergency Medical Technicians. They waited in the hall, the room already as full as it could get.

"Freawin, can you take your sisters and Dwalin out in the living room for a while so these medics can check out Stephanie?" Bob asked the Valkyr.

Freawin nodded to him, then gathered her sisters with a glance. As the Valkyr left the room, Dwalin laid a hand on Stephanie's and gave it a small squeeze. Then he joined the exodus. Freawin looked at the woman EMT as she moved toward to bed. A hand on the EMT's shoulder caused her to turn and look up at the blonde warrior.

"You will aid our sister," she stated.

The EMT smiled and nodded. "We'll do everything we can," she promised.

Freawin looked down at her for a moment then nodded and turned to the hallway to join the rest of the Asgard crowd.

"Sister?" the male EMT asked with raised eyebrows.

Bob Fuller shrugged. "They're a sorority. My daughter is something of a mascot with them. It's a long story."

"Hmph," the man answered then joined his partner at the bed.

"Her BP is normal but her body temp is depressed," the woman stated. She turned to Bob and his wife. "Has she been out of bed?"

"Yes. She must have been sleep walking or something like that," Fuller answered. "Her sisters just found her wandering on the road about a mile from here."

The EMT shook her head. "Outside, in this weather, in just a night-gown from the looks of things." She lifted one foot and examined the dirt and small gravel still stuck in the skin of Stephanie's sole. "And barefoot, too." She looked up again. "How long was she outside?"

Fuller shook his head. "We don't know. She was in bed at three a.m. when I checked in on her and she seemed to be resting comfortably. When my wife checked again at about seven, she was gone. She's been down with a fever all week and only made it to school one day. No doctor we've seen seems to know what it is so they've just been treating it with bed rest and fluids."

The EMT nodded and turned to her partner. "Get the thermal blanket and the gurney." She turned back to the Fuller's. "It looks like on top of whatever else was going on, we may have the beginnings of hypother-mia. If we get her body temperature back to normal soon, she should be okay, but given that she tried to walk off on her own, I think we need to transport her to the hospital so we can keep an eye on her. We'll take her to Lehigh Valley Hospital and one of you can ride with her. The other can meet us there with your car so you can get home."

There was some commotion in the hallway and the gurney appeared with the male EMT at one end and Freawin at the other. Dwalin followed behind and stepped into the room when the man pulled the blanket off the gurney and walked over to the bed. The two medics quickly and efficiently wrapped Stephanie until only her head was clear of the blanket. The EMTs turned around and looked at the growing crowd in the room.

"Ah, folks, you really need to give us some room so we can get this youngster on the gurney and out to the ambulance," the young man stated.

"I take Stephanie to moving bed," Dwalin said as he walked up to the bed and picked up the girl.

"And we will take her to your transport vehicle," Svala said as she moved aside for Dwalin.

"Really, we need you people to let us do this. I mean there are regulations and liability and—" He stopped as he found himself face-to-face with Svala.

The Valkyr didn't say anything. She just looked the young man in the eye and waited.

"On the other hand, we always appreciate it when people make our jobs easier," he said. He stepped out of the way.

"Smart move," Bob Fuller murmured.

Dwalin laid Stephanie on the gurney and the young woman EMT fastened the straps to hold her in place. Freawin and Svala each picked up an end and started toward the stairs.

"Um, it has wheels," the male EMT said as they moved away.

Dwalin looked at him. "Is light. Stephanie too important to take chances with," the dwarf said. "Valkyr will carry her."

"Sure. Whatever." The EMT just shook his head as he watched the gurney move swiftly down the hall, down the stairs and out to the vehicle. He had to run to catch up in order to show the Valkyr how to seat the gurney into the floor of the ambulance and lock the wheels.

The female EMT gathered the cases of equipment and tried to pick up all three before Dwalin gently took two of them from her.

"I will bring," the rock dwarf.

"Thanks," she said, then turned to the Fuller's. "Okay, who's riding and who's following?"

"I'll come with you," Stephanie's mother said.

The EMT nodded. "Let's go." She led the way down to the ambulance.

"I called it in. They're waiting for us in emergency," the young man said to his partner as she stowed the cases in the back of the vehicle.

She nodded and stepped inside, giving Stephanie's mother a hand up. "We'll meet you there," she said to Bob Fuller as she closed the doors.

The male EMT glanced at the Valkyr, who stood alongside the ambulance trying to see in the small windows, and at Dwalin, and looked up at Bob.

"Strange sorority," he said.

"You have no idea," Fuller answered.

The medic shook his head and walked to the front of the vehicle. It drove off with lights flashing but no siren, since they didn't need to break any speed limits to get Stephanie to the hospital.

Bob turned to the Valkyr and stopped as he saw Freawin speaking into a small communication disk. He had spent enough time around the Aesir and their friends to recognize some of the equipment. Freawin finished her conversation and smiled at Fuller.

"They have located Eric, as well. He is in much the same state as our sister and they take him to the same hospital, from what Albert John's Son reports. He said he will meet you in the E.R., whatever that may be." She laid a hand on Bob's shoulder then placed the communication disk in his hand. "Take this. You may need our aid again. My sisters go to Eric's home to await news while I join you at the healing place, since we would be too many with no purpose and only in the way if we all came. Sky Stepper and his brothers are as worried about our sister as are we. They will aid in any way they can."

"Thank you," Fuller answered. He slipped the disk into his pocket and started for his car. As he slid into the driver's seat, the passenger door opened and Dwalin slid his heavy bulk into the vehicle.

"Dwalin come to place of healing," the dwarf stated. "Many dwarf miners hurt. I help to heal them. Maybe I help heal Stephanie."

"Belt in, my friend," Fuller said as he started the car. "I'll take all the help I can get."

* * *

It was a short drive to the hospital, but by the time they reached the emergency room, Eric's aunt and uncle were already there, along with Thor, Sudri and Freawin. How the Valkyr had beaten Bob to the hospital on a horse was a mystery he left for another day. Sky Stepper waited patiently in a parking space, gaining some strange looks from people going into the hospital. He and Dwalin moved into the emergency room and up to the Johnsons.

"Where did you find him?" Bob asked Uncle Al.

"Pretty much the same as the Valkyr found Stephanie, walking along the road in his bare feet and in a sort of trance. The doctor is checking him out now, but from what Freawin has been telling me, they don't know any more than they do with your daughter." Aunt Cindy gripped his hand and he reached over to pat hers without looking. "I have to wonder if there's something going on here that might involve the Vanir." He looked up at Thor. "Do you have any way to tell if the Giants have infected the children with something?"

Thor looked off into space for a moment as he considered the question. Then he looked at the Valkyr leader. "Have you a micro-integrator in your saddle kit?"

Freawin nodded. "I'll get it." She was out the door before she finished the sentence.

It was about thirty seconds when she returned at a run. The nurses at the desk looked up as if expecting to see blood or broken bones. Freawin handed the sensor to Thor and the group watched as he adjusted several settings. Then the blonde Aesir look at Uncle Al.

"Can you get me onto the room where Eric is kept?" he asked.

Uncle Al nodded. "The rest of you stay here for now. We'll let you know what we find." He motioned to Thor and started down the hallway.

The emergency room was as busy as could be expected for a Saturday morning. Accidents from careless use of tools while doing chores around the house shared space with the results of too much partying and careless driving. They turned a corner and found Eric in a room with a young doctor leaning over him as he checked his vital signs.

"No change, Mr. Johnson," the doctor said. "His temperature is stable but he isn't responding to anything we've tried so far." He looked at Thor. "And you are?"

"Theodore Olson," Uncle Al stated. "He's a friend of the family and just happened to be nearby when Eric was found. He's been doing some special medical studies and may be able to help us out."

Thor stepped toward Eric's bed and the doctor stepped out of the way of the large man. When Thor took the sensor out of his pocket and started to run it over Eric's body, he smiled.

"Oh, great. He has a tricorder," the doctor sneered.

"No," Thor stated. "A micro-integrator." He ignored the doctor and continued his examination of Eric as Uncle Al moved closer to the doctor.

"He's been doing some specialized work in Europe with polarized viral components. He thinks he might be able to pinpoint the problem with Eric, based on the symptoms I was able to explain to him." Uncle Al looked over at the Aesir as he moved across the body with the sensor. "At least I hope so," he said more to himself than to the doctor.

"Polarized viral components," the doctor repeated. "Pretty fancy stuff. The last I heard most of the deep research in that kind of stuff was being done over in Europe. With immunosuppressive diseases, if I recall correctly."

Uncle Al smiled. "And that's where Dr. Olson has been for the last five years, working with folks at Heidelberg University and some places in Sweden and Denmark."

The doctor stepped a bit closer and tried to watch what Thor was doing but the Aesir turned to him and motioned him back.

"You are contaminating the readings," Thor stated. "Please stand clear. I have shielded myself, but it is a narrow range in order not to read more than one body."

He completed his scan and frowned as he looked at the sensor. Then he looked at Uncle AL. "As we feared. The Vanir have tampered."

"Vanir? Is that some type of virus I haven't heard of?" the doctor asked.

"A disease in truth," Thor agreed. He looked back at Uncle Al. "We will need to reverse the polarity of the load. Have you a way to generate a large scale magnetic field?"

"We can run him through an MRI unit," Uncle Al suggested. "It generates a high intensity magnetic field we use to see into the human body. You won't need to take any readings, but putting him through the field would disrupt any magnetic polarization in his body."

The doctor looked from 'Dr. Olson' to Uncle Al and back. "He's a doctor and doesn't know what an MRI is?" He shook his head. "Well, okay, if you say so and you can pay for it. We'll schedule him for an MRI first thing Monday morning."

Thor shook his head. "If this illness is what I fear, we must give the treatment now or there will be irreparable damage."

"But we don't have a team to run the unit, and the power was knocked out yesterday in a short circuit," the doctor said. "The best we can do is Monday when things are powered up."

"Take me to this machine," Thor directed. "Perhaps there is something I can do with it."

"What? You're mechanic as well as a doctor? You don't even know what an MRI is and you're going to fix it?" the young doctor asked.

"If need be," Thor answered. He gave the doctor's shoulder a gentle shove. "Shall we go?"

The doctor moved down the corridor with Thor close behind. Uncle Al suspected Thor's size had as much to do with the doctor's cooperation as his supposed knowledge. The MRI unit was separate from the emergency building and shielded as much as possible due to the magnetic fields generated by the scanning unit. Thor walked through the doorway into the scanning room and saw the control unit in pieces on the floor. The smell of burned electrical circuits filled the air. He walked over to the large tube used to project the field and took some readings with his sensor.

"What is that thing he has?" the young doctor asked.

"Something that's going to help my nephew," Uncle Al said. "And I suggest you leave it at that."

Thor turned back to the two men. "We can use this for what we need. Bring Eric here and I will prepare the unit."

"Hey, wait a minute. I can't just let you play with a multi-million dollar piece of equipment. I need security here." The doctor moved toward the phone on the wall outside the shielded room.

As he cleared the doorway, Thor pointed the sensor unit at him and pushed a button. A spark jumped the distance between the Aesir and the doctor, and the doctor stopped dead in his tracks. He turned and walked back over to Thor.

"How may I help you?" he asked the Aesir.

"Please bring the young boy here and place him in this small cave so we may heal him," Thor answered.

The doctor bowed and answered, "Right away." Then he turned and walked back down the hallway toward the emergency room.

Uncle Al looked at Thor as the Aesir frowned.

"We don't like to use those methods on your people," Thor stated. "It is too much like what the Vanir do to control their minions. But we have no time to waste if we are to help Eric and Stephanie." He turned back to the MRI unit and said to himself, "In the meantime . . ." He began to connect wires to various sections of the unit.

By the time the doctor has returned with Eric on a gurney, Thor was ready. He picked up Eric and slid him into the MRI chamber. Then he led the young doctor and Uncle Al out of the room before returning to connect his micro-integrator to the main unit. He walked out the door and closed it behind him.

Uncle Al looked at the doctor as Thor touched a bracelet on his wrist and a loud humming permeated the hallway. A paperclip lying on the floor flew through the air and stuck to the doctor's leg, but the young man didn't react at all. As the humming stopped, Thor opened the door and went into the room. He pulled Eric out of the unit and held him in a sitting position.

Eric gasped, blinked and looked up.

"Thor, what are you doing here?" Then he looked around and realized he was not in his bedroom. "Okay, what am I doing here? And where are we?"

"You've been sick, Eric, and Thor has been helping you get better," Uncle Al said. "What do you remember?"

Eric shook his head for a moment, his hands pressed to his eyes. "The last thing I really remember was coming home from the tournament yesterday." He looked up at Uncle Al. "What happened?"

"Well, for one thing, the tournament was a week ago, and you've been in and out of a fever that whole time," Uncle Al answered.

"But now you are well," Thor stated. "And we shall deal with Stephanie as well."

"Stephanie? Is she sick too?" Eric asked.

"Yes," Uncle Al said. "But she's going to get better real fast, I think."

"Please bring the young girl here as well, for treatment," Thor directed the doctor.

"Of course," the doctor answered and turned back.

Thor looked back over at Uncle Al. "And once that's done, we shall take steps to assure the Vanir do not attempt this again."

"Vanir!" Eric exclaimed. "Have the Giants been fooling with me?"

"We think so," Uncle Al said. "But Thor fixed things."

"This time," the Aesir said with a sigh. "But can we continue to do so?" He looked down at Eric. "And can we keep those who require it safe from our enemies?"

"That's always the question, isn't it?" Uncle Al answered. "We just have to be ready for them."

"And we will be," Eric added.

Thor laughed. "Well, with a warrior such as you on our side, how can we lose?"

Chapter Eight

To anyone else, the group sitting on top of the ridge in the afternoon sun would have seemed a bit strange. Two young boys, a young girl and two rock dwarves sat on sections of a large log cut in pieces and placed on end for seats. Behind the girl, a large white stallion nudged her shoulder until she reached up and stroked the scarred cheek. Behind one of the boys, a dragon loomed over the entire group. When the stallion pushed harder, trying for more scratching, the girl laughed.

"Behave, Mist Walker. I'm paying attention to you," she said, patting the cheek.

"Valkyr steed afraid you go away from him, like his last rider," Sudri said. The rock dwarf was only slightly shorter when sitting than when standing, as his feet barely touched the ground even on the low seat of the log. His flinty skin gave off a pale gray glow in the afternoon sun, overwhelmed by the gleam from his bright Hawaiian shirt and neon green sneakers, his standard attire when visiting Midgard, or Earth as his friends called it. The chill in the air made the Bermuda shorts seem a bit out of place.

"Stephanie's friends also afraid for her. Think she should spend more time with Aesir friends so we can watch out for her," Dwalin said. He was also a rock dwarf, but dressed in the tunic and trousers of an Aesir artisan, a worker in metals and gems. Sudri had been trying to get him to adopt his "disguise" when visiting Earth, but the rock dwarf just smiled and said this was how Stephanie and her family saw him first, so he preferred to stay in character.

"Eric also needs to be more careful who he spends time with," Fornir suggested.

The huge wyrm, the last of the Vanir-created breed of giant dragons from Jotunheim, was the reason their meeting was here on the top of the ridge, since he could not have fit into a tunnel of Enigma Caverns, and to land in the Johnsons' back yard would have been too exposed. Eric's neighbors were already commenting on the number of people and the group of white stallions who came to their property each time the Valkyr dropped in to visit. While horses were not an uncommon sight in farm country, the Valkyr mounts were not common horses, and their special nature showed to anyone who paid attention when they saw them. As for Fornir, he stayed away from the house and called Eric to the ridge by communicator when he wished to visit.

"Come on, guys," Eric protested. "Even Thor admits the Giants were sneaky in using to Earth kids to carry their bugs to Stephanie and me. If he didn't spot it after all the years he's been fighting these guys, how were we supposed to spot them?"

Sudri and Dwalin shrugged. Fornir pushed his head a bit further into the circle.

"I admit the manner of the Vanir's attack was different," the wyrm said. "But we must be even more vigilant than in the past. Based on what Mimir has been suggesting, the Vanir have reached a point in their struggle with the Aesir that they have little left to lose and much to gain. After centuries of searching, they now know where Mimir is, and how to get to him. He has closed off all access points on Jotunheim, which limits the Giants' options to here on Midgard. And he has stopped trying to hide from them, as he did for so long, since he now has contact with the main Aesir force. He once thought he was alone, as did all the cousins of Sudri and Dwalin who were separated with the computer when the battle ended so long ago. Now that he knows he has allies, he can take a more active role in the conflict."

"So what do we do?" Tommy asked.

"Freawin and the Valkyr are going to run regular patrols through a wide area," Stephanie said. "Mist Walker and I will help with some of those, but Svala has me wrapped up in bubble-wrap to keep me away from any possible meeting with Giants. And Dwalin has been a regular fixture in the cave. Some of the people coming for tours have started a rumor we found him buried in a deep chamber and are keeping him around as a mascot." She smiled at the dwarf. "They started calling him the Rock Man."

Dwalin shrugged. "Is true. Did find me in cave. And am made of rock, sort of."

"Yeah, well, Sudri has moved into the guest room at our place, and I don't think it's just for Aunt Cindy's cookies," Eric said.

"Aunt makes good cookies," Sudri stated. "Besides, need to learn more about Midgard so can help Aesir fit in better when they visit."

Eric looked at his friend with a smile. "I don't think re-runs of old sit-coms and cartoon shows counts as research, Sudri."

"Work for me," the dwarf answered.

"Gee, I feel left out," Tommy said. "All I have at home is my parents, who I can't even tell about you guys."

"You have one of the most important jobs of all," Fornir said. He looked down at Tommy and puffed a bit of smoke from one nostril, a sign of his excitement and concern. "I have been a friend of Mimir for many years, living deep in the caves and helping the dwarves stay free from the Vanir. Now you will be working with him as well, helping to adapt Aesir technology to this new battlefield. It may well be that your work is the key that brings this battle to a conclusion."

Tommy looked up at the huge wyrm. "Do you think so?" he asked.

"Almost certainly," Fornir answered. "This battle will not be one of massed armies meeting on a battlefield. It will be one of deception, disguise and confusion on the part of the Vanir. Your work will be needed to break through that wall of confusion to find the grain of truth that leads to the defeat of our enemies. Do not think you are playing less than a major role in this battle."

"Like Uncle Al says, these days techno-nerds get the big bucks," Eric added. "And you're being trained to be a top notch Norn, from what Thor tells me."

"Well, I've got to admit some of the stuff Vili has been teaching me is really interesting," Tommy said. "I still have a lot to learn, but we've been working on some old equipment sent over from the command ship on Jotunheim. The dwarves have set up a workshop at their village over there." He waived a hand toward the old Giant compound now owned by the dwarves. "Vili is working hard to keep busy and keep his mind off what he went through all those years on Jotunheim."

"How's he doing?" Eric asked.

Tommy shook his head. "I had a long talk with Thor when we started this project. He warned me that Vili might have some sort of flashbacks to his time with the Giants. But Odin thought being here on Earth would make it easier for him to get over some of that stuff. And being with the dwarves rather than the other Aesir makes it easier to keep his mind on other things, Thor said." Tommy shrugged. "Plus if he does snap out, the dwarves can handle him a lot better than even the Aesir, with a lot less damage to themselves or to Vili. They're pretty tough little guys."

"Who is little?" Sudri asked.

Tommy put up his hands to ward off a dwarf attack. "Hey, compared to Fornir, all of us are little."

Sudri looked up at the dragon, then back at Tommy. "Well. Okay, if you mean that way."

"Good save," Eric murmured. He gave Tommy a wink and a smile as his friend wiped imaginary sweat from his forehead.

"But that still doesn't really answer what we're supposed to do to find the rest of the Giants," Stephanie said. "We can look around the cave, because we know they want a way to Mimir, but they have the whole planet to run around on if they want. And they still have Jotunheim to go back to if they really want to stay away from the Aesir."

Fornir puffed smoke again. "While there is truth in what you say, Mimir believes the Vanir will stay near to the cave, at least for now." The wyrm looked around the circle of friends. "While the Vanir have often laid plans that have taken many years to complete, they are not by nature a patient people. Mimir believes they are already working to find a way into the cave, either by direct assault or by subterfuge. This is the only way the Vanir know of to access the information stored in Mimir's memory, since all the access tunnels on Jotunheim have been collapsed and sealed with force screens. The Vanir may be able to travel to Jotunheim using their synthetic crystals and the power of their command ship, but there is nothing there for them, other than a place away from the Aesir. What they truly desire is an end to this conflict and a return to their home dimension, so they may bring their new knowledge to bear in that battle."

"Does Mimir really think the information he has will let the Giants travel between dimensions?" Eric asked. "By our calendar, it's been centuries since the Aesir appeared on Earth. Can he really get them back to when they left?" Eric spoke of the command computer as a person, since the artificial intelligence had developed a distinct personality in the centuries is had been buried on Jotunheim.

Fornir nodded and puffed. "Indeed. Observations of the time shifts between Jotunheim and Midgard have permitted Mimir to calculate the manner in which the dimensions warp time, just as they warp space. The Aesir have already calculated what it would take to return to their own time and place, but they stay only to complete their defense of Midgard against their foes, the Vanir. Once the battle is done, it is thought some of the Aesir will return home. The information the Vanir have accumulated is also available to the Aesir, since it was stored in many of the machines captured when Jotunheim was opened after Eric's rather dramatic return from the dead."

"Aw, gee. You'll make me blush," Eric said jokingly.

"Just don't go pulling that stunt again," Tommy ordered. "You did it once before I met you when you first met Thor, and again after I met you when you got thrown in the Lost River. The third time you might not come up for air in one piece." Tommy glared at his friend. "If that happens, who will I spar with?"

"Probably somebody who can beat you as often as I do," Eric answered with a smile.

Tommy shook a finger at Eric. "You just wait until your uncle says you're ready to spar again," Tommy warned. "I've been watching the dwarves practice and picking up some tips about fighting people bigger than you are. I might give you a surprise or two."

"Yeah, some surprise. You'll fall harder and farther after all that training," Eric said. "But I'll go easy on you since you helped find me when I was sick."

"Still are sick, it looks like," Tommy suggested.

Sudri stopped what was quickly becoming a friendly tussle with a hand on each boy's shoulder. "Play later. Need to figure out how to find Giants before they turn Midgard into slave camp for experiments."

"Would they really make all of us slaves?" Stephanie asked.

"You betcha," Sudri answered. "If not believe, just ask brother Suori. He spend more time with Vanir since created by them. But be ready for not so nice stories if you ask him. Vanir definitely not nice people."

"To say the least," Fornir agreed. "While Mimir is very concerned about what plan the Vanir might be hatching to gain entrance to the command data banks, he is just as concerned about what the Vanir will do while they are waiting. Mimir believes the Vanir will have at least one if not several additional plans as diversions. And those plans will certainly be to the detriment of those Aesir here on Midgard, as well as all of your people." He looked from Eric, to Tommy, to Stephanie.

"Aw, crap," Eric said. "There's no way we're going to keep this quiet if the Giants start doing things all over the world. Or even if they start doing things on a larger scale here in the Lehigh Valley. Uncle Al and Lieutenant Harris had to do come fancy talking after all those dogs attacked the cave while they kidnapped Aunt Cindy. If that's the Giants' idea of a diversion, we're in for big trouble."

"Exactly," Fornir said. "The Giants have no care for the people of this world other than tools for their using. And while they have been willing to keep their battle with the Aesir quiet up until now, there is little chance they will continue to do so if they feel they are either close to their goal of access to Mimir, or likely to lose if they don't escalate the battle and force things into the open."

"And if they do reveal themselves to people on this planet, it's going to get real weird real fast," Eric suggested. "Aside from all the nuts who really believe in the Norse gods, who will want to come and worship Odin and the Aesir, there will be just as many nuts who want them all destroyed because they identify with the Frost Giants. Then there are all the other governments on the planet who will want a piece of the action when they find out a super intelligent race of alien beings has been here for who knows how many centuries. The fact that they pop up in the United States will drive some of those guys over the edge. And don't even want to think about the religious wars that will erupt when real gods start walking the earth."

"Aesir not gods," Sudri stated. "Just very powerful people. Good people, too."

"I know that, and you know that," Eric said, "but people who haven't met them yet will only think about the legends and the mythology. They won't care about anything else but keeping America from getting all that knowledge for themselves. I'll be surprised if we don't get a couple of hundred nuclear missiles fired at us as soon as the first television story hits the airwaves." Eric shook his head. ""I don't think even Mimir has a shield that can protect the whole country."

"So how do we hide what the Giants are doing and who they are, if all this breaks loose?" Stephanie asked.

"No clue," Eric answered. "All that Norn training give you any ideas, oh wizard of warcraft?" He looked at Tommy.

"Sorry. No magic shields. No atomic ray guns to kill only Giants. No flashy memory wiping gadgets to cover our tracks." Tommy shrugged. "We're going to have to do this the hard way."

"There's an easy way?" Stephanie countered. "After what happened when the Giants tried to close the cave with that planted toxic waste, the people around here are going to be very easily confused about anything that happens. After all, they still think that Eric and Sudri's little carnival at the skinhead's camp a year or so back was a localized tornado. If they believe that, we can get them to believe anything!"

"I hope so," Tommy said. "But I'm afraid that with what I've learned working with Vili, and since the Giants still have all their stuff from their own command ship, we're going to be in a lot of trouble soon. We really need to find out where they are and stop them before they have a chance to start something."

"Well, just run back to the lab and rustle up a handy Giant Detector and we'll go to work," Eric said.

"Actually, we've been working on something pretty much like that." Tommy pulled something that looked like a fat ink pen from his back pocket. "Vili has been trying to get something like this to register on some the main frequencies that the Giants use so we can trace them to their hiding places. But it keeps going off at weird times and we haven't been able to figure out why. Vili thinks that either the Giants have a lot of stuff scattered all over the place, which makes tracking any one place tough, or the unit is tracking something that's supposed to be here on Earth that is like what the Giant's use." He pushed a button on the side and a red light lit up on the top of the pen, blinking like a warning signal. "See. We know there's no Giant stuff up here and this thing is telling me there's Giant stuff nearby." He turned it off and stuffed it back into his pocket. "But we're working on it. Vili keep trying to do something about what he calls focus."

"Maybe I should send Uncle Al over to help," Eric suggested. "He's always telling us to focus when we train. Maybe he can give the machines a few katas to learn and get them on track."

"Funny man," Stephanie said as she punched Eric in the arm. "But this isn't a game." She shuddered. "When Tommie and I were in that building after the Giants took us, I was sure we were dead. Then you and your uncle came through the wall with that magic sword and the Valkyr dragged us home, and I thought it was just a bad dream. Then Svala got shot and it was a really bad dream. And then the government people at the cave . . ." She shuddered again. "We can't let the Giants do to the people on this planet what they did to Dwalin and his people. We have to stop them."

"Hey, we'll find a way," Eric said softly.

Mist Walker nudged Stephanie from behind and laid his muzzle on her shoulder. She leaned into his head and started to cry.

"We'll find a way to stop them," Tommy promised. "I won't let them get you again."

Stephanie looked up through her tears at Tommy. "Promise?" she asked.

"You betcha," Tommy answered. He stuck out a hand in the middle of the circle. "To stopping the Giants."

"To stopping the Giants," Eric agreed, his hand on top of Tommy's.

"You betcha," Dwalin and Sudri agreed, their hands joining the pile.

Fornir lifted his head and roared a call up into the sky, echoed by the shrill scream of the Valkyr steed, Mist Walker.

"Fear us, Vanir," Fornir taunted. "For you have roused the sleeping warriors of this world. And your days are numbered!" he challenged.

"You betcha," Stephanie agreed, adding her hand to the pile.

Chapter Nine

Loki walked down the dark corridor. He didn't know how he had arrived at this place, but he knew he had to do something important. The walls of the corridor were smooth metal, like the corridors of the command ship he and the rest of the Aesir had traveled in prior to coming to Asgard. In his hand was a weapon, not the sword or hammer he was used for so many centuries, but an Aesir hand weapon capable of firing blasts of energy at an enemy. But even the presence of the weapon did not stop the waves of fear that washed over him with each step he took. He moved cautiously, stopping to listen at each intersection of the corridors. Somehow he knew what direction he had to go, just as he knew he had a mission to perform.

Suddenly, he reached another intersection and turned to the left. He was not alone. Four Vanir stood across a wide section of the hallway, waiting for him. He raised the weapon and fired, again and again, at each of the Vanir. He screamed out as he fired. The fear made his chest tight and his ears ring like a thousand small bells. But the weapon had no effect on the Vanir. Loki fired again and watched as the bolt of energy washed over the tall, white-haired creatures without effect.

The Vanir laughed at Loki, pointing at him and shouting challenges. Loki tried to move closer to the enemy, but his feet were locked to the floor, as if they were a part of the metal. The Vanir continued to laugh and pointed behind Loki. He turned carefully, so as not to fall with his feet locked in place, and a wave of blackness fell over him, swallowing his last scream.

Loki awoke again.

He was walking down a corridor sheathed in metal like the hallways of the Aesir command ship. In his hand was a war ax, a favorite weapon of his. He listened carefully at each intersection of the hallway, watching for Vanir. He had a mission to perform, but he could not remember what it was. No matter, he would know when the time came. He moved forward and fear grew within him as each step carried him closer to his goal.

He turned a corner and suddenly faced four Vanir. With a scream of defiance he started down the hall at a run, his ax raised high to strike. But his movements were slowed, almost frozen and each step seemed to carry him away from the Vanir rather than closer. Fear tightened his chest and his blood pounded in his ears as he screamed out a challenge to the Vanir. But the sound died on his lips. The Vanir stood, not caring that they were being attacked. Arms crossed on their chests, they laughed at the Aesir warrior and pointed at him as they called out challenges and insults. Their words were lost in the sound of his own heartbeat, but Loki knew what they were saying. He tried harder to move forward, until one of the Vanir laughed and pointed behind him. He tried to turn his head, but the world went dark as a wave of viscous evil washed over him and dragged him down into the night.

Only he heard the scream that echoed in his mind.

Loki awoke.

He walked down a corridor of his old command ship toward Odin's office. In his hand he carried a message tube with important information that could end the war with the Vanir. He was afraid, an emotion he seldom permitted to rise further than his own dreams. He knew there was danger aboard the command ship, and that the danger was focused on him. But he had to get this message to Odin. MMR, the command computer, was not communicating through the ship as usual. Somehow the Vanir had closed down all communication channels aboard the command ship.

Loki turned a corner and faced four Vanir armed with energy weapons as well as swords and axes. Before Loki could move another step, the Vanir fired and a wave of blackness engulfed Loki, smothering his as it drained away his life. He screamed into the night as he realized the Vanir had won.

* * *

Bor watched the tall Aesir on the treatment table. Loki's eyes were open but they saw only what Bor's computers transmitted through the metal cable fastened to the cap locked around the Aesir's head. Again and again, Loki was thrust into the middle of a conflict, only to have every effort blocked or turned aside as they would the blows of a child. No matter what Loki did, he was defeated, crushed, and drawn down into the darkness that sucked away at his very soul.

"How goes the conditioning?" Bor asked Hrolfr, the Vanir in charge of the conditioning room.

"It goes well," Hrolfr answered. "Loki is strong. But the time he spent with us long ago is still in the depths of his mind. The Aesir have buried it deep, and placed walls around it as thick as a world. Every time we push him into a conflict, then crush him as if he were a weak child, we bring him closer to that deep memory. Once we have tapped that hidden fear, he will be ours again."

"How soon?" Bor asked.

Hrolfr looked down at several monitoring devices attached to Loki's table. "If there is a hidden flaw in the conditioning the Aesir put him through perhaps as early as tomorrow. Otherwise not later than the day after." He looked up at Bor. "You commanded he be of sound mind, for the most part, so we could use him against Odin. If that were not the case we would have broken him before now. But the results would have been little more than a husk of an Aesir, with no mind to guide it."

Bor nodded as he watched Loki writhe in pain on the table. "Good. Well, within our time schedule." He turned to Hrolfr. "And the human subjects? How goes that project?"

Hrolfr shrugged. "The first group went out a month ago. We have replaced key personnel in various government and law enforcement positions across the state. The second group will go out starting tonight and into tomorrow, depending on who they are to replace. By the end of the week, we will have control of the communication facilities for this immediate area and most of the surrounding area. Once we initiate the shutdown, we should have at least three days of total control before either the government or the law enforcement teams from outside the state start to try and enter." He looked at his leader. "Have you decided whether you wish to try the terrorist plan or the plague?"

Bor smiled. "The terrorist plan has much to benefit. We would be able to destroy several key Aesir sites we have located, as well as dispose of some troublesome humans. But the plague scenario will give us more flexibility and will actually permit more control of the government forces should they try to interfere. I believe we will use that method to access what we want."

Hrolfr bowed. "As you wish. I will set the proper programs for our controlled subjects." He leaned down for a moment to tap notes on a recorder mounted on the panel in front of him. "Do you still plan to make use of the weather control units to add to the confusion?"

"Will that change the programming for our subjects?" Bor asked.

Hrolfr shook his head. "Not initially, but as this proceeds, we will need to exercise specific control of some aspects of the government response to both the weather and the plague. Coordination of these two threats will make our response more efficient as well as more devastating for the humans. I merely ask so I can prepare the proper commands."

Bor nodded. "Excellent." He stopped and stood, deep in thought for a moment. "Set the controls for the weather device to start now. Plan on a first release of the plague three weeks from now. We will have our tunnel in place one month from now, since we must move slowly to avoid Aesir sensors. As the plague and the weather peak in effect, the humans and the Aesir will be too concerned with keeping this planet from turning into a ball of ice to stop us from gaining the memory of their command computer."

Hrolfr nodded and made additional notes. "And the two children?"

Bor smiled. "Where are they now?"

"In storage," Hrolfr answered. "They were placed in cold stasis as soon as you commanded, since you stated you might have need of them again."

"The Aesir fell into our trap very easily," Bor stated. "Passing the John's Son boy and the cave girl through the magnetic field stopped the initial nanocites. But it also triggered the reserve commands. The secondary contaminates will come out of dormancy just in time for the plague to begin. With the two children we have in storage able to carry the disease to other places, our two controlled subjects inside the Aesir camp will permit us to devastate the Aesir ranks as well. Finding a disease that would affect Aesir was difficult, but not impossible for Vanir."

He tapped the top of the control console as he thought. "With the two children to carry the disease to the Aesir, and with control of the local government and law enforcement, we will be able to finish the tunnel to the river and deploy the contact modules. We will be able to penetrate the computer's defenses and bypass the command security. We know the computer has an access in the cave, but the dimensional fold make contact difficult. We will need time to confirm a breakthrough of the security. We will move our ship on Jotunheim back to the location above the computer and go through the tunnels once we have control." He looked at Hrolfr. "And once we have access, you can turn your creatures loose to feed upon the humans at their leisure. This world will be yours to play with."

Hrolfr smiled in return. "It will be good to have a world to experiment with again," he said. "There are many things I would like to try that will expand the abilities of a creature under our command. But the failure rate will be high until I can perfect my implant methods. A world of such creatures will give me ample subjects for experimenting."

Bor laid a hand on the shoulder of the trainer. "You have done much for us in the past. I expect your future experiments to be just as successful." He turned toward the table and watched Loki squirm, his mouth open in a silent scream. "Finish with the Aesir. We will need him for the final assault." He looked back at Hrolfr. "And prepare yourself for a world at your feet, ready to serve you."

"As you command," Hrolfr answered. He turned back to the controls and Loki arched in pain.

"Gently. Gently, my friend," Bor said. "Don't break him." He laughed as he looked at the Aesir. "Yet!"

And the two Vanir joined in laughing at the squirming victim on their table.

* * *

The launch of the Vanir weather probes was hidden deep inside a late season thunder storm. The three small satellites flew into the upper atmosphere and hung deep in the jet stream. Between them, they build a web of energy that filtered the stream and changed its temperature, while directing its movements as well. Normally, high and low pressure system across the continent below would have determined the flow of air across the continent. But with the devices of the Vanir in place, the stream's path was altered. What had been a balmy winter in the

Northeast United States up until the middle of December suddenly dropped in temperature to well below freezing. Nobody suspected anything out of the ordinary at first, since there had been winters like this in the past. And when snow fell the week before Christmas, the only reaction was pleasure from many people at a traditional holiday.

But the snow kept coming. By the time schools closed for the year-end holiday, everyone was glad to keep the students off the highways.

Many businesses had closed for a day or two to permit road crews to plow the growing mounds of snow. In many places, front end loaders took the snow from massive piles pushed into convenient places and loaded the snow into dump trucks for removal to someplace less problematic for traffic. Local governments restricted dumping the snow into rivers and streams, since the snow tended to freeze immediately and cause massive blockages in the water flow. The first overflow of the Lehigh River turned a large section of Easton into a skating rink as the water poured out into the streets and froze solid in the below zero temperatures. A bridge further up the river collapsed after snow dumped in even further upstream turned into icebergs and slammed into the supports, cracking them and twisting the road surface above into a checkerboard of holes and cracks. The resulting traffic congestion was annoying but not deadly, although it took quick work by rescue crews to free several trapped people before their cars slipped from the road surface into the icy water below.

State governments all up and down the eastern seaboard declared a state of emergency in their area, limiting travel to essential vehicles and emergency crews. Schools were closed for the duration of the weather pattern. Meteorologists poured over satellite photos of the weather and tried to predict when the weather would break. But every predicted date of change they made passed without a single degree increase in temperature.

The only good thing to come out of the discussion, from the point of view of some scientists, was an end to the complaints about global warming. As the cold winds continued across the Atlantic Ocean from North America, more and more of the world felt the drop in temperature. News crews in the Sahara Desert filmed a six-inch snowfall for the first time in recorded history. Ecologists across the world warned that plants all along the equator would start dying soon if the temperature did not begin to rise. Tropical plants were more used to temperatures in the eighties and nineties on the Fahrenheit scale, than the swiftly dropping temperatures outside. There were concerns that some traumatic shift in the temperature was the cause for the beginning of a new Ice Age. But no cause could be found.

The Vanir satellites continued to shift the flow of the jet stream as well as lower the temperature of the air. Very soon, most of the world would be covered by a slowly moving glacier, which was exactly what the Vanir had planned.

The legends had come true. Fimbulwinter had come to Midgard. The time of Ragnarok was at hand!

Chapter Ten

Tommy waved goodbye as Mr. Johnson pulled away from the entrance to the dwarves' compound. He turned to the wall of snow and pulled his scarf tighter across his face. At the side of the entryway, a tall pole held a small rectangular box and Tommy pushed the button at the bottom of the box. It was less than a minute before a dwarf voice answered.

"Who is?" the dwarf questioned.

"It's Tommy and it's getting pretty cold out here. Open the door," he called out through his scarf.

The laugh of the dwarf cut off as the circuit closed and a doorway opened in the wall of snow. Tommy stepped inside and waited for a minute for the door to close before he pulled the scarf off his face and draped it around his neck. As the lights came on in the snow tunnel, Tommy walked over to the beginning of the entry slideway. A huge wheel stood at the end of two tunnels, with a cable leading down both passages. Tommy knew the procedure and stood on a section of carpeting at the entrance to the left tunnel and grabbed the cable.

"Okay. I'm ready," he called out.

There was a hum of machinery and the wheel started to turn slowly. As he hung on to the cable, Tommy started to slide along the floor of the tunnel. He gained speed as the cable started to move faster, until Tommy was moving fast enough for his scarf to flap in the breeze of his passage. Less than two minutes later, he reached the end of the mile long tunnel and let go of the cable. He slid across the floor and grabbed onto one of the poles set in the snow for travelers to use as brakes. He managed to stay on his feet again, since he had used this mode of transportation for several weeks now.

"Hey, Tommy," Suori called from the side tunnel leading to the workshop. "Good slide this time. Stay on feet again. Pretty soon you be as good as dwarf in the tunnels. Then we give you pick and shovel and put you to work."

"No thanks, Suori," the boy answered as he set his pack straight. "I'll stick to working on that Norn stuff with Vili." He looked up at the tunnel roof. "What are you going to do when the snow melts in spring? You'll need something to slide on other than packed snow."

Suori held a finger along his nose and winked. "Dwarves have idea. Use same cable and pathways we have now and use small boards with wheels we see at trading place. Young people ride them everywhere. No reason dwarf not do same."

"Hey, that's a good idea," Tommy said. "But you'll need a bigger skateboard than the kids use. You guys are a lot heavier."

Suori shrugged. "No problemo, kemo sabe. Vili say he can make easy. Maybe you help?"

"I don't see why not," Tommy agreed. "We can probably whip up a bunch of them with Mimir's help in a day or so." He paused and thought for a moment. "Maybe Mimir has something that will work better than wheels so you don't have to pave the driveway."

"Already have something, Vili say," Suori stated. "Put strip down on pathway and board stay above with this much space between," he said as he held his fingers a few inches apart. "That way not dig into ground and keep travelers on pathway. Board only work above strip."

"Sounds like a plan," Tommy said. "Well, I better get to work before Vili thinks I don't want to come any more."

"No problem. He know you here."

Suori pointed up to the corner of the tunnel room and Tommy saw a small tube pointed at him.

"Hey, you got the security system running. That's great." Tommy looked up at the small tube. "And it's barely noticeable. That will help a lot." He looked over at Suori. "You have them all around yet or just here at the tunnel?"

Suori waved a hand. "All over. Make sure Vanir not come close that we not see them. This winter good to hide Giants. Dwarves not want to go back to Jotunheim and dig in tunnels. If going to dig, would rather dig on Asgard."

"I'm sure Sudri would be glad to have you there." Tommy looked up at the camera and waved. "I better get to the workshop and get to work. Vili said something about a special surprise today."

"Okay. Go play with Norn toys. Build good stuff to fight Vanir." Suori waved back and strode off down another tunnel in the direction of his home.

Tommy shook his head. All those centuries living underground and the first thing the dwarves did when they had a chance was build tunnels to get from one place to another. He headed down the tunnel to the workshop and opened to the door to the heated building. A small entry-way protected the inside from the weather and Tommy made sure the outside door was well closed before opening the inside door. He knocked the remaining snow off his boots and pulled a pair of sneakers out of his pack before he sat down to change his footgear.

"Greetings, young Norn," called a voice from deep inside the room. "When you are properly attired, come back to the large work area and see what we will be working on today."

"Okay, Vili. Be right there."

Tommy slipped off his boots and pulled on his sneakers, slipping the fastenings closed with a quick pull. Then he stepped into the silvery suit hung by the door and fastened the closures at wrist and ankle. A quick touch of the front sides together closed the suit to protect him from spilled caustic materials, burns and the occasional energy flare. Then he stepped quickly between the tables and headed for the work area. No running in this workshop, he had learned the hard way. Vili was just as demanding an instructor as Mr. Johnson, and just as fair. But he had his rules and he expected them to be followed.

As he passed through the open area of the workshop, Tommy saw new boxes piled on most of the tables. One box held several rows of silver-gray spheres that looked like the web grenades Eric had brought back from Mimir. Another box held a dozen or so of swords Tommy suspected had the same ability to cut through anything on this planet as the one now hanging over Mr. Johnson's mantle piece. That sword was a souvenir of the rescue of Mrs. Johnson and Vili.

The large number of new boxes meant the dwarves had finished setting the crystals for the new gateway to Mimir. The connection Tommy and Dwalin has set up on top of the ridge, when Eric returned from Jotunheim with the dwarves and the great wyrm, Fornir, was fine for large deliveries that needed room. But for day-to-day stuff, the dwarves suggested a new connection here in their village. Since the Giants had already set up one connection to Jotunheim, which they had used to escape after Eric and several hundred dwarves dropped in on their plan to capture or kill Odin, Thor and Loki, the dwarves merely retuned the crystals to go to a different part of that dimension. As a result, they now had a direct line to Mimir and all the supplies aboard the command ship.

Tommy reached the edge of the large hanging tarp that protected the area of the workshop used for energy related projects. A tall Aesir stepped around the end of the barrier and smiled at him.

"Welcome, young Norn," Vili said to the boy.

They greeted each other in the Aesir manner, grasping wrists rather than hands, and Vili thumped Tommy on his right shoulder with his free hand.

"I had thought you would bring your companion today," Vili stated. "I still have not properly thanked Eric John's Son for my rescue from the Vanir. We have spoken only briefly since my return and I still owe him a weregilt."

"Weregilt? What's that?" Tommy asked.

Vili stepped back and looked down at the boy for a moment, then nodded. "I forget that you were not raised with the same customs as the Aesir." He leaned back against one of the tables lining the room and frowned. "Weregilt has many forms and as many names. A strict translation might be something like 'blood price.' One can incur weregilt if their life is saved by another, or if some great deed is done that benefits another person, or an entire community, should the deed be great enough." He shook his head for a moment. "But there is also a darker side to weregilt. Taking the life of a warrior can incur weregilt from the warrior's family or followers. Or taking a life outside of fair combat incurs weregilt to the survivor. Many warriors have spent their lives running from weregilt. Some of those warriors ran from nothing at all, since there was no weregilt to face other than their own belief. In other cases, the weregilt chased them from planet to planet."

"Kind of like what was happening between the Aesir and the Vanir," Tommy suggested.

Vili nodded. "In truth, much like our battle with the Vanir. The Vanir have incurred weregilt from so many lands, so many planets, that they have little room left for their own people. They travel the spaceways, hoping to find a planet where they can rebuild their race. But the Aesir have sworn that such a rebuilding will not take place. And that is why we fight here, to save Midgard."

"Well, that certainly explains why you guys are fighting each other," Tommy stated.

"But it does not explain why you are without your companion, Eric," Vili answered.

Tommy shrugged. "They've closed the schools for the holidays and because of the weather. Kind of like two birds with one rock. So Odin though it might be a good idea for Eric and Stephanie to come to Asgard for a scan of their bodies, to make sure all the Vanir bugs are out of their system. They'll only be a couple of hours on Asgard, but with the time difference it will be about a week here on Earth. This is the first chance Odin had to take them to Asgard without them missing a bunch of school and causing a lot of questions. He had enough trouble cleaning up after Thor ran the two of them through the machine at the hospital. There were a lot of confused doctors after that day, let me tell you."

"So, I have you all to myself today," Vili said with a grin.

"Um, well, yeah, I guess so," Tommy answered. "Is that a good thing or a bad thing?"

"I will let you decide which it is," Vili answered, his smile growing wider. "I promised you a special project today, and it is here for your labor."

"Um, okay." Tommy still wasn't sure what the Aesir had in mind. "Is this going to hurt?"

"No more than our other projects have pained you," Vili answered.

"Yeah, well some of those left me too sore to walk for a couple of days," Tommy said, rubbing his shoulder. "And my arms weren't too good for a while either."

Vili laughed. "Come, young Norn, and see your future in combat."

"Uh, okay," was all Tommy could say as Vili took him by the shoulders and led him around the end of the tarp.

On the other side of the barrier, eight tables had been lashed together by twos, edge to edge. But it was what was on the tables that immediately drew Tommy's eyes. Lying across all eight tables was a metal giant. The shiny forms of its limbs stretched at least fifteen feet, and the arms and legs were articulated like a suit of armor. The strangest part, from where Tommy was standing, was that there was no head to the creature, if that's what it was. All that sat on the shoulders was a hump of metal, like a small dome.

"Wow, what's that? A suit of Vanir battle armor?" Tommy walked closer and reached out a hand, but stopped and looked back at Vili before he touched the amazing construction.

"It will not bite," Vili assured him. "All power systems have been deactivated while we repair much of what is left."

"What it is?" Tommy asked again.

"Your suggestion of battle armor is almost correct," Vili answered. "This is the latest generation of Aesir ground combat augmentation. The warrior slides inside this unit and gains not only a height to match that of the largest Vanir, but also gains augmentation of strength and senses. There is an array of sensor units in the dome on the shoulders that gives the warrior inside communication with all battle units as well as the ability to see what is all around him or her. Even to the rear, the warrior now knows what threat approaches."

Vili patted the armor suit like he would the shoulder of an old friend. "Loki and I wore this type of armor when we went down to rescue the dwarves. There were three of us that day who went ahead of the main force, so the dwarves would be ready to leave when the Aesir attacked. Our job was to clear the way for the dwarves while the rest of the Aesir kept the Vanir occupied in battle. The Vanir had no suspicion the real purpose of our mission was the rescue of Suori's people. They could not believe Aesir would die in battle trying to rescue mere creatures of another race."

"Yeah, the Giants have a couple of blind spots," Tommy said. He moved toward the table and looked at the articulated form lying there.

"So this gives you super strength and lets you know what's going on all around you. Does it fly, too?"

Vili laughed. "No, my young friend. It does not fly. But the addition of an Aesir flight unit would be no great task." He smiled at the young boy. "Would it please you to aid in restoring this unit? I had thought it lost after the battle to rescue Suori, but Mimir had it placed in storage while we were aflight. When the dwarves started to bring supplies here from the ship, Mimir sent this with the other materials."

"That's right, Tommy," a voice said from the corner of the work area.

Tommy spun around.

"Mimir! How did you get here?" he asked. "I thought you were still on Jotunheim!"

"And so I am, young Norn," the computer answered. "I asked the dwarves to place a transfer unit at the local gate juncture, and that gives me access to this compound. I also have a communication unit at Enigma Caverns. I have smaller units for your use and for you to pass to Eric John's Son, as well as a small unit for Stephanie Robert's Daughter, so we may all stay in close communication."

"Hey, that's great. Kind of our own personal walkie-talkies," Tommy said. "And I could talk to the dwarves and Vili on it as well, right?"

"Indeed so," Mimir answered. "We believe we will need to be in close communication. The Vanir certainly plan something soon. We must be ready to stop them and we can only do that if we are prepared and if we can quickly communicate with each other."

"Can the Giants break into this communication system?" Tommy asked.

Vili shook his head. "Both the Vanir and the Aesir have their own communication systems and neither have been able to break into the others' system in all the time we have been fighting. Although this is something we still work on, and you will be aiding me in the search for a way to listen to the Vanir transmissions."

"Okay. At least that is one good thing, to be able to talk and not have the Giants hear stuff." Tommy looked back at the battle armor. "So what else does this do?" he asked Vili.

The Aesir laughed. "Come, my young friend. Time we work on defeating the Vanir."

He led Tommy to the top of the metal skeleton and gave the dome a quick twist to remove the helmet. "This is the sensor dome and contains all the information connections down into the rest of the suit. Here is what I need you to do . . . "

Tommy and Vili both leaned over the battle suit and began to work. Tommy used Aesir instruments to trigger the sensors so Vili could test the results further down in the unit, then used Tommy as a test subject inside the suit to make certain all the neural connections were working properly. By the time they were through the morning hours, both Vili and Tommy were tired and sweating. The two turned at the sound of a door opening in the workshop on the other side of the tarp and Vili looked at the monitors to see who had entered. Tommy was strapped into the skeleton and unable to turn his head far enough to see the screen, since they were checking neural feeds to the armor's arms when the sound stopped them.

"Norns work hard but need to take time to eat," came Suori's voice from behind the tarp. The dwarf walked around the end of the partition with a large tray of various fruits and meat on platters. The dwarf had made the trip from the communal kitchen fast enough the meat still steamed in the cool air of the workshop.

"Hi, Suori," Tommy called from inside the suit. He raised the right arm of the suit and waved to the dwarf.

"Ho, get battle armor working well," Suori answered as he set the tray on an empty table. "Good that you do. Might be needing to fight Vanir soon if Odin and Mimir find place Vanir hiding."

"We're getting there," Tommy answered.

Vili helped unfasten the neural connections of the suit and Tommy climbed out and jumped down to the floor. He stretched to work out the kinks from lying in the armor all morning.

"Jeez, just testing that stuff works up an appetite," Tommy said.

"But it was a good morning's work," Vili stated. "And I could not have made the progress I did without your aid, young warrior." He laid a hand on Tommy's shoulder. "I value your skill and you grow wise in the ways of the Norns. You will be a warrior to be feared when you reach your full growth."

"As long as I don't have to fight any Giants before I get bigger," Tommy answered. "Right now I couldn't do more than kick one in the ankle and pray he doesn't fall on me."

"A small blow at the right time may have more effect than the largest weapon used too soon or too late," Vili said.

"That's sounds like something Sensei would say. Eric's uncle used the same sort of confusing comments when he's trying to sound like an old master."

"Albert's John's Son is not old in terms of years but he has gained much wisdom, I have found," Vili said.

"Right," Suori added. "Could not have found place for all dwarves to live without his help." He waved a hand around to indicate the entire compound. "Now dwarves have nice home with plenty of room and many friends. Much better than Jotunheim."

"Well, that wouldn't take much," Tommy suggested. "But I agree, Mr. Johnson is a smart man. I just wish sometimes—"

Tommy sentence was buried under the scream of an alarm.

The three turned toward the monitors Vili set up to watch the cameras set all around the compound. As they watched, six screens flashed with movement as Mimir sounded the alarm throughout the dwarf village.

"They are attacking," the computer called out to the three in the workroom. "The hounds of the Vanir are here and Fenrir leads them."

On the center screen, Tommy saw the form of the huge wolf, genetically altered by the Vanir as one of their helpers here on Earth. Tommy remembered the story Eric told about meeting Fenrir the day he, Thor and Loki had stormed the skinheads compound and the battle they fought with the feral dogs led by Fenrir. It looked like the wolf had gathered all the dogs that had recently attacked Enigma Caverns and brought them here to attack the dwarves.

Tommy looked at the screen and a cold wave of fear washed through him.

"Oh, crud," was all he could think to say.

Chapter Eleven

Vili grabbed a staff from the side of the doorway and followed Suori out into the main area of the compound at a run.

"Stay inside," he said to Tommy.

Tommy walked over to the monitors and watched as the dogs swept into the compound and rolled over the few dwarves outside in the frigid weather. Fenrir stood in the center of the open area and howled commands to his pack. The huge form of Fenrir dwarfed even these genetically enhanced dogs, and as Tommy watched, the dogs started to dig at the snow covering the doorways of the buildings. But the dwarves were not idle. The short, solid rock dwarves looked like children against the dogs, but there were many more of them and they swarmed the beasts. The dwarves' attack pushed the dogs back from the doorways. A half-circle of armed defenders at least three thick surrounded each door and the dwarves swung ax and war hammer with fearful effect. The dogs were fast, and dodged most of the dwarves' swings. But the few times the dwarves connected with a dog, it went down and lay still, unconscious or dead. Tommy couldn't tell.

Fenrir looked from doorway to doorway, directing the dogs with howls and growls. Tommy watched the giant wolf. It seemed Fenrir was looking for something, but the boy could not guess what it might be. Then a break in the fighting opened the area around the door outside the workshop. Vili stood at the front of the circle, his staff whirling in his hands like a six-foot sword, building a web of blows all around him to keep the dogs back from the door.

Fenrir saw the Aesir and howled again. At the command, the battle shifted and the dogs focused on the door to the workshop.

"Now, slave, our masters will have you back in your pen as you deserve," Fenrir called to Vili.

"Never!" Vili screamed in answer. "Never will I return to that foul hell-hole. Death will take me first."

"This, too, can be arranged," Fenrir replied. The wolf howled and the dogs surged forward, attacking the dwarves in a frenzy to reach Vili.

Tommy watched the battle rage in the compound and wished he could help his friends. But he knew that while he was making progress in his fighting skills, he was far from being the kind of warrior needed for this type of battle. His own abilities would be about as effective as throwing snowballs at the dogs.

"Snowballs! That's it!:

He dashed around the corner of the tarp and pulled a box of metal spheres from one of the tables. Then he looked around.

"Something to throw them with," he muttered. "Don't want to get too close." He knew his own throws would force him get too close to the dogs, and he didn't have the rock dwarves' hard skin or Vili's speed and skill with weapons to defend himself.

He raced back around the tarp and looked through the materials he and Vili had been using earlier in the morning. He remembered seeing a lever arrangement . . . ah, there it was. He reached down and grabbed a part of an arm assembly he and Vili had replaced from the metal giant on the table. Something in the gearing had jammed and the arm "spasmed" each time the servomotors were triggered. The end result while it was still attached to the shoulder was the arm slamming back into the chest like an open hand slap.

But if Tommy pointed it in the right direction, it would also act like a catapult. He grabbed the arm and his pack and went back to the spheres. He slipped a tray of the balls into his pack, and slipped the pack onto his shoulders. Then he picked up a second tray and slid a covering across the top to hold them in, picked up both the second tray and the metal arm and raced up the stairs to the second floor of the workshop. He quickly found the windows looking out on the open area. He was high enough that the snow had not piled up to this level, but the packed drifts made a slippery ramp up to the opening. He knew he had to be careful or the dogs would be in through this window and have him for lunch. Not a good thought. But he had to do his part to help the dwarves and Vili.

He dragged a table over to the window and laid out his equipment. His work with Vili had ingrained fast and efficient work habits, which were already a benefit at school. But today it would help his friends. Tommy pulled the spheres out of his pack and set them aside for the moment. Then he pulled out a few tools he carried all the time, now that he was doing so much work with Vili.

He laid the arm on the table and oriented it so when the "muscles" were triggered, it would throw out of the window. He looked around for something to anchor the arm to the table but all that was in the room were boxes of Aesir equipment and clothing. There might be something in one of the boxes to help, but he didn't have time to search. Then he remembered something else and reached into the bottom of his pack and pulled out a roll of duct tape. He quickly ripped off several strips to hold the arm down, grinning at the story he would tell Eric about this one! They kept joking that duct tape could fix anything, and now Tommy added one more story to the list. It took almost half the roll before Tommy was satisfied the arm would stay in place when activated.

With the arm anchored down, Tommy opened the window carefully. The smooth operation of the window made little noise and the battle in the compound covered a lot more than Tommy made. The fighting had moved away from the door as the dogs drew Vili away from the doorway and into the open. The Aesir and dwarves were now ringed by dogs, who dodged in and out of the massed warriors to reach Vili. But the dogs were beat back by the swings of ax and hammer and the whirling staff of Vili.

Tommy hadn't been in many fights before, if you didn't count a couple of kids in school who picked on him before he started to travel with Eric. But he could see that Vili was totally caught up in the fight. The Aesir was screaming at the dogs and at Fenrir, and he surged forward to reach the wolf and attack him directly. But Fenrir dodged as well, and used Vili's own movements to direct the battle out into the open where the dogs' speed would be more effective. For the moment, the battle was a stalemate, but Tommy could hear Fenrir's howls as he gave new directions to his pack.

Tommy laid out the spheres in their trays next to his improvised catapult. He took one of the medium-sized spheres and laid it in the palm of the hand, then stood to the side and reached into the arm with a slender probe. With a gentle push, he triggered the arm and it "spasmed." But the movement threw the ball out of the palm and up into the air. Only a fast catch by Tommy prevented the ball from impacting the floor and filling the room with webbing, which would have effectively ended Tommy's part in this battle. He laid the ball back in the tray and muttered a few choice phrases he had heard from Vili, usually when he hit his hand with a tool while they worked, which the boy's mother would have been appalled to hear from her son.

He picked up the roll of tape and quickly formed the fingers into more of a cup, then held them in place with the tape. He carefully laid the sphere back in the hand, stood to the side, and inserted the probe. This time the arm worked and the ball arced out into the compound. Tommy had aimed the arm to the side of the battle, where there were only dogs and no dwarves. The ball landed on the ground and burst with a pop to cover one dog and part of another in webbing.

"Yes!" Tommy hissed to himself. He didn't want to call out and call attention to the open window if he could help it. He carefully loaded another ball into the hand and fired again, with a similar effect.

It only took four shots with the catapult for Fenrir to realize he was losing pack members to some new threat. The great wolf looked around the compound and spied the open window just as another ball shot out to capture more of the dogs. He howled a command and three dogs broke off from the battle and raced across the snow. They started up the packed drift toward Tommy.

"Oh, crap," Tommy said as he saw the dogs move up the packed snowdrift.

Their claws dug into the packed snow and ice and slid with every step, but they were moving father forward than back with each step. The dwarves were too far away to help, and Tommy's only other option was to close the window and keep the dogs out. But that would mean he would be unable to help Vili and the dwarves. That was not an option. He pulled the table away from the window and grabbed one of the spheres in each hand as he moved around the barrier. He stuck his head out of the opening and the dogs howled as they saw their prey appear.

With a quick toss, Tommy threw one sphere against the dog in front. At that range even he couldn't miss. The ball impacted against the dog's chest and the webbing exploded out to catch the front paw of the next dog to the right along with his target. Tommy shifted the second sphere to his right hand and threw it. He caught the second dog in the side and now both dogs were wrapped tightly in webbing. He reached back for another sphere as the third dog howled and lunged forward, almost to the edge of the window. As Tommy turned back to the opening, a hairy snout appeared and fierce jaws opened to bite down on whatever was available of the boy.

Tommy triggered his Aesir shield, a bracelet given him by Thor that opened into a circular buckler of Aesir steel. He slammed the shield into the dog's face with all the weight of his body behind it. It was enough to knock the dog loose from his grip on the icy snow and make him slide back several feet. Before the dog could get a better grip, Tommy slammed the sphere at the dog and the webbing enveloped the beast and threw it back into its companions. The three dogs wrapped in webbing effectively blocked the way up to Tommy's open window. He smiled and pumped an arm in success, then moved away from the window to push the table back into position.

He had the range now, and knew the direction the arm would throw. With careful precision, Tommy worked spheres back and forth across the edges of the crowded battle, capturing at least one dog with each throw. As the number of dogs started to thin to the point where a group of dwarves circled each one, Vili moved toward Fenrir. The Aesir swung the staff in a steely arc, back and forth in front of the wolf. Fenrir dodged in to attack, then drew back quickly as the staff slammed down toward him. Back and forth, the two warriors worked their way around the open compound, until they were right below the window where Tommy watched the combat. Tommy pulled the table away, since the combatants were too close together to use the catapult, and stepped closer to watch the fight. Suddenly, Vili slipped on the ice as he swung the staff again at the giant wolf. Fenrir darted in and took hold of the staff in his enhanced jaws, as Vili tried to gain his balance. The staff was ripped out of the tall Aesir's hands and Vili slammed down on the ice with a loud crack.

Several dwarves raced to aid Vili and their cries pulled Fenrir to one side, up against the snowdrift below the window. But Vili was now only a few feet from the wolf, and barely conscious from the impact with the ice. Fenrir looked at the dwarves, then down at Vili.

"My masters wished you alive, but they will be satisfied with your blood instead, I think," the wolf growled through bloody jaws. He opened his mouth to snap down and tear the life out of Vili.

"No," Tommy screamed. He jumped up out of the window and onto the drift. He fell to one knee as he hit the slick surface and immediately started to slide toward Fenrir.

The great wolf whipped around. He saw the boy sliding down the bank toward him and casually opened his jaws and waited to end the boy's life at the end of the slide. But Tommy rolled over and slammed a sphere into the open jaws. The webbing exploded across the wolf's face to fill mouth, eyes and nose with the viscous substance. As Tommy hit the bottom of the drift, Fenrir rolled on the ice, unable to do more than grunt in anger as the web held him securely. His army of dogs, those few that were left un-webbed, immediately left the compound at a run, howling in frustration.

Tommy watched as Vili picked up his staff and got to his feet. He walked over to the bound wolf and raised the staff over his head. His face was a mask of rage and Tommy drew back in fear, even though he was not the target.

"No more will the Vanir plague me!" Vili screamed. "No more! No more!"

"Vili, no!" Tommy called out. He scrambled to his feet and moved toward the Aesir.

Vili stopped, his arms shaking in his rage as he wavered between slamming the staff down on Fenrir's head or permitting the wolf to live.

"You can't," Tommy said. He walked up beside the Aesir and laid a hand on his shoulder. "We have him. He's not going anywhere. And you can't just kill him, no matter what he's done. Not like this. Maybe if you killed him while you were fighting. But not like this. That's not the Aesir way."

Vili wavered for another moment. Tommy wasn't certain the Aesir had heard him, but he had to believe Vili wasn't lost in battle madness, or some other kind of madness left over from his time as a Vanir captive. This was one of the things he was supposed to help watch for. And Vili was on the edge of madness, closer than he had been since his recovery from Jotunheim.

With a scream that tore across the compound, Vili spun around and slammed the staff down on the frozen ground. Again and again, he slammed the solid Aesir steel into the frozen earth, and chunks of ice and frozen earth flew away from the impact of the staff. By the time his anger was spent, the staff was bent, which Tommy had never seen happen to battle steel. He shuddered as he thought of the strength, or energy, or pure madness, Vili had released that gave him the power to bend that steel bar. Vili dropped the staff and turned to Tommy. His face was not calm, but the glimmer of madness was gone from his eyes. He reached out his right hand to the boy.

"I owe you thanks, young warrior," Vili said. "Thanks for your aid in battle. Thanks for capturing a great foe of the Aesir," he said as he looked over at Fenrir. Then he looked back at Tommy and smiled. "And thanks for reminding me I am a warrior of the Aesir, and that none control this body but me."

Tommy smiled back and grasped Vili's wrist. "That's what friends are for, Vili. To help each other. You've helped me a lot. I guess it was time to pay back some of it."

"And well you did, my friend," Vili answered. He looked down at the captured wolf. "This great beast reminded me all too well of the time spent in the hands of the Vanir. That is not a place to which I can return." Then he turned toward Tommy. "And you reminded me why that will not be needed. Here among the people of Midgard are warriors the equal of the Vanir. Even the young of this place are warriors the equal of any saga told through the ages. What you have done this day will be a tale worthy of a skald. How a young boy was the bane of the Vanir's greatest tool on this world. What say you to that, Tommy Fenrir's Bane, for that is how you will be known in ages to come."

The crowd of dwarves cheered and waved their weapons in the air. "Fenrir's Bane! Fenrir's Bane!" they chanted.

"Ah, well, um . . . " Tommy looked at the web-covered wolf, chanting dwarves and Vili's smile and shrugged. "What can I say? It seemed like a good idea at the time."

Vili threw back his head and roared in laughter. Then he joined the chant.

"Fenrir's Bane! Fenrir's Bane! Fenrir's Bane!" the warriors chanted.

Tommy just smiled.

Chapter Twelve

Eric slammed his right fist into the heavy hanging bag with a grunt of effort. The bag moved almost eight inches from the blow and Eric shifted his shoulders to slam his left fist into the same spot. The bag did not have time to drop back into position and moved away from the second blow and to the side. Shifting from left to right, Eric slammed blow after blow into the bag and the bag danced from side to side as the energy of the punches shifted the heavy weight. Again and again, Eric struck and each blow was matched by a grunt of effort that grew in volume until it was a scream that echoed thought the basement. Finally, Eric stopped his punches and stood with his arms down at his sides, completely exhausted.

"Feel better?" Uncle Al asked from the doorway to the basement dojo. He leaned against the doorway and watched.

Eric grunted an answer and started to kick the bag with the same intensity as his punches. Kick after kick slammed into the bag and Eric kept up his attack, as if the bag was every enemy he had ever had in this world, and probably several others, to judge by the passion of his attack.

When the last kick bounced off the bag, Eric slumped to the floor, totally exhausted.

"You want to talk about it?" Uncle Al asked as he moved into the room. He pulled out the small stool he kept there to sit on while he watched Eric and Tommy train. He placed it so he could lean against the wall as he sat. Then he just waited for Eric to answer.

The silence grew to several minutes. Eric breathed hard from his efforts, and sweat dripped from his hair, even in the cool of the basement. Finally, he stood again and faced the bag, ready to begin again.

"Shift your right foot a bit counterclockwise," Uncle Al advised. "Your stance is too narrow."

"Is that all you can do?" Eric screamed. "Pick on me and tell me what I'm doing wrong?"

Uncle Al sat for a moment without responding. A flash of pain crossed his face as Eric's comment hit home. Uncle Al stood and walked toward the door. "Let me know if you want to talk," he said over his shoulder.

"Wait," Eric called out.

Uncle Al stopped and turned.

"I'm sorry," Eric said. "I shouldn't have said that. You didn't do anything wrong."

Uncle Al nodded and returned to his seat at the side of the room. Then he waited again.

Eric turned to the bag and started to throw light punches. The bag barely moved as it was hit. Then he stopped and looked at Uncle Al.

"Odin said there was still some Vanir stuff in my system but it's inert," Eric said, still facing the bag. He started to throw light punches again. "He doesn't think it's a problem, but even he admits he's not sure."

"Uh-hmm," Uncle Al murmured in agreement. He had has his own discussion with Odin, with a lot more details than Eric had just stated.

"So I'm still being watched to make sure I don't do anything crazy again." Eric continued to punch the bag, shifting from left to right and from straight punches to backfist strikes to palm strikes.

"Do you mind having Sudri here in the house?" Uncle Al asked quietly.

Eric shook his head. "Sudri's a good guy. He really likes cartoons and old comedy shows. Research, he calls it."

Uncle Al nodded but again did not speak.

"Tommy's a real hero after what he did at the dwarves' compound last week. He's getting to be a real warrior now that he's working with Vili all the time." Eric's punches were harder now, with more emotion behind them.

"Does that bother you, that Tommy is the hero now?" Uncle Al asked.

Eric stopped and looked at his uncle. His face was twisted with anger. "You mean that he's the hero and I'm not? That after all I've done for the Aesir and the dwarves all they can do now is follow after Tommy like he was some kind of superhero? That they keep me penned up in my own house like some kind of caged animal?" Eric spun back to the bag and slammed another punch into the tough leather. The bag moved at least eight inches with the impact. "No, it doesn't bother me at all!"

"Ah," Uncle Al responded. "Good."

Eric spun back toward his uncle. "Good? Is that all you can say? Good?" Eric waved his arms at the walls of the basement. "All this stuff going on. The weather a mess because of who knows what the Giants are doing. Dogs the size of school buses attacking people out of snowstorms. And all you can say is good?"

Uncle Al smiled. "I could say 'very interesting' with a German accent, but I doubt you'd get the reference."

"Jeez, now you're making jokes." Eric spun back to the bag and slammed another fist into the leather. Then he stopped and shook his hand from the pain of the impact.

"Keep your fist tight when you hit," Uncle Al said.

"I know that!" Eric spun again to look at his uncle. "I know what I'm supposed to be doing. I'm supposed to be out hunting Giants, so I can get the rest of this stuff out of my body. So I can be me again!" Eric sank down to the floor and dropped his head on his knees. "So I can be me," he sobbed.

110

"Ah, so that's what's bothering you," Uncle Al said softly. He got up from the stool and walked over to Eric. He sank down to the floor next to the boy and pulled him into a hug. "You're you, Eric. You're still you and you always will be."

"How can you know that?" Eric sobbed into his uncle's shoulder. "How can you know what the Giants have done to me?"

"Do you trust Odin and the Aesir?" Uncle Al asked.

"Yeah. Sure. Of course," Eric said with a sniff. "But this is all new stuff the Giants have built since they've been on Earth. Odin said they didn't know what it did, just that it appeared to be inert." Eric looked up at his uncle. "How am I supposed to know it won't jump out and take over like it did before? And I'll wind up walking in snowdrifts higher than my head this time, instead of just cold weather."

Uncle Al shrugged. "To be honest, you don't know. Nor do I. Nor does Odin. But you can't spend all your time worrying about it or you'll tie yourself up in knots and get nothing done."

"You mean like now?" Eric said with a little laugh.

Uncle Al smiled. "Something like that."

Eric laughed again. He sunk back down onto his knees, his head buried in his arms. "Ah, crap. So now what do I do?"

"Well, my first suggestion would be a shower. You're pretty stinky and Aunt Cindy would prefer something that smells better at the dinner table." He wiped a hand off on his shirt. "And it looks like I might need one, too, after this little session."

"Yeah, okay," Eric said with another sniff. "But what am I supposed to do about this Vanir stuff swimming around in my body?"

Uncle Al shook his head. "I really don't know, Eric. You might try talking to Vili about it. He knows more about what the Giants have been doing recently than anybody else, even if he was in stasis most of the time. Maybe he and Tommy have some suggestions about how to get the stuff out of you without ripping things apart in the process."

"That's a pleasant thought," Eric said. "Gee, maybe I can just empty everything out from inside, pick out the bad stuff and put it all back afterward."

Uncle Al shrugged. "You can try. But I think you might want to wait until you can do better than an eighty-seven on your biology test. Otherwise you might wind up with an eyeball somewhere around your kneecap."

"That might be useful in searching under the bed for loose socks," Eric replied. "But not much help searching for Giants."

"True," Uncle Al agreed.

Eric paused, then looked up at his uncle. "Uncle Al?"

"Hmm?"

"Can we stop the Giants? Can we keep them from getting the stuff from Mimir and going back home to destroy Odin's people? Can we stop them from destroying this planet? And if we can't stop them, what can we do to save some of the people?"

Uncle Al sighed. "All very good questions, Eric. Very good questions. The problem is we're running a bit short of answers." He stood and moved back to the stool and sat. He leaned against the wall and looked back at Eric. "Odin has brought additional sensor units from Mimir to the dwarf compound to help in the search. The units from the ship were designed to be functional in space for a range of several light years, from what he told me. But in the atmosphere of a planet, their range is severely limited. Or, to be more precise, their range and sensitivity is so good that the planet itself gives off too much information. Trying to pick out what might be Vanir influence or machines at work is very difficult. The Aesir, and Vili, and Tommy for that matter, are trying to find a way to locate just the Giant stuff here on Earth. Part of the problem with that is the Giants have been using Earth materials for so long that anything they build on this planet won't register properly on the sensors, and the Giants know that so they have been using Earth stuff more and more, Odin told me."

"Can the police help?" Eric asked. "I mean can they help look for Giants around here, or stuff that doesn't belong, of maybe people doing stuff that doesn't make sense?"

Uncle Al nodded. "Again, all good questions. Part of the problem with that is my contacts with the local police have dried up. Lieutenant Harris has been transferred to another unit in a different part of the state. A promotion, he told me, but more a case of getting him out of the way. I think the Giants know he's worked with us in the past and they want him somewhere else other than close to me and the cave. Unfortunately, that also means the Giants have their own control of the state police, at least at the higher levels. And that also suggests they have infiltrated some of the local government as well."

"When you think about what they did when they tried to close down the cave last year with that fake toxic waste complaint, I guess that makes sense. That they have people in the government and the police, I mean." Eric thought for a moment. "Do you, or does Odin, think they have Giants in place in some of these offices or just people they control? I mean with what they can do to disguise themselves, it could be either."

Uncle Al nodded again. "The Aesir have been running sensors at all the local government buildings, and moving further out into the state with their probes. So far they have not caught one disguised Giant. Which means the people in those places must be controlled by the Giants in some way."

"So how do we find them?" Eric asked.

"We can't," Uncle Al answered. "Not unless they do something that shows they are under the control of the Giants or if we catch them with a Giant."

"Crap," Eric said. "To bad we can't just round them all up and give them a lie detector test or something."

Uncle Al smiled. "Which is the same problem we have trying to round up any type of criminal. In this country, people have the right to privacy and we have to respect that until we are sure they are doing something wrong. Not just suspect, but know they are doing something illegal."

"And I'd bet working with Giants isn't illegal right now," Eric said.

"Not right now," Uncle Al agreed. "But some of what they are doing almost certainly is illegal under other laws than working with aliens from outer space."

"Yeah, I guess we don't have too many laws about working with aliens," Eric said with a laugh. He lay back on the floor and exhaled loudly. "If there was just some way to track them down. If there was something about them that the Aesir could trace. That's what we need to find."

"You figure out a magic spell to find that and the Aesir will make you as much a hero as Tommy is right now," Uncle Al said.

"No magic, Uncle Al. Science. That's what Thor and Loki have been teaching me and what Vili is teaching Tommy." He exhaled again. "But there has to be some way."

"Well, you keep working on that idea and when you get something, let Odin know. In the meantime, how about that shower? You're leaving a puddle on the floor."

Eric rolled over and came up on his knees. Where he had lay was a large damp spot. "Jeez, I'm a mess," he said.

"Just go take a shower and put on clean clothes. Your aunt is making something special tonight: a recipe she got from Sudri's wife, I think."

"From Ioreth? That's going to be something different, all right. Where did she get the ingredients?"

"Sudri brought them back with him the last time he stopped home. I think it's a partial payment for all the chocolate and new spices we've been sending over to Asgard lately. Ioreth thought we might like to try some Aesir recipes."

"Well, that's fair," Eric said. "I remember the last time I ate Ioreth's cooking. I was full for a week."

"Earth time or Asgard time?" Uncle Al asked with a smile.

"Both," Eric said with a smile.

"Well, we'll just have to see if Aunt Cindy can live up to those standards." Uncle Al answered. "Go take a shower."

"Yes, Sensei," Eric said with a bow. He started across the basement for the stairs, then stopped and turned back. "Uncle Al?" he said.

"Yes, Eric."

"Thanks," Eric said. "Just . . . thanks."

"No problem," Uncle Al said in a soft voice. Then he cleared his throat. "Go shower!"

"Yes, Sensei," Eric said, already halfway up the stairs.

Uncle Al shook his head and followed after the boy.

* * *

Behind them on the floor lay a wet patch. As the light went out, the patch shifted in shape. Slowly the moisture came together until it was a single spot the size of a quarter. Just as slowly, the spot moved across the floor and toward the basement and the stairs. The movement of the spot of moisture changed as the spot pulled into a small ball and rolled across the floor. It stopped at the bottom of the stairs, as if listening to the sounds from above, then rolled up the stairs in defiance of any law of gravity known to mankind. At the top of the stairs, the ball stopped. The kitchen was a busy place as Aunt Cindy prepared dinner for the family. Uncle Al stepped into the room and helped move plates and bowls from the counter and stove to the top of the table. A hint of steam from the oven suggested something was baking there as well, but neither of the adults moved in that direction just yet. As the ball waited, Eric and Sudri entered the room and sat down at the table. The rock dwarf had his back to the doorway to the basement, and as soon as he was firmly in his seat and starting to load his plate with the food suggested by his wife, the ball rolled across the floor in his direction. Under the chair, the ball moved from leg to leg, as Sudri's feet waved in the air above. The rock dwarf was just a bit too short for his legs to reach the floor in a normal human chair. But the ball finally stopped its search for direct contact with the dwarf, and rolled up a front chair leg to the seat. There it moved closer to the dwarf and soaked into Sudri's pants with only a small wet spot to show it had ever existed. Sudri scratched his leg as he continued to eat. He felt a wet spot but didn't think much about it. His table manners were not the best in this world, or any other for that matter, and a stray spot of moisture was to be expected from time to time. He finished his meal, complimented Aunt Cindy on her prepa- ration of the foods, even as he praised Ioreth's cooking of the same rec- ipe, and stuffed himself with cookies from the oven as dessert. By the time he went to bed later that night, after he checked on Eric to make sure the boy was securely tucked in, the wet spot on his pants was not even a fragment of thought in the back of his mind. The dwarf sat down to watch late night television with the sound turned low enough not to disturb the Johnson family. He absently scratched his leg as he laughed quietly to himself.

He never noticed the flakes of rock that came off on his hard finger-tips and dusted the seat of the chair. And when he finally fell asleep, he also never noticed that the rock dust gathered itself into a ball and rolled across the floor to his pack, where it waited to be carried to Asgard.

Chapter Thirteen

Loki Odinsson sat at the table and worked on a small piece of electrical apparatus. Using Vanir and Aesir tools, he assembled the small unit and turned a switch. With a shimmer of displaced air, a small globe appeared on the top of the table with several shining points indicating powered units.

"Ah, excellent," the other Aesir in the room stated, looking at the different points of light. "Are you certain these are all the Aesir compounds? We wouldn't want to go looking for friends and find the enemy instead. There seem to be so few of them."

Loki nodded. "It's the different power systems we use than the Vanir." He pointed to the globe as is slowly shifted position to display the full planet. "Because we try not to disturb the environment, or provide something the Vanir could use to locate the encampment, we have only these few units. I'm sure once we escape from this place we can find one of the Aesir sites with no difficulty. And if all else fails, there are always our friends here on Midgard we can hide with until we get word to Asgard."

"Excellent," the other Aesir repeated. "But we better turn that off and hide it until we're ready to leave. We're almost ready to escape this place. We don't need any last-minute errors."

"Agreed." Loki shut down the display. He handed the unit over to the other Aesir and watched as it disappeared inside an air duct low on the floor. With a chair strategically placed in front of the duct, it would take a full and detailed search to locate the unit. Loki looked out the window at the blowing snow and frowned.

"Soon, my friend," the other Aesir said to Loki. "Soon we will be out of this place. Now it is time to rest." He motioned Loki over to the bed and the dark Aesir lay down with uncharacteristic obedience. "Soon," the other Aesir repeated, and Loki dropped off to sleep, locked in Vanir hypnosis.

The other Aesir watched for a moment then turned and went to the locked door of the room. He placed the palm of his right hand against the upper right corner of the door and it clicked and slid aside with a whoosh of displaced air. He left the room with Loki still asleep and stepped into another small room just outside. Once the door to Loki's room was closed, he reached down to his wrist and touched a bracelet. With a shimmer, he changed from a moderately tall Aesir to a much taller Vanir, complete with long white hair and black eyes with no pupils. He stepped through the next door and looked to his left. Bor stood at the wall and looked through a panel into the room where Loki lay on the bed, now asleep.

"He seems well within your control, Aurnir," Bor said, looking at the Aesir asleep on the bed. "How close are you to complete control?"

"Close enough, if we are careful," the Vanir replied. "We have managed to get him to believe I am an Aesir and he does not question that I have been here for so long and know so much, but have not attempted to escape. We have also managed to get him to tell me certain things about the Aesir here in this valley and at the cave." The Vanir smiled. "To borrow a phrase from this world: I have some good news and some bad news."

Bor growled. He knew this would alter his plans. "Very well. Tell me," he said.

"First the bad news. The plan to use the river to journey to Jotunheim and enter behind the guards at the command ship will not work, for two reasons. First the river does travel to Jotunheim, but in an irregular manner. One reason there has been so little sign of passage from that site, even when we were searching the cave for information, is that the junction through the river is variable. We would likely lose most if not all of the Vanir to attempt the passage. It was almost miraculous that the boy managed the passage alive, according to the stories told by Loki."

Bor frowned and nodded. "And the second reason?"

"The river does not lead behind MMR's screens. According to the story the boy told the Aesir, he came out in a cave and was led behind the command ship's screens by the wyrm. We would be no better off than the attempts we made at the pool on Jotunheim."

Bor growled again. The team was almost through constructing the tunnel to the lower reaches of the cave, which he had thought would permit them to access MMR and the command ship. Now all that work was wasted.

"And the good news?" he asked Aurnir.

Aurnir smiled. "There is another access to MMR which will permit us to enter the command ship itself inside all the defenses of the Aesir and without going through any of them."

Bor straightened. "Indeed? And where is this place?"

"At the top of the ridge not far from our old compound," Aurnir answered. "When the boy brought the rest of the dwarves to Midgard from Jotunheim, as well as the last of the wyrms, they created a new gate on the ridge for that purpose. They have maintained that gate as a reserve while they have transferred the main transport unit into the area to our old compound. They retuned the gate that permitted us to escape back to Jotunheim, since it was already tuned to the proper dimension. The gate on the ridge is set to only a few security codes, and Loki's is one of those. It is unlikely they would have altered the code to that gate, since it would require much effort to power the gate and permit access to the command ship by anyone not Aesir. But we have the materials needed to let Loki go through directly inside MMR and access the data banks for us. He will think he is aiding a team of Aesir going home to bring reinforcements for the battle against the Vanir."

"Excellent!" Bor exclaimed. "An entry inside the ship will be even better than our original plan, and to use the Aesir to obtain the knowledge will be a fine jest on Odin One-Eye!" He looked at Aurnir. "How soon can you prepare Loki to escape from here and go through the gate?"

Aurnir paused for a moment in thought. "To be certain he would go through and do what we need, I would suggest not less than two weeks. We will need to let him go through alone, since even with our disguise units, MMR will recognize a Vanir as soon as I would step through the gate. We must be certain he is fully under our control."

Bor nodded. "Well, enough. By now, the disease is loose on Asgard, and we can release the similar disease here on Midgard. By the time you are ready with Loki, the Midgarders will be so concerned with how to save their people, and the Aesir will be so weak, Loki will think if he does not look for help from the home dimension, the battle will be over."

Aurnir nodded. "A good plan. I can easily lead him in that direction with bits of talk from the Vanir guards outside our cell. By the time you are ready for him to escape, we will know where all the pieces are for him to open the gate."

Bor nodded and paced the room as he thought. "We will need to arrange for guards to follow you and keep Loki under the belief we want him here. We will also need to guide him to the ridge and arrange it so only he can go through to MMR. Once he is through and inserts our virus into the command ship, the gate will open for us."

"If I may make a suggestion," Aurnir said. "I have had some time to think on this as I watched the Aesir fall deeper under our control. I believe I have a way that will work."

"Go on," Bor said.

"If we move Loki to someplace else, and tell him we need other machines to help break his security blocks, then fly near the ridge to get to the new site, I can arrange for the flyer to crash near the ridge. All that would be needed is a small team of Vanir to stay on our trail and keep Loki headed toward the gate. I'm certain he would get the idea to use the gate to escape, and if not I can suggest it to him as we grow near. At the appropriate time, I can pretend to be wounded by fire from the guards behind us and force him through the gate to bring back help for me. He will think he needs to move quickly to save me and will pay even less attention than normal to any attempt by MMR to stop him. He will have a data crystal with our viral program and will insert it directly into the computer core. He will think it has information needed to stop us. He will insert the program and within seconds the computer will be ours to command. Its first action will be to stun Loki, then open the gate for us to use, with all the security systems turned off."

Bor considered the plan. "Yes. Good. But we will use Midgard vehicles rather than a flier. It will be less suspicious and less control will be needed. We will release the two children now in storage. With them infected with the disease, we will have them walk through any crowded area and infect as many people as they can. By the time the disease is fully involved in the Aesir, humans will be fully infected all across the state. We will also take the children to other places and spread the disease there as well, so there is no sign this is the central focus of the disease. In fact, we will do that first, so it does not start here. The humans will look elsewhere for the start of the disease and give us even more time to work."

He looked through the window. "When Loki is ready, we will break through the tunnel in the cave and create a diversion. With any Aesir who can still stand in the cave to try and stop us, we will set Loki on the course you have described." He paused and smiled. "An excellent plan.

I will be certain to tell our superiors of your good work when we return home. You will be promoted, perhaps to command your own battle squadron."

Aurnir drew up straight and saluted Bor. "My thanks, Commander. I have always tried to do my best for our people."

"And you have succeeded. Now prepare the children for release. We need to spread the disease as far as we can and that will take time, especially if we release it away from here first." Bor stood at the window and watched Loki sleep. "Soon, dark one. Soon. You will provide us with a doorway home."

* * *

The young boy and girl stood in the center area of the mall, near the escalator leading to the top level. They stood at the edge of the crowd and smiled at the people as they went past, then stepped out to shake hands with as many of them as they could. Both of them wore blue jeans, sneakers, and a deep blue T-shirt with a large snowflake design and crossed skis. The sign behind them stated they were with the new Lehigh Valley Olympic skiing team and were raising money for the next Olympic Games. A lot of folks smiled back as they shook hands with the two children, and more than a few suggested the ski team had done too good of a job asking for snow this year. The children smiled in answer, shook hands, and laughed at the jokes.

After several hours, the boy sighed and turned to the blonde woman seated behind the table.

"How much longer do we have to do this?" he asked.

The woman frowned and tapped on a small keypad sitting on the table in front of her, next to a laptop computer. When she had finished the adjustment, she looked up at the boy and smiled.

"Ready to go for a while?" she asked him.

He straightened as she spoke and smiled back. "Oh, yes. I'm good for a long time yet."

He turned back to the crowd and continued smile and shake hands. The woman looked at the computer and frowned.

"The control should last longer than that," she murmured to herself. She shook her head. "Have to fix that when we get back to base."

After a day at the mall, the two children were very tired when the woman drove them into the large warehouse. As the doors closed behind them, the woman tapped a control on her bracelet and the children immediately dropped unconscious. She tapped another control and the air around her shimmered. Now behind the wheel of the mini-van sat a tall Vanir. He opened the door of the vehicle and stepped out. Aurnir walked up to him.

"It went well?" Aurnir asked.

The Vanir driver shrugged. "These humans are so trusting. The children must have infected hundreds. And by the time they get home and pass it along further, there will be thousands of infected humans here in the valley."

Aurnir nodded. "Good. There have been reports from all across the states about this disease, as well as reports from several other countries. The humans will search for many years before they find the source, if they are not all dead by that time."

Both Vanir laughed and opened the back of the van to transfer the children to gurneys and wheel them off to the lab. They would be kept in stasis until Bor decided where the next outbreak would take place.

* * *

Over the next two weeks, the newspapers and television were full of reports of mysterious outbreaks across the state of some unknown disease. People were told to stay in their houses. Businesses closed down.

Roads and highways filled with snow as the drivers of plows fell ill with the disease. Across the entire Lehigh Valley, and much of the Northern Hemisphere, a blanket of white covered the ground, with almost no movement of any living creature.

Chapter Fourteen

Eric watched as Sudri lay on the bed, barely breathing.

"Isn't there anything we can do?" he asked Uncle Al.

Uncle Al sat on the bed and laid a hand quickly against Sudri's forehead. The rock dwarf was hot with fever, almost at a level that would melt rock, which was not surprising since the dwarf seemed to be part rock. Uncle Al shook his head.

"He really should be on Asgard, since they know more about his people than here on Earth," Uncle Al said. "But Odin said the dwarves on Asgard are just as sick, and so are many of the Aesir. They haven't found any medication that helps the symptoms and Odin is afraid that if the dwarves or the Aesir get any weaker, they'll die. We'll just have to the best we can here for him."

"You know, it's weird this all started on Asgard just after Sudri and Dwalin went back this last time for a visit," Tommy said. "It's almost like they took the disease back with them. But they weren't sick when they went home."

"Incubation period," Uncle Al said. "A lot of diseases have a period of time right at the start when the patient doesn't feel sick, but have the disease and can pass it along to someone else."

"But this isn't like the disease that's affecting the people around here, is it?" Eric asked.

"Actually, it is. And that worries me," Uncle Al answered. He turned and looked at the two boys. "I find it very interesting that the dwarves over at the compound with Vili and the other Aesir who have been tracking the Vanir, are all healthy. Only the dwarves who have been either here or at the cave have been sick. And all the Aesir who are sick can trace their movements back to either here or the cave or both."

"You think Stephanie and I are the reason they're all sick, don't you?" Eric asked in a quiet voice.

Uncle Al nodded. "I do. But I don't think it's your fault. I think this is something the Giants planted in both you and Stephanie to come out later, after we seemed to cure the both of you."

"But Eric's been to the compound with me since he's been sick," Tommy said. "If he has the disease to give to other people, then why aren't those dwarves sick? Or for that matter why aren't you and Mrs. Johnson, or me, or my parents sick? He's been around us a lot since then."

"I have a theory, but I'm not sure how valid it might be," Uncle Al said. "I think whatever the Giants put into Eric to make him sick and left that residual reading when Odin ran his scans, has come out and gone on to Sudri and the rest of the dwarves and Aesir. And I think it's something different than what is making the people around here sick."

"Two diseases?" Eric exclaimed. "You think there are two different things making everybody sick?"

"Makes sense," Tommy said. "Odin said the Aesir don't get sick the way people on this planet get sick. Maybe they have special immune systems or something. Anything the Giants could make that would make Aesir sick, probably wouldn't work on humans. But that means they would need a different way to make people sick, especially in as many places as this thing has popped up."

"The girl!" Eric exclaimed. "That must be how they're getting the disease out to other people. They used the girl to infect me, and the boy to infect Stephanie and now they're using them to make other people sick with a different disease."

"Makes sense, guys," Uncle Al agreed. "Now the problem is figuring out why the Giants are doing this. What could they want that they can get if all the dwarves and Aesir are sick?"

"Mimir," Eric stated. "They want Mimir and the information about how to get back to their home dimension." He looked from his uncle to Tommy and back. "If they get control of Mimir, they not only get what they need to go home, but they can use Mimir to either kill all the Aesir or keep them locked up wherever they want. All of this is just so they can get to Mimir."

"One heck of a diversion," Tommy said. "But it makes as much sense as anything else the Giants have done. But just how can they get to Mimir?"

"The only ways from Earth to Mimir are along Bifrost, which they would have to shift to take them to Jotunheim, the gateway at the compound which is currently the best guarded spot on the planet, the river at Enigma Caverns which gives them just as good a chance of ending up dead, or through the Crystal Chamber at the cave. Maybe we need to get Vili and his team to make sure all those places are as well protected as the Aesir can make them." Eric frowned. "Something about all of this still doesn't make sense to me. The Giants don't care about what they do to people here on Earth, and they already have control of a lot of stuff that would let them get to either Asgard or Jotunheim. So why are they playing around and don't just attack and try and get what they want? Why all this confusion and deception?"

"Odin believes there is a basic flaw in the Vanir mentality, something that has only gotten worse with all the years they have been on Jotunheim and here on Earth," Uncle Al said. "If the Giants just attack and kill everyone in their way, they won't have won by playing by their rules. They have to find a way to do as much damage as possible before they make their play for the computer. Also, Odin thinks the Giants are really afraid of the Aesir, especially since the Aesir have begun to make friends here on Earth. He said something about seeing the same sort of thing on other planets the Vanir attacked in their home dimension. The people on those planets began to fight back and help the Aesir when they arrived and between the two groups—people fighting for their own planet and the Aesir—the Vanir were defeated in every case, except when they completely destroyed the planet. And in those cases, the Vanir lost anyway because they had to destroy what they wanted to keep the Aesir from getting whatever it was on the planet that would have helped them. Odin told me the Vanir have gone sort of crazy since they started playing with their own genetic material, and nothing the Aesir have been able to do has helped so far."

"And the war has gone on for thousands of years, at least here on Earth," Eric said. "They must be crazy to keep a fight going for this long. You'd think they'd either give up or go somewhere else."

Uncle Al nodded. "But Odin thinks the Giants have something planned. He also thinks that whatever the plan is, it includes the weather problems we're having here on Earth, the people getting sick here, and the Aesir and dwarves getting sick on Asgard."

"So what can we try to make Sudri better?" Eric asked.

"I don't know," Uncle Al answered. "His people don't react to antibiotics from Earth, and since the disease was constructed by the Giants to affect both Aesir and dwarves."

"Thirsty," Sudri whispered.

Eric looked at the glass next to the bed. It was empty. He picked it up and started for the door. "I'll get a drink for him."

"I just wish there was more we could do to help him," Tommy said. "This is just as bad as when Eric was sick and he wouldn't let anyone help him."

"I know," Uncle Al said, laying a hand on Tommy's shoulder. "But we're here for him, just like you were here for Eric. Right now, that's all we can do."

They sat for a moment and watched the dwarf as he lay in the bed. Small pearls of liquid formed on Sudri's brow and Tommy wiped the off with a towel.

"Eeww!" Tommy exclaimed as he looked at the towel. It was covered with a fine gray ash.

Uncle Al just shook his head. "It's as if the rock he is made of has begun to dissolve. I'm afraid if we don't do something quick, he'll be in real trouble."

Eric walked back in and moved to the head of the bed. He put the end of a straw in Sudri's mouth.

"Go ahead, Sudri. This should help a bit. It always helps me when I'm sick," Eric said.

Sudri took a suck on the straw. Then, as the liquid passed his tongue and hit his stomach, he gave a stronger drink, then another. Within a few moments, the glass was empty.

"Wow! He was thirsty," Eric said.

"I guess so," Tommy agreed.

"Well, he must have needed it," Uncle Al said.

Suddenly, Sudri seemed to shake. He arms and legs moved, only a small amount, but much more than he had moved in the past several hours. His eyes opened for the first time that morning and he reached a hand up to his mouth.

"Up. Stuff come up. Help!" he said around the hand over his lips.

"The wastebasket, Eric!" Uncle Al exclaimed.

Eric set down the glass on the night table and quickly picked up the wastebasket. He reached the side of the bed next to Sudri just as the dwarf turned toward the floor and opened his mouth.

"Gross," Tommy said.

It was not the most pleasant of sights, but Sudri seemed to dump everything he had eaten for the last two days into the wastebasket.

Finally, the dwarf finished and slumped back to the bed as Tommy handed him the towel to wipe his mouth.

"I guess you need some more to drink," Eric said. Then he looked at the wastebasket. "And I think we want this out of here." He left the room with the wastebasket at arm's length.

"Feel better," Sudri said. He looked at Tommy and Uncle Al. "How long been sick?"

"About two days," Uncle Al answered. "And we were worried about you."

Eric came back in and handed Sudri another glass with a straw. "Here. Try and keep this down a while longer this time."

Sudri sipped through the straw then lay back on the bed and sighed, the glass propped on his blanket covered chest. "Feel much better now. Good medicine. Maybe get some for other dwarves?"

"What was in that glass, Eric? Sudri does seem to have made an amazing recovery." Uncle Al laid a hand on the dwarf's forehead. "His fever's lower than before, and in only a few minutes."

Eric shrugged. "Ginger ale, that's all. The stuff you get from some local guy made the old way with real ginger and stuff, you said. Aunt Cindy gave me some the other day and I seemed to feel a lot better afterward. But I did spend a bit of time in the bathroom. Not like Sudri did, just had to sit for a while was all."

"Could it be that simple," Uncle Al said, more to himself than to the boys. He looked at Eric. "What did you do with the wastebasket? I need to check something."

Eric looked down at the floor. "Well, I knew we'd really need to clean it good before we brought it back up here, so I just set it on the back porch for now so I could get back up here with the drink for Sudri."

"Good. I'll be right back." He left the room at almost a run.

Eric and Tommy looked at each other and both shrugged. Sudri sipped on the straw of the glass on his chest.

"Good stuff," he said. "Real good stuff. What is?"

"Just a soda we have around here. Actually we have it a lot of places," Eric said. "It helps settle your stomach when you don't feel so good, which is why Aunt Cindy gave me some. But I've never seen it work like it did on you. And not so fast either."

Sudri sipped again and smiled. "Real good stuff," he repeated.

Uncle Al walked back on the room. "Gentlemen, I think Eric may have just hit on the cure we need," he said.

"You're kidding?" Eric asked.

"No. Actually, in a strange sort of way, it makes sense," Uncle Al said. He picked up the now-empty glass from Sudri and held it aloft. "This drink, well the drink that was in here, is made from a plant that probably doesn't grow on Asgard. And since the Aesir and the dwarves don't really drink soda and other sorts of stuff from here on Earth, they probably haven't had any before now."

"I noticed the dwarves seem to drink of lot of milk, water, fruit juice and some alcoholic stuff, and not a lot else," Eric said. "So what's special about ginger ale?"

"The ginger, actually," Uncle Al said. "The medicinal properties of ginger have been known for some time here on Earth. The Eastern healers have been using ginger in many forms for years to heal a variety of illnesses. The ginger ale I buy is from an old Pennsylvania Dutch recipe, one that I prefer to the newer, more commercial varieties. That means it has more ginger in it that the other stuff. I think something in the ginger reacts with the stuff the Giants created and neutralizes it."

"Neutralizes? You sure you don't mean blows it out of the water, or maybe out of the body!" Tommy exclaimed.

"Not a bad description," Uncle Al agreed. "I have a feeling that this might be the key to helping the Aesir and the dwarves, and maybe our people as well. But I'm going to try a bit of an experiment first."

"You're not going to give Sudri the disease again, are you?" Eric asked.

"No. Nothing like that," Uncle Al assured him. "I'll call Bob Fuller and suggest he either give Dwalin some ginger ale, if he has it, or maybe some ginger tea. Stephanie's mother is a pretty good cook and I'm sure she has some powdered ginger in her spice rack. If that works, it will be a simple matter to get some ginger to Asgard and cure all the Aesir and the dwarves."

"Which assumes it will work on the Aesir as well as the dwarves," Eric said. "How do we know the medicine will work for them? They're two completely different people!"

"Because of what you said about what happened when your aunt gave you the ginger ale," Uncle Al said. "You had to go sit in the bathroom for a while after you drank the ginger ale. That probably means that since this is a created disease, it's similar enough in form that the ginger affects all the different types of it, not just the one that makes the dwarves sick." He turned and headed out of the room. "I'll be back soon," he said over his shoulder.

"Eric help dwarves again," Sudri said. "And help Aesir. Odin be very pleased."

"Yeah, well, it was just a lucky break," Eric said. "Don't make a big deal about it."

"Is big deal. But Giants not be too pleased with Eric," Sudri warned.

"Aw, crap. Here we go again," Tommy whispered.

"No kidding," Eric agreed. "All we need now is for the Giants to come looking for me to take me out of the picture."

"At least we'll know where they are," Tommy said.

"You're not helping this," Eric said to his friend.

Uncle Al walked back in with the cordless phone in his hand. "Bob should call back soon. I warned him he better have a bucket handy after he gives Dwalin the drink. Hopefully this will be the answer we need."

"Hope so too," Sudri said. "Not want wife Ioreth to be sick anymore."

"I just need to see where I can get enough ginger . . . " Uncle Al was interrupted by the phone. He hit the button and raised it to his ear. "Bob?" he asked, then paused to listen. He smiled at the boys and Sudri and nodded his head. "That's great. Give him a little more and he should settle down soon. That's what happened with Sudri. By the way, do you know any place we can get a lot of powdered ginger, or a lot of the good ginger ale from the old Dutch recipe?" He paused again. "You do? That's great. Give him a call and see if I can swing past and pick up a couple of cases of both. We need to get this to Asgard as soon as we can."

He listened again as Mr. Fuller spoke. "Yes, I think that's a good idea. We think that a dose of ginger to our people works to either give a cure or like a vaccine. Make sure Stephanie drinks some especially, but be ready for her to spend some time in the bathroom." He listened again. "Okay. I'll swing past then get it over to the dwarves so they can send it to Odin with some instructions. Talk to you soon."

He clicked off the phone and looked at the other three in the room. "It worked for Dwalin, too," he said with a smile. "And Bob knows where we can get a supply of both powdered ginger and some of the good ginger ale. A friend of his has a health food store in Hamburg. That will make it easy for me to pick up the supplies and get it over to the dwarves' compound to take to Asgard, especially with the way driving is right now." He looked down at Sudri. "How are you feeling? Up to some travel? You are the best one here to take the stuff to Asgard."

Sudri threw back the covers and swung his legs down to the floor. He wobbled for a moment then stood straight. The shorts he wore when he came to Earth looked strange on his body without the Hawaiian shirt covering his chest. He looked up at Uncle Al.

"Feel okay. Need to get stuff to Asgard and fix up wife, other dwarves and Aesir. We go now." He reached for his shirt.

"Saddle up, boys," Uncle Al directed. "We're off to play cavalry again. I just hope we're in time."

"So do I, Uncle Al," Eric agreed. "So do I."

Chapter Fifteen

Loki looked over at the other Aesir prisoner who shared his room and nodded. Within a few seconds, the door to the room opened and a Giant entered the room with a tray.

"Time to eat, slaves," the Giants said. "Enjoy the meal. It will be the last you have for quite some time, I think."

He laughed and turned toward the door. Just as the door opened, Loki and his companion shot from their bunks and slammed into the Giant, pushing him out into the hallway and into the second Giant who stood guard outside. After weeks of submissive behavior by the prisoners, the Giants were overwhelmed by the vicious attack and were quickly knocked unconscious. The only damage to the two escaping Aesir was a cut on Loki's left hand as he shattered a mug against the head of one of the guards. The sharp-edged shard felt good as it cut into the angry Aesir's hand. Loki and his companion stripped the guards of everything that could be used as a weapon, then turned and raced down the corridor. Their goal was close, but neither of them believed they would reach it without a fight. The Giants had every hallway covered with monitoring devices, just as any prison on Earth would do, and they knew their attack on the guards had already been spotted.

They were almost to the outside door when the alarm went off. The sounds of many feet echoed in the hallways and five Giants appeared at the doorway just as Loki and his friend reached the entryway. The two Aesir slammed into the Giants with all the ferocity of attacking lions and three Giants were down before the others could react. The buzz of Vanir energy weapons filled the hallway and Loki grabbed the wrist of the Giant in front of him and held the muzzle away from his body. The two men strained against each other, dancing across the hallway as they tried to gain possession of the weapon. The Giant's greater height gave him an advantage in leverage, but Loki fought with the desperation of a man who had been captive for much too long. Then, with a movement that took advantage of his shorter height, Loki slipped under the Giant's arm and pulled him down to the floor. With a twist of the wrist in his grasp, Loki slipped the weapon out of the Giant's hand and turned it on its prior owner. The weapon buzzed and the Giant slumped to the floor unconscious.

Loki turned to his companion and found him on the floor next to his opponent. A bloody knife and a pool of blood on the side of the Aesir's tunic showed the Giant had fought hard and almost won the battle. Loki turned the Aesir over and looked into his eyes.

"Can you travel?" he asked softly.

"I will not stay here any longer," the Aesir answered in little more than a whisper.

Loki smiled and helped his companion to his feet. They made it through the doorway just as the sounds of footsteps echoed behind them. Reinforcements were coming for the Giants, but Loki closed the door and shoved a previously prepared metal wedge under the edge of the door to jam it closed. Then he took his companion's arm and looped it over his shoulder. The two warriors made their way to one of the vehicles in the garage they had entered, their goal since they had left the room. Loki slid his companion into the passenger seat of a large truck and then climbed into the driver's seat. The truck's large wheels and four-wheel capability would be needed in this weather if they were to get far enough away quickly enough to escape the Giants.

* * *

As Loki slammed the truck through the door of the garage and out into the snowstorm outside, the cloth held to his companion's side to stop the bleeding never got fully saturated with blood, as if the wound had either stopped bleeding, or was never more than just a thin layer that looked much worse than it was. He also never noticed the small red light under the dashboard of the truck, connected to a device that let the Giants know where the two escaped slaves were, and pinpointed their every move toward their goal, the same goal the Giants had: Mimir.

* * *

Uncle Al slid the last case of ginger ale onto the dolly and pushed through the doorway into the tunnel. As the door closed and cut off the wind, he breathed deeply in relief and pulled his snow-encrusted hat from his head. The wind had picked up again just as he, the boys and Sudri reached the compound. The four cases of ginger ale and two cases of powdered ginger would be enough to cure all the dwarves and Aesir on Asgard. The ones cured quickly by the drinks would be able to make ginger tea for the others and make sure everyone was dosed and cured. Bob Fuller's friend had been told about how the ginger helped Eric and cured the humans who had received doses of the drink. He would call all the newspapers and TV stations he could reach and tell them he had stumbled across the cure by accident. Uncle Al didn't want any more attention brought to Eric and the dwarves at the compound that necessary. It made sense for a health food store owner to have found this cure. To announce a thirteen-year-old boy made the discovery would prompt more questions than Uncle Al wanted to answer. He pushed the dolly down the tunnel to the old office building of the Giants, where the gate was located. He watched as dwarves quickly loaded the boxes on a pallet Sudri could move through the gate in a single trip.

"Have all drinks and spice ready to go to Asgard, once this stuff added on," Suori said to his brother.

"Make sure keep some spice for people here and they drink soon," Sudri answered. "Not want last place here on Midgard sick now that we know answer to problem."

Suori nodded. "Make tea now. Have some to all dwarves and Aesir within hour. Not want to be sick like you, even if you are weaker brother."

Sudri slapped his brother on the shoulder with a huge hand. "When come back from Asgard have wrestling match and show you who is weaker brother. You spend too much time in caves while dwarves on Asgard work hard all these years. We see who is stronger."

Suori answered with a hand on his brother's shoulder. "Go. Save Asgard. Make Ioreth better. Then get back here so we beat Giants."

Sudri nodded. "Good idea. Time to kick Giants' butt."

"You got that right, Sudri," Tommy said. "I'm pretty tired of all the problems here on my world. We need to stop these guys as soon as we can."

"You and Vili find Giants, dwarves go and stop them," Sudri promised.

"It's a deal," Tommy said. He reached out a hand to the dwarf and they gave the standard double-pump handshake all the dwarves used.

Eric laid a hand on the clasped hands of his friends. "I'm in on this too, guys. I have a really big bone to pick with the Giants. I don't like being used like they used me, and it's time for payback."

"Okay, you get piece of action," Sudri agreed. "Now get to work so you be ready when come back with more dwarves to help."

"You betcha, Sudri," Tommy agreed. "Piece of cake."

Sudri shook a finger at the boy. "If so easy, why not do before now?" he asked.

"Ah, well . . . " Tommy stammered.

"Because he was too busy catching Fenrir," Eric answered and he gave Tommy a punch in the shoulder.

"Hmmph," Sudri grunted as he looked from one boy to the other. "Okay. Is good reason. This time." He shook his finger at both of them. "But now go find Giants. Okay?"

"Got it," Eric replied.

"Yep," Tommy agreed.

"Hmmph," Sudri repeated. Then, with a wave to his brother, he turned and pushed the loaded pallet on its wheeled base through the gateway.

Just then, Vili appeared in the doorway of the tunnel. "Come quickly," he called. "We have found part of the answer."

He turned and raced back down the tunnel with Uncle Al, Suori, Eric and Tommy right behind. They all followed to the workshop and Vili led them over to the consolees that held a variety of Aesir communication and sensor equipment. Vili pointed to one of the consolees.

"Here is the reason for the weather problems on Midgard," he stated.

On the screen was a pattern of lines indicating altitude and temperature, if the information at the bottom of the screen meant what Eric thought it did. The temperature seemed to hold steady until it reached a certain point on the screen, then dropped considerably.

"That's one heck of a cold spot," Tommy said mostly to himself as he read the screens. He knew more about the Aesir equipment than Eric and could read the information better as a result.

"A cold spot!" Eric exclaimed. "You mean a cold spot caused all this snow and stuff?"

"It's in the jet stream, in the atmosphere," Tommy stated. "Just like the normal winter weather we have when the jet stream drops closer to the equator, a colder air flow makes the weather even colder."

"Well, thank you Mr. Weatherman," Eric said as he looked at the screen and tried to make sense of the readout. "So what do we do about it? Or can we do anything about it?"

"How much of a temperature drop is it? And is it natural?" Uncle Al asked Vili.

"At least three degrees, with some variation so it appears not to be a constant factor, and it makes the same three degree drop each time it passes the same point in the atmosphere," Vili answered.

"That's crazy!" Tommy exclaimed. "Air doesn't do that!"

"Correct, young Norn," Vili agreed. "And to answer your teacher's other question: no, it is not natural." He pointed to two other screens with similar readouts. "These screens show the same type of temperature drop and are at two different locations from the first readings."

"Three temperature drops?" Tommy asked. "Now that's really crazy!"

"Unless it's caused by something. Or by someone," Uncle Al stated.

"Giants," Eric said with certainty. "The Giants put something in the jet stream to make the temperature drop. And each time the air goes around the world, it gets colder and colder. And we end up with Fimbulwinter."

Vili nodded. "As you say, young warrior. Fimbulwinter is indeed upon us, and brought by the Giants themselves, rather than the forces of nature."

"Do you know what the Giant have put there to cause this drop?" Uncle Al asked the Aesir.

Vili shook his head. "Not exactly. But there are several units available that could cause this amount of a temperature drop over a small area. With three units placed across the jet stream, with a variable effect rather than a constant change, the Giants have been able to hide the effect for a time, and make it look like the weather itself has shifted. But we were able to trace the effects over a long period and pinpoint the locations."

"And do you have anything that can stop these units from working?" Uncle Al asked.

Vili shook his head. "If we had the full resources of MMR here on Midgard, we could use one of our smaller reconnaissance units to carry a deactivation device closer. Or even with some of the larger energy weapons mounted on the command ship could blast through the shields on the units and stop them. But without some way to either shoot them from a distance or fly close enough to deactivate them, we are at a loss for answers."

"Do we have anything here on this world that can shut them down?" Uncle Al asked.

"I fear not," Vili said. "The Giants have shielded these units well. Your flying machines would find them only if we gave them sensors to see the units, their weapons would not be able to penetrate the shields."

"Fornir and I could do it," Eric said.

Everyone turned and looked at him. Uncle Al started to speak and Eric raised a hand to stop him.

"Look, I know it sounds crazy. But Fornir can fly close enough for me to use one of those deactivation units Vili talked about." He looked up at Uncle Al. "If we don't do this, the entire planet is going to be one big icicle. I'll bet the Aesir have some sort of suit I can wear to keep me warm enough while we fly close to whatever is up there and shut it off. All Fornir has to do is get me close enough, then we can shut those things down and let Mother Nature bring the temperature back to normal."

"I fear it will not be quite that simple, young warrior," Vili stated.

"Why not?" Eric asked.

"Because even if we shut down the Giants' temperature units, there has been enough damage done to the weather that the cold will continue on its own. Right, Vili?" Uncle Al asked the Aesir.

Vili nodded. "I fear so. Unless we are able to not only stop continued damage to the airflow, but reverse what has already been done to a large degree, I believe there will be little but snow and ice for many centuries on this world. We could take you and your families to Asgard and you would be safe, but I fear most of the people on this world will perish."

"Well, crap. That's just not good enough," Tommy said. "There has to be some way to make those things heat up the air rather than cool it down."

"Perhaps, young Norn. Perhaps. But it will take time to compute the instructions needed to make the changes even with Mimir's help. And that may well be time we do not have." Vile looked around at the group. "We must prepare for the worst, even as we strive to correct the problem."

"I agree," Uncle Al said. "Do what you can to work out some way to reverse the effects of the Giants' machines," he said to Vili. "Eric, you call Fornir and ask him to come and help us out. I know he's been staying further south with all this cold weather, but ask him if he will come here and take you to where you need to go if we can find a way to shut these things down. Even if we can't use those units to reverse the effects, we can stop them from making things worse. Maybe the Aesir have something we can put in place to heat things up after we take care of the Giants."

"Good idea," Eric agreed.

Uncle Al turned to Suori. "Get your people ready to move, my friend. I know we have just given you this new home, but if we cannot find a way to stop the Giants plan, Asgard will be the only safe place for you to go."

Suori bowed. "Dwarves be ready to travel or fight. But prefer to fight. No good for Vanir to destroy this world. Nice place to live. Not just give up and run."

"I understand," Uncle Al answered. Then he turned to Tommy. "You have the tough job, I'm afraid."

"How's that?" Tommy asked.

"Well, the short version is: you have to find a way to reverse the controls of the Giants' weather machines, figure out how to give Eric what he needs to carry that Fornir can handle, give him a way to stay warm while he does it, and then . . . " he said with a raised finger, "Help me come up with a story that will satisfy all the people on this world who don't know about the battle between the Aesir and the Vanir. Got all that?"

"I guess an attack from aliens from outer space isn't a good idea for a cover story?" Tommy suggested with a smile.

"Not unless you want to explain why they landed in Pennsylvania rather than Washington, D.C.," Uncle Al answered.

"Because they forgot to ask for directions?" Tommy offered.

Uncle Al shook his head and smiled. "Keep at it. The jokes need to be better than that before we talk to people." He waved Tommy over to the consolees to start to work.

"And while we're doing all of this stuff, what will you do?" Eric asked.

Uncle Al sighed. "I'll make some phone calls. The way things are right now, there's a very good chance the Giants will attack. We don't know where, we don't know with what, and we don't even know what they really want, other than Mimir. All we know is that it will be fast, hard and will not matter how much damage they do or who gets killed in the process. I think I want a few local people in on this. They deserve to know what's going on here, even if they can't do much about it."

"People like Lieutenant Harris?" Eric asked.

Uncle Al nodded. "Exactly. I think it's time he knows all of the story, including the part about how his superiors are part of the problem rather than the solution."

"Okay, let me see where Fornir is and Tommy can get started on the other stuff. We have a lot to do and not a lot of time to do it," Eric said with a shrug. "Just like is usually the case where Giants are involved." He looked at his uncle and his friend. "Any chance we can take a real vacation when this is all over?"

"Tahiti is a bit cold this time of year, I hear," Tommy said with a smile.

"I was thinking like maybe another planet," Eric suggested. "Some place without Giants."

"And what makes you think the problems on another planet wouldn't be just as bad as Giants?" Tommy asked.

"You're just a ray of sunshine today, aren't you?" Eric groaned. "Okay, no vacation. But we make sure the Giants are all packed away someplace safe."

"Works for me," Tommy agreed.

"And for all of us, I believe," Vili stated as he moved closer to the group. "Perhaps it is truly time to end this battle with our ancient ene-mies. Perhaps it is indeed time for Ragnarok!"

"I was afraid you were going to say that," Uncle Al said with a frown. "The ground under a battlefield is never the same afterwards, and a battle of this magnitude could well destroy the Earth."

"We shall strive to assure that does not happen, my friend," Vili said as he laid a hand on Uncle Al's shoulder.

"I know you will, Vili. You and all the Aesir care about this world." He looked at the Aesir. "But will the Giants care if they blow up the planet in the process?"

Chapter Sixteen

The workshop at the dwarf compound was a madhouse of activity. Vili, Tommy and several of the Aesir were in deep discussion with Mimir, trying to find a way to disable the Giants' weather satellites, and then reverse the problems with the jet stream. The storm was interfering with many of the communication devices used by the Aesir command ship, but there was still an audio-only line that worked most of the time. Kind of a Viking telephone, as it was explained to Eric.

Uncle Al had been on the phone for at least two hours with several different people in an attempt to get at least some of them to understand what was really going on with the weather and the sickness affecting so many people in the area. Lieutenant Harris was able to understand because of what he had seen when they rescued Aunt Cindy and Vili, but even he had some trouble with the idea the Giants were causing a worldwide weather problem. Some of the other people Uncle Al called did not believe much of what he told them. But something strange was behind all the problems and any excuse gave people a place to start. There were already mass evacuations in places around the world as people moved closer to the equator, but this still left all too many people stranded in the colder areas. And even the Aesir weren't sure they could correct things enough to keep a new Ice Age from happening. Uncle Al left Eric at the compound while he went home to let Aunt Cindy know what they were doing and to pack for a trip to Asgard. They may not be able to save everyone, but Eric was glad his aunt would be safe someplace the Giants couldn't get her this time.

Eric worked with the dwarves to prepare for a large number of evacuees at the compound. Several of the old Giants' barracks were still empty and they just needed to be cleaned before they could be used to hold people before they were sent to Asgard or Jotunheim. Eric had suggested that since the Giants were pretty much all here on earth, why not use their old home dimension as a place to keep people safe from the weather.

The dwarves placed special crystals in all the buildings to keep them warm. But each time any of the doors opened to let people in or out, the wind sucked a lot of the heat out into the storm. The dwarves worked hard to make secondary doorways attached to the buildings to limit the heat loss, but it was hard work in very difficult conditions and Eric hoped Tommy could help find a way to fix things so it wouldn't be needed.

Eric stopped for a minute to wipe the sweat from his forehead. Even in the bitter cold of Fimbulwinter, the sweat poured off him as he moved beds and boxes in the empty barracks. He looked over at the far side of the compound, where Tommy and Vili worked in the depths of their workshop on an answer to their problems. Tommy had changed in the last year Eric had known him. The smaller boy had followed Eric around almost like a lost puppy when they first met. Now, and especially after the capture of Fenrir, Tommy was much more sure of himself. Eric decided he liked it. He might not be able to push Tommy around any longer when he chose to, but now he had a partner in his adventures. Which was even better.

"Eric feel okay?" Suori asked as he looked up at the boy.

Eric smiled and shook his head. "Just thinking about how much things have changed since I first met Thor. Not quite the way I planned to spend the rest of my life."

"Better or worse?" Suori asked with a smile the size of a compact car's grille.

Eric laughed. "I don't know, Suori. Maybe just different."

"Different okay too," Suori stated. "Dwarves are different and we pretty good people."

"Yes, you are," Eric agreed and slapped his friend on the shoulder with a crack of rock-hard skin. "Definitely pretty good people. Now we just need to help some other pretty good people."

"Then Eric need to get to work and stop waste time," Suori said handing the boy a large box.

Eric took the load and woofed as the weight almost slammed his hands to the floor. Suori just smiled.

"Good people but lousy jokes, Suori," Eric said as he straightened up.

"What joke? Just box that need moved." Suori tapped Eric on the shoulder. "Need to toughen up young Aesir so sword work not be so hard."

"With friends like you—"Eric started to say.

There was a blast of air from the courtyard and a loud roar like a steam engine. Eric set the box on a nearby bed and raced to the window.

"Fornir's here!" he yelled and raced for the doorway.

"Put on coat," Suori yelled after the boy. Then he shook his head and grabbed the coat from the bed near the door and followed Eric out into the cold.

By the time Suori was out into the courtyard, Eric had his arms wrapped around his friend's neck.

"Boy, am I glad to see you," Eric called out over the roar of the wind. "Let's get you inside someplace and out of this wind."

Suori draped Eric's coat over his shoulders and pulled to boy toward the workshop. He looked up at the great wyrm and pointed. "Have place big enough for you to get out of wind and snow, with door big enough to get through."

"Excellent, my friend," Fornir called back. "Let us move quickly."

Fornir pushed ahead, and he used his great bulk to open a way through the drifts that appeared and disappeared in the open courtyard as the wind-driven snow piled up and moved aside in the gusts. As the wyrm reached the far side of the yard, a large door opened in the side of the workshop and he moved quickly inside, followed by Eric and Suori. As the door closed behind them, snow sifted through the open door and piled in corners of the room, then quickly melted as heat crystals shifted in to high gear to heat the area. A smaller door opened on the far side of the room and Tommy came in, followed by Vili.

"Hey, Fornir! How's it going?" Tommy called out to the wyrm.

"Rather cold, actually, young Norn," Fornir answered. "Even so far south as the middle of this world, the temperature is much less than normal and people fight with each other for places of warmth. Has the cause of this problem been found, as Eric suggested in his call to me?"

"Indeed," Vili stated. "And is so often the case with our people, the Vanir are behind the problem once again."

Fornir growled and the vibration shook the building. "There must be an end to this insane behavior."

"We agree," Eric said to his friend as he laid a hand on the dragon's leg. "And we think we might have a way to put an end to at least part of it."

"Well and good," Fornir answered. "What is it you wish of me, my friends?"

"You and I will knock out the Giant's weather controls, if Tommy and Mimir can figure out a way to do it," Eric said.

"We think we have a way to reprogram the satellites," Tommy interjected. "At least Mimir thinks he has it figured out."

"Good. Then the weather can return to a more normal temperature," Fornir stated. "How are we to do this thing?"

"Well, you have to fly within fifty yards of the satellite and stay there for at least thirty seconds for the download to sink into the computer in the machine," Tommy said. "The Giants used computer stuff from here on Earth and that's the quickest we can get the info loaded. Aesir or Vanir technology is faster, but I guess the Giants wanted to use something that wouldn't be so obviously from some other planet."

"Or if it was found, they could blame it on some other country or maybe some terrorist group," Eric suggested.

"Well, that sounds good, but they missed a big point when they put those things together," Tommy said.

"What do you mean?" Fornir asked.

Tommy smiled. "They used Earth equipment and computers, but they built a Vanir antigravity unit into the satellite. As far as I know nobody on this world has that kind of technology."

"Neat," Eric said. "Maybe we can take one apart after this is over and get antigravity for ourselves."

"No need, young warrior," Vili stated. "The Aesir also have this technology, and now that it has been seen on this world, we can share it with you without fear of contamination."

"This is going to be so cool," Eric said.

"But first we must stop the Vanir machines from harming this world," Fornir reminded him.

"Are you kidding?" Eric said. "We have a dragon, a computer that's alive, enough rock dwarves to build a mountain to the sky if we need to, and all the Aesir to guard our backs while we do this. What could possibly go wrong?" He smiled at Tommy and winked.

Then both boys broke down in laughter as the Aesir and dwarves joined in.

"Not really going to be that easy is it?" Tommy asked his friend between gasps of air.

"No. Not really. But we're in better shape than we were, and in a lot better shape than the Giants think we are," Eric answered. "We just need to get this done before they find a way to stop us and then we need to find all of them and put them somewhere so they don't do this anymore. Piece of cake."

"I'm glad you think so," Tommy said. "But you get to ride a dragon while all this is going on. Us other poor slobs have to stay here on the ground and wade through ten feet of snow everywhere."

"Dig tunnels," Suori suggested. "Dwarves good at dig tunnels. We get to where you need to go, no problem."

"I think I'll stay above the snow, as long as you guys have some way for me to keep warm up there," Eric said. "Fornir's back gets kind of cold in good weather, much less the kind of stuff we have now."

Tommy laughed. "You'll love this." He darted back into the workroom and retuned almost as quickly with a silvery suit and a large helmet. "Aesir Space Legion general issue. One gen-you-wine space cadet package."

Eric groaned. "And you'll never forget that part of it, will you?"

"Nope!" Tommy's smile was as wide as his face. "I owe you a few yet. But this goes a long way toward an even score."

"All right. Let's see if it fits," Eric said as he reached for the suit.

"It'll fit," Tommy assured him. "Mimir picked the size for you. He knows you better than you know yourself. Not that it takes much."

"Funny. Real funny."

Eric slipped his feet into the suit and closed the front with a simple press of the seams together. He took the helmet from Tommy and slipped it over his head. The seals clicked into place with a solid sound and Eric heard the climate controls activate with a whoosh of air. He walked around the floor of the workshop and tried to move in the suit.

The Aesir unit was made for space combat and Eric found it easier to move in than his karate gi.

"Pretty neat," he said. Then he looked up to see if the others had heard him.

"The suit has built-in speakers that permit the people outside to hear what you say," Vili explained. "And if there are other combat suits close by, the suit automatically activates a communication system that permits speech in airless space. And it has an internal air supply for four hours in case you start flying too high."

"Cool," Eric said. He turned toward Fornir. "Well, friend. Any problem with me on your back dressed like this?" He held out his arms to show off the suit.

Fornir puffed smoke. "Indeed not. If we are able to stop the Vanir and return your world to its rightful green, then a shining bauble like yourself on my back is a small price to pay."

Eric shook his head. "A bunch of jokesters. That's what you all are."

"Ain't it great," Tommy said with a slap on Eric's shoulder.

"Yeah, great," Eric answered. "So what do we need to take with us to fix these Giant machines?"

Vili nodded and stepped back into the workshop to return almost as fast as Tommy had. He held a small, flat box that he showed to Eric and Fornir.

"This will fasten to the belt of your suit. Once you are close enough to the Vanir machines, it will automatically begin to transmit the signals needed to change the programming. Merely stay close enough for the transmission to complete and your job will be done. But Mimir said you can't use your Uni-Shield while you are close to the satellites. The shield blocks the transmissions from this unit."

"Oh, crud," Eric said. "We'll just have to make sure we stay away from any planes they may have protecting those satellites. And speaking of the satellites, how will we know where those things are?"

Vili pointed toward the helmet. "There is a screen inside this unit that will provide the information you need. Follow the signal and the directions given and you will have no difficulty finding the machines."

"Piece of cake," Eric said. He looked up at Fornir. "You ready to do this?"

Fornir looked down at the young boy. "As you say, my friend, piece of cake. Come! We ride the skies to stop the Vanir's plans and avenge my clan's honor!"

He held still for a moment to permit two of the other Aesir to attach a series of straps to his neck, a safety harness for Eric. Then the wyrm spun around and almost clipped Eric with his tail as he waited for the door to open the whole way. Eric was glad of the suit's warmth as the cold wind whipped into the workshop. He clipped the flat box to the suit's belt and moved out into the courtyard to mount Fornir. His head jerked up as a voice echoed in his ears.

"Hey, Eric. Can you hear me?" Tommy asked though the communication unit.

"Loud and clear," Eric replied. "Put on a pot of hot chocolate. We'll be back as soon as we can."

"With the little marshmallows?" Tommy asked.

"I think we deserve the big ones this time, don't you?"

"Big ones it is," Tommy agreed. "Remember to block," he added, one of Uncle Al's favorite lines during training.

Eric laughed. "Yes, Sensei."

Eric climbed into the saddle formed by Fornir's neck spines and the scales around his shoulders, then fastened the straps in place to clips on the suit. He tapped his friend on the top of his head to get his attention.

"Okay, Fornir. Let's go take care of some bad guys."

"Indeed, my friend," Fornir answered.

With a powerful thrust of his legs, the wyrm bounced into the air and spread his wings. As he reached the top of his jump, the huge wings swept down and thrust the wyrm and his rider higher into the wind. Fornir used the force of the wind to aid his climb into the sky and in a short time the two were headed west toward the first of the Vanir machines.

* * *

Tommy watched the dragon disappear into the storm and headed back into the workshop. He moved toward the consolee showing what was happening in the air over most of this part of Pennsylvania and spotted the tiny moving dot of Fornir. For a brief moment he wondered what the airline pilots and control towers would make of the strange flying creature. Then he turned his attention to the rest of his consolees and the information they contained.

"Do you wish you were going with him?" Vili asked the boy.

Tommy shrugged. "Part of me does. Another part of me is very glad I'm not out there in this storm. We still have a lot to do here."

"But you want to be part of the battle?" Vili asked. It was part question, part statement.

Tommy sighed. "Maybe. Yes. Well, I don't know." He turned and looked over at Vili. "I'm just a kid. I know that. But all the stuff that's happened to me over the last year . . . well, I'm not the same kid I used to be. The training with Mr. Johnson, working with you and Mimir and the dwarves, and all the Aesir . . . all of that has changed me, a lot."

Vili nodded. "As it should, young Norn."

"Yeah, well, that's kind of what I mean. All those changes, and what am I turning into? I mean, am I a human, or an Aesir, or what am I?" Tommy asked his friend.

"You are you," Vili answered, laying a hand on the boy's shoulder. "The questions you ask are the same ones every person asks as they grow older." He looked down at Tommy and smiled. "Are you the same person you were? No. Are you an Aesir? No. You are human. You are not the same person you would have been had you not met Eric Johnson and joined him in his travels. But you are a good man, Thomas Kuhns, and will be a better man with each passing day. This I know." Vili patted his shoulder. "I have trained a great many warriors over the years, my young friend, and I tell you in all truth, there are few of them who would be able to match you when you reach your full potential."

"Really? You mean that?" Tommy asked.

Vili smiled. "You will not be as strong as Thor, but few are. You will not be as quick witted as Loki, but few want to be, for it causes as many problems as it solves. But you combine many qualities together in a way uniquely your own. And that makes you a warrior any commander would want under his command, and is often the basis of making a proper commander in your own right."

"Me? A commander?" Tommy said in astonishment. "No way! Nobody would follow me anywhere."

"You think not?" Vili answered. "How is it then, many of the dwarves here at this place come to you with questions? I do not say you know the answers to all questions, but you find those answers and pass them to those that require the information. This is one of the marks of a good commander. Not that you know all, but that you know how to find what you need and direct the men under your command in what they need to do with those answers."

"Jeez, I never thought of it that way," Tommy said.

"You are still young, my friend. There is time yet to grow into your skills. Perhaps some other task will be for you in the future. But for now, do not be displeased with your progress. Continue to work as you have, and the future will be open to you. Perhaps even the stars themselves."

"Hey, now there's an idea. Go to the stars," Tommy said. "I like that idea."

"Then we will go together, young Norn," Vili said. He held out a hand to Tommy and the two grasped wrists in the Aesir manner. "And I would be proud to have you in my service," Vili added.

"Thanks, Vili," Tommy said. "I appreciate everything you've said. I won't let you down."

"I do not doubt it," Vili replied. "Now, finish those scans on Vanir activity in a one hundred mile area."

"Aye, aye, Captain," Tommy said and saluted his friend.

Vili laughed and walked back to his station.

Tommy shifted through the information coming through his screens for the next half hour, before something caught his eye. He touched the controls and fine tuned some of the information coming into the screen.

"Uh, oh," Tommy said.

Vili turned to look at the young boy.

"What?" the Aesir asked.

Tommy leaned back in his chair and shook his head. "It just got worse," he said. He turned and looked at the Aesir and dwarves in the room. "You know how we've been trying to track down what the Giants are doing? And how we've put Aesir sensors at all the places we know of that they might want to attack?" He pointed at the readout in front of him. "Well, it looks like we know the first place they'll attack."

He shook his head and looked at Vili. "They don't know what we found out from Mimir and Fornir. The Giants are digging a tunnel to the Lost River! And it looks like they'll break through in about two hours!"

156

Chapter Seventeen

"No, Steph. I'm not kidding. The Giants are coming through the west wall of the lower chamber, down below the Hall of the Giants. You, know, the one Dwalin found that we really can't get to."

Tommy almost yelled into the phone as he spoke. "They're using some sort of high energy drilling stuff. Vili said it's something both the Aesir and the Vanir use when they want to dig tunnels. They must have been using some kind of dampers on it until now or we would have seen it sooner. It looks like there about six of them in the bunch."

"So what do we do? We can't keep them from digging into the cave!" Stephanie wailed.

"Wait a minute. Let me put you on speaker. Vili has an idea." Tommy pushed the button on the phone and set the receiver in place. "Okay, can you hear me?"

"Yes, I hear you," Stephanie answered. "You're on speaker phone here, too. Svala and a couple of the Valkyr came by a while ago to check up on me."

"That is well," Vili stated. "Well come, battle sister. I fear it yet again time to face our ancient foe."

"Well met, Vili Norn-smith. I am glad you are with us in this fight," Svala answered. "What wisdom do you have for us?"

"The Vanir will enter the caverns lower down than the main chambers, from what we see in Mimir's mirror," Vili said. "They will be unable to use their tools to open many passages up to the river for if they do they may well flood their own doorway. This will limit the ways they can come into the cavern. If strong warriors were to block the passages, the Vanir would have great difficulty reaching Mimir's Well."

"A good plan," Svala said, "did we but have more than three Valkyr, a dwarf and an untrained and much too young battle maiden."

"Hey, I can help," Stephanie said.

"But you are no match for a Vanir in full battle gear," Svala warned, "especially without Mist Walker to carry you away to safety should the battle turn poorly for us."

"Have more than those to help," Suori said, heard by Stephanie and the Valkyr.

The dwarf had entered the workshop as Tommy, Vili and the other Aesir tuned the sensors to see what the Giants planned with the cavern. The dwarf listened carefully and now smiled as he looked at Tommy and Vili.

"Can have troop of dwarves ready to go in two shakes of daglin's tail," Suori said. "No problem." He waved his hand casually.

"Well, that will work, but how can we get you there in time?" Tommy asked. "In this weather it would take half a day to drive to the cave, if we even had enough cars to get there."

"Pffft!" Suori puffed. "Why go hard way? Go through cave, through Dwalin's gate."

"Jeez, I'm a nidiot," Tommy said as he slapped a hand to his forehead, repeating one of his father's favorite phrases.

"Well, yeah," Stephanie agreed from the other end of the call. "But you're my nidiot, so just keep on doing this stuff so good."

"Excellent!" Vili said. "We will have enough help to protect the cave from the Vanir, and keep Stephanie safe as well." He turned to the dwarf. "Once again we thank you, my friend." He held out his hand and grasped wrists with the dwarf. "It was one of Odin's better decisions to save you and your people. You have been of great aid to us."

"It what we do," Suori said. "Now go get dwarves ready to fight Vanir. You tell Mimir to change setting on crystals so we go through to cave."

"And so I shall," Vili agreed. "And we shall watch carefully to assure the Vanir do not try to attack from outside the cave as well as in."

Suori turned and headed back out of the workshop at a surprisingly fast pace for such a short man.

"Sounds good," Tommy agreed as he turned back to the phone. "Steph, you behave yourself and stay out of the fighting."

"And just what will you be doing while I'm staying out of the way?" she asked her friend.

"I'll work with Mimir to see if we can find all the Giants around here," Tommy said. "If they're really attacking the cave, there must be more of them around here than just the ones down near you. Or else the Aesir have done a lot better job or rounding up the bad guys than we think they have. Last time I talked to Thor he said there were still about a hundred Vanir left unaccounted for. You don't want them to appear out of left field in the middle of some other fight, do you?"

"No, I don't," Stephanie stated emphatically. "So you go find them for us."

Tommy hung up and turned back to Vili.

"Something about this doesn't seem right," he said to the Aesir.

"How so, young Norn?" Vili asked.

"Well, we know the Giants aren't stupid. A little weird maybe, but not stupid." Tommy shook his head. "They have to know they're coming into a cave that's going to be wired for all kinds of alarms. So why are they coming in like this?"

Vili nodded. "This is true. But the Vanir would not have been able to use sensors to find a better place to enter without setting off the alarms the Aesir have set into the cave. They may not know the chamber they enter will not provide them with easy access to the river. There is a limit to what they may have found out as they tried to tour the cave, before Odin set the warnings at the entryways. And they may believe all Aesir and dwarves are disabled by their created disease."

Last year, before the cave was so well covered with warning alarms, Tommy, Eric and Stephanie has discovered the Giants were coming into the cave and going through the tour, and that sometimes they left sensors in the tunnels and chambers to send information back to some main communications site of their own. The Giants had used the tunnel for travel through to Jotunheim for many years without Stephanie's family knowing there was anything different in the Crystal Chamber other than some very energetic crystals. But Dwalin's appearance had alerted the Aesir to the Giant's activity in the cave, and with their free access back to Jotunheim cut off, the Giants realized there was more to the cave than just the Crystal Chamber. That was when one of the Giants tossed Eric in the Lost River, where he thought he would freeze or drown, or both. But Eric wound up instead on Jotunheim, where he met Fornir and Mimir, the Aesir command computer. It was that computer the Giants wanted, to find their way back home and back to the battle that had brought them here in the first place.

"So as far as the Giants know, the river is a way to get to Jotunheim and to Mimir. They don't know about the shift in the dimensional stuff that could cut them to pieces if things shift just a bit." Tommy looked up at Vili. "Right?"

"And this does not seem right to you, that the Vanir would tunnel in from below to try and follow the river to Mimir?" Vili asked.

Tommy waved a hand as if he was chasing the idea away. "No. Not that. If the Giants think they can get in that way, why send in such a small bunch of Giants. Unless they have something else planned to go with the attack through the tunnel they're digging."

"Your suggestion has much sense in it," Vili agreed. "But do not forget the Giants have brought Fimbulwinter upon this world, and have begun a plague in both your people and mine which has dropped many of both our people to their knees and to their beds. Were it not for the discovery of this strange elixir in a bottle Eric John's Son has brought to us, there would be almost none to stand in the way of the Giants. They will be most surprised to find Valkyr and dwarven warriors at the cave when they first break through. The river will not be an easy goal to reach, and they will know this as soon as they open the doorway they now build."

"Which reminds me," Tommy said. "Shouldn't we send some people to the other end of the tunnel to catch the Giants if they try to go back after they find out they can't get to the river?"

"An excellent idea, young Norn," Vili said with a smile and a slap on the back for Tommy that almost knocked him out of his seat. "We will advise Suori of this and some of the dwarves can brave the snow and wind of Fimbulwinter to block the far end of the tunnel as well. Should they be able to cut the power supply to the drill unit, they will be able to block the end of the tunnel with rock and turn it into a fitting prison for those Vanir inside."

"Good," Tommy agreed. "But I still get the feeling there's something we're missing. I think the Giants have something else they're trying to do. Not just the attack on the cave. But something else."

"Then let us turn to our devices and see what we can find," Vili suggested. "We have sensors in many places that we know are of interest to the Vanir, and many more places we know are of concern to your people as well. Perhaps we will discover what they have planned."

"I just hope we're not too late already," Tommy said. "The Giants have had all this time to plan out what they want to do and we're playing catch up."

Vili smiled. "How can the Vanir hope to defeat Eric John's Son, Stephanie Valkyr's Daughter and Thomas Norn-Smith. Our enemies are truly outnumbered from the start."

"I just hope we can say that in a couple of days," Tommy said as he turned back to his consolee. "Let's see what we can find in this storm that might help us." As he started adjusting the sensors, he muttered to himself. "And one of these days I have to find out what a daglin looks like."

Vili smiled again and nodded to the other Aesir to begin their search as he turned to his own consolee and began to work. The Aesir and Tommy searched through all the places they had access, and by some adjustments to the system supplied by Mimir over the audio link, they managed to tap into some of the human communication equipment systems. Tommy smiled as he heard a couple of airline pilots discussing with the ground directors the strange thing that had passed their plane at about twenty thousand feet. Nobody was admitting it was a dragon, but the descriptions could be very little else than that mythological creature and the pilots knew it. They also knew that if they started reporting dragons flying around in the sky, their own days in a plane as anything other than a passenger were in short supply.

"They do not believe in dragons?" Vili asked Tommy. "Has it been so long since Fornir's kin have traveled this world?"

"It's been so long nobody ever saw a dragon and recorded it as anything other than a legend or some tale told after too much to drink at a party."

"Indeed," Vili replied. "This is a very strange world you live on."

"And it's a lot more strange than people think, since they don't know about Giants and Aesir," Tommy answered.

"Good point," Vili agreed.

They continued to study the information coming into their con-solees, but with no success for many long hours. They each took a quick break for something to eat, as dwarven cooks arrived with trays of food that could be eaten with fingers while working. Tommy walked back over to his consolee and bit down into the leg of an Aesir bird like a chicken, but three times the size. It made a really big leg to eat and tasted even better than his mother's fried chicken, Tommy decided. As he wiped grease from his chin with a napkin, Tommy taped a button on his consolee to change the view in one area. He glanced down at the screen and almost choked at what he saw. The chicken leg dropped to the floor and he wiped his hands on his shirt before he adjusted the view again.

"Hey! I think I have some good news for a change!" he called to the Aesir in the workroom. "I found Loki."

Tommy adjusted the view in the screen as Vili and the other Aesir gathered around behind him. The view showed the road leading up to the top of the ridge where the amateur observatory was located, the spot where the first gate between Mimir on Jotunheim and the Aesir here on Earth was created. Loki had opened the door of the truck he was driving and turned back to the inside of the vehicle for a moment.

"It's really tough to tell with all the interference from the storm, but it looks like he's talking to someone in the truck," Tommy said.

"Then some other Aesir was with his when he left Asgard," Vili stated.

"But didn't Odin say nobody else was missing?" Tommy asked as he looked back over his shoulder at Vili.

Vili nodded. "It is possible he has found some aid from your people here," the Aesir suggested. "After all, Loki does have much experience with your people, more than most Aesir."

They watched as Loki opened the back door of the vehicle and took out a blanket, then started up the road toward the location of the gateway to Mimir. The tall Aesir braced himself against the winds of the storms.

"He's headed for Mimir's gateway. Maybe we should shift him here, so we can give him some ginger tea before he goes to Asgard," Tommy suggested. "He may not have been exposed to the disease the Giants created and we don't want him to get sick."

"An excellent idea, young Norn," Vili said. He directed one of the other Aesir to send the signal to adjust the gateway.

"But I wonder where he's been?" Tommy said, more to himself than to anyone else.

He focused the sensors on the Aesir as he moved slowly up the hillside. Loki looked tired. A bandage on his left hand suggested he had been injured, and with everything Tommy had seen lately, that probably meant a fight with the Giants. He knew Loki had been looking for the Giants when he left Asgard, but the Aesir was smart enough to call in if he found anything. Unless he was caught off guard and taken prisoner.

"I'll bet he's been a prisoner of the Giants," Tommy stated. "I think that's why nobody's heard from him for so long." He looked up at Vili. "He went looking for the Vanir but they found him first. He's been their prisoner for months."

Vili considered the boy's words carefully. The he nodded. "You may well be correct, young warrior. And that would explain many things, not in the least Loki's arrival at this place at this time. The Vanir would have conditioned him to go through the gateway to Mimir and place a controller that would give the access to Mimir's memory units."

"You mean he's been brainwashed?" Tommy exclaimed.

"Most likely true, I'm afraid," Vili said. "And that means we cannot just bring him through the gateway to Dwarvenheim. He will know the settings have been changed and will try to change them back before he goes through."

"But if he's trying to get to Mimir for the Giants, why aren't there any Giants with him now?" Tommy asked.

"Because Mimir would sense them as the gate opens and block their passage, as well as Loki's, before he reached his goal," Vili answered. "The only way Loki can reach Mimir is on his own, with no Giants nearby. There will not be any Vanir within a great circle of area as Loki opens the gate." Vili watched the dark Aesir trudge up the roadway toward the gate. "The gate will permit him to open and reach Mimir. We must stop him before he tries, else the security protocols on the ship will destroy him when they sense his mental state." He looked down at Tommy. "Loki will be conditioned to keep trying, no matter what happens, to open the gateway to Mimir. If he persists in his attempts, the computer will realize he is under Vanir control and destroy him rather than risk him reaching the command ship."

Tommy looked up at Odin's brother. "You know about this stuff, about the Giants' conditioning, don't you?"

Vili nodded. "Such as was done to me for many years, and only the great skill of our healers and the assistance of Mimir has permitted me to become almost what I was before."

"Can you stop Loki? I mean without hurting him?" Tommy asked.

Vili smiled at the boy. "I can but try. And I owe Loki blood debt. He saved my life at the final battle that brought us to this world. Only the fact that I was placed in a section of the command ship with other wounded warriors, a section thought lost by those who reached Asgard, put me in the hands of the Vanir so long ago. I would save him from what the Vanir would have him do."

"The gate can take you to the top of the ridge before he gets there," Tommy said. "After we send the dwarves through to the cave, we can send you through to the observatory. Then you can bring Loki back here so we can help him."

"I believe that will be the best plan," Vili agreed. He turned to the other Aesir in the workshop. "It is best that I go alone. If Loki sees many warriors at the gateway, he will think the Vanir have disguised themselves to look like Aesir in order to go through with him. He will fight. If I am alone, I can speak as one Aesir to another. He will remember me, I think." Vili smiled. "And perhaps my coming back from the dead will give me some time to convince him I speak truth."

"And if you cannot convince Loki Odin's Son you speak truth?" one of the Aesir asked.

Vili leaned over and opened a compartment on the side of the console. He took a slim rod from the small compartment and held it up. "Then Loki will sleep until he can be brought to a place of healing."

Chapter Eighteen

Fornir flew high, well above the clouds where the air was thin and moved fast. But it was also cold, and Eric was glad for the Aesir space suit. The small amount of cold that seeped along the edge of the faceplate gave him a good idea how cold the air was at this altitude.

"You okay, Fornir?" he asked his mount.

"Well enough, young warrior," Fornir answered, his words almost whipped aside by the wind of their passage. "How far yet to our goal?"

"Tommy, give me a readout of the distance to the satellites," Eric directed his friend. There was no response for several seconds. "Tommy, you there?" Again no response. "Any Aesir at Dwarvenheim. What's going on there, you guys?"

The communicator crackled as Tommy came on line. "Sorry about that, Eric. We're pretty busy here with some new stuff."

"What new stuff? What's going on there?" Eric asked.

"Not your concern, young warrior," Vili answered. "You have a task to complete and it must be done as soon as you are able. You are approximately one hundred leagues from your first target. At your present rate of speed you will reach it in about one half hour." There was a pause. "I have activated the tracking unit in your suit. You should see a small dot high and to the right in your helmet screen."

Eric looked through the screen and focused at the close faceplate. In the upper right corner glowed a dot, its steady pulse shifting as Eric turned his head.

"Got it, Vili," Eric said. "Okay, we're on course and headed for the first satellite."

"Excellent." There was another pause before Vili's voice echoed in Eric's helmet again. "I have activated the display unit in the suit and will maintain a constant feed from our other tracking units. If there are any other aircraft in your area, you will know."

"Thanks. We've given a couple of pilots some strange stories to tell already," Eric replied. "It might be better if we can stay out of their way, even if there aren't that many planes up here now."

"I will also be feeding you information as it becomes available," Mimir's calm voice said in Eric's helmet.

"Glad to have you along, Mimir," Eric answered.

"I am more concerned about the possibility the Vanir will have some sort of protection for their satellites," Vili stated. "This is an important battle for them. They will not permit you to destroy their work without a fight."

"Oh. I didn't think about that," Eric mumbled. "Well, we'll just have to do the best we can with what we've got."

"I have great faith in your skill, young warrior," Vili said, the smile in his voice very clear to Eric. "And the aid of such a fighter as Fornir will make this a battle for the sagas."

"Except we can't tell anyone," Tommy said. "So you'll just have to put up with my sagas about Eric Vanir's Bane."

"Oh, great," Eric groaned. "I've read your poetry. It stinks. You can't write a saga."

"So I'll get Sudri to help me," Tommy joked. "He'll have a lot of good stuff to say, I'm sure."

"With friends like you . . . " Eric started to say.

"Oh, crud," Tommy's voice came through the helmet speaker. "You got bandits, six o'clock low and climbing. Looks like the Giants know you're there."

"Okay, we're heading for the first satellite to try and take it out before we have to deal with the bad guys," Eric said. "Wish me luck."

"Kick some butt, dude," Tommy said.

"Fight well. Be safe," Vili offered. "We will monitor and aid as much as we can."

"As will I," Mimir added.

"Okay, Fornir," called to his friend. "Looks we've got company coming. Let's see if we can get to the first target before they catch us. Turn just a bit to your right and let's go for it."

Fornir answered with a roar heard over the wind as he stretched out his neck and pumped his wings for more speed.

So what are the Giants sending against us this time, Eric wondered as he leaned against Fornir's neck to cut the wind.

* * *

"Falcon Leader to base, no sign of hostiles. Fifteen minutes to target one."

"Copy that, Falcon Leader. Be advised hostiles have new stealth technology according to intelligence reports. Contact may need to be by eyesight rather than instruments. Also, be advised their stealth units have unusual configurations. Once target it confirmed, you have release on your weapons for free fire."

"Confirm base. Once we eyeball target we have weapons free. Falcon Leader out."

The two fighters climbed through the heavy cloud cover toward their target. The high winds buffeted the planes from side to side as they tried to get above the storm clouds that covered the earth below. But the pilots were excellent, the best in the area and used to flying in poor weather.

"Falcon One to Falcon Two. Coming up on location for target. Keep an eye peeled for something different. Radar may be ineffective."

"Roger that, Falcon One. Falcon Two has eyes wide open."

The planes broke through a layer of clouds and raced through the clear air toward their target site. A blinking icon on their screens showed the satellite they were to protect, something their commander had advised was supposed to stop the cold weather blanketing the planet. Whatever was up here with them, its job was to destroy the satellite, according to the mission brief. And their job was to stop it.

"Falcon One, I have . . . something on my screen. Just a shadow, but it could be our bogie. Two o'clock low."

"Got it, Falcon Two. Not much of a signal, but there's nothing else up here. Let's check it out."

The two fighters shifted position slightly and moved in on the shadow. They were close enough now to see it by naked eye if it appeared, but whatever it was, it seemed to be staying just below the edge of the clouds. Suddenly, the screen in each fighter pulsed with a signal and the target they were here to protect appeared on their screens, still about five miles away. But that the speeds they were moving, that was much less than a minute of flight time. And just then, the bogie they were tracking appeared from the clouds.

"Jeez, it's a freakin' dragon," Falcon Two whispered over the circuit.

"Tighten up, Falcon Two. We're here to protect that satellite. Stay focused."

"I'm focused, Falcon One. But the guys are never going to believe this one."

"They will when we bring it down," Falcon One answered.

Just then the bogie slowed and dropped back under the clouds and the two fighters flew past with a wash of hot air across the clouds.

"Lost him, Falcon One. He's back in the clouds and whatever stealth he's got just cranked up a notch or two. I don't even have a shadow anymore."

"Come back around and we'll see what we can find. If he's after the target, he'll have to come out of the clouds."

In a patch of clear air that extended for miles, a silver ball of light floated in the air at the position noted by the radar screens in the two fighters. That was the target they needed to protect, locked in position in the upper atmosphere by some new kind of technology. But when they swung back around for another pass, they saw a strange shaped craft at the satellite, gliding around it in a slow circle. By the time the planes returned to the satellite, the bogie was gone, back into the clouds, and the satellite floated in the air just as it had before.

"I guess we scared him off," Falcon Two suggested.

"Yeah, looks like it," Falcon One responded. "I wonder . . . " There was a pause. "Whatever. Let's do a sweep and make sure it's not hiding in the clouds. Then we can go home."

"Roger that, Falcon Leader."

The planes found no sign of the strange craft they had seen so briefly. All they saw was the wall of clouds spread out from the satellite as the air currents shifted. Their planes weren't equipped to read the outside temperature, or they would have realized the air was now a few degrees warmer than when they first arrived.

* * *

"Jeez, we were lucky," Eric said to Fornir. "We managed to get the signal through and didn't have to fight those planes."

"What would that matter?" Fornir answered. "They were just the two and not even fully my size. They were no match for a wyrm warrior."

"Um, Fornir, remember that talk we had a while ago about guns and rockets?" Eric asked.

"What of it, my friend?" the wyrm answered.

"Well, those two planes carry enough rockets to turn a fairly large mountain to gravel. And their guns could poke enough holes through your skin that you would whistle as you flew, if you could still fly."

"Hmm. Perhaps it were best we avoided conflict," Fornir suggested after a moment of thought.

"I kind of thought the same thing," Eric agreed.

* * *

"The first satellite has shifted output, Commander" Keyes said to Bor.

Bor sat behind his desk as he read the report on the spread of the disease among the humans. At this point, if their calculations were correct, most of the humans in the United States, and many others around the world would be infected with the disease. Bor was almost ready to release the rest of the nanites he had prepared, which would give him control of all the humans on the planet as soon as the infections reached everywhere. And that would be soon.

"Is it a malfunction?" Bor asked his minion.

The human shook his head. "No. We detected a change in the input parameters, then were locked out by a change in the command codes."

Bor slammed a fist down on the desk. "How? How did this happen?"

Keyes backed away a step. "We received a report from the airfield covering that satellite that some sort of stealth equipped aircraft flew near the satellite but was chased away. That's all we know at this time."

"And the other two units?"

Keyes shrugged. "At this time they appear to be working properly. We can maintain the temperature drop with what we have left, even with the change in output from the third unit."

"Can you lock out their input from the satellites?" Bor asked.

The human shook his head. "We designed them to accept only close range input. We did not believe the humans would have any means of getting close enough to reprogram them."

Bor cursed. "Contact our controlled humans in their military. Those other two units are to be protected at all costs. I don't care how many humans it takes to protect them. They will do it or die." Bor half rose from his seat. "We are too close now to permit victory to slip through our grasp." He slammed his fist down again. "We will not fail."

"No, Commander," Keyes said as he backed out of the room.

Bor slammed back into his seat with a growl. So close. They were so close to finally getting off this poor excuse for a planet and back to real civilization. With all the setbacks they had this past year, they could not afford another failure. He could not afford another failure.

Bor reached out and pushed a control on his desk. A small screen lit up in the air over the center of the desk. In the screen, Bor saw the leader of the tunnel unit at Enigma Caverns.

"Report," Bor ordered.

"We will be through to the lower chamber in a few minutes, Commander."

"Excellent. And do you have the explosives with you?"

"They are in the house at the end of the tunnel, Commander. The vibrations from the drill would have set them off prematurely."

Bor nodded. "When you are through the cave wall. Bring the explosives into the cave and collapse it. We have found another way to our goal that is more certain."

"As you wish, Commander. And the humans in the cave?"

Bor shrugged. "It matters little. Just be certain to collapse the cave and close it away from the Aesir."

"It shall be done." The screen went blank and disappeared.

Bor reached out to touch a different control and the screen reappeared.

"Prepare an assault team from the humans we have trained. Give them weapons and send them to Enigma Caverns. They are to commence an attack as soon as they reach that location."

"Yes, Commander," the Giant on the other end of the transmission answered.

"Then prepare an assault team of all the remaining Vanir warriors. We will breach the computer's portal soon and I want to be ready to attack at a moment's notice. Once we are through we will close off the portal and destroy all that remains of this location. No reason to permit the humans to have our technology. We may need them as slaves in the future and they will be easier to conquer if all they have to fight with are their own puny weapons."

"It shall be done, Commander."

The screen blanked and disappeared again.

Bor clenched his fists. "Ragnarok, indeed," he whispered to the empty office. "The end of all of them, it shall be."

* * *

Eric and Fornir flew through the clouds toward their third goal. The second satellite was reprogrammed as easily as the first but without the visit by jet fighters. Eric hoped they reached the third satellite before they had any other "help" from humans or trouble from Giants. As they came closer to the third satellite, he realized it wasn't going to be that easy.

"Fornir, we've got company," he called to his friend.

"So I see," the wyrm answered.

The air around the third satellite was crowded. Jets buzzed over and under the unit's position, searching for the strange aircraft the pair of

174

jets had seen at the first satellite. There was no way to approach the satellite without several of the jets spotting them. Suddenly there was a musical tone sound in his helmet.

"Mimir what's that sound?" Eric asked.

"The aircraft are trying to lock onto your position with their weapons," the computer answered. "I will attempt to divert their signals."

"I sure hope so," Eric muttered. "Okay, Fornir. Let's see if we can get close enough to knock out this one."

The wyrm dropped into the clouds below the satellite and flew closer under cover of the condensed moisture.

"Mimir, can we tap into their communications?" Eric asked.

"Easily," the computer answered and there was a hiss in Eric's speaker as he heard the chatter between the pilots.

"It's dropped into the clouds, Eagle One. I have no visual sighting and nothing on radar."

"All Eagles, go to infrared and see if you can spot their exhaust," Eric heard the flight commander order.

"Oh, oh," he muttered. "Fornir, do you give off a lot of heat?"

"My muscles work very hard to keep us aloft," the wyrm stated. "I am grateful the air is cold enough to draw the heat away or I would have problems flying by now."

"I was afraid of that," Eric answered. "Well, they're going to spot us any minute now."

"Got it," Eric heard over the radio. "Low and east of the target position, in the clouds. Eagle Six and Eight are in position. Use heat seekers to target lock."

"Roger that," two pilots echoed.

Eric twisted his head and looked behind them as two flares of light appeared in the clouds.

"Fornir, they're shooting rockets. Look out," Eric called.

"Hold on," Fornir replied and rose out of the clouds.

Eric held onto the spines on Fornir's back and the straps the Aesir fastened to the wyrm. As Fornir dodged from side to side, the straps kept the boy tight to the wyrm's neck and he saw two icons in the helmet display he knew were the rockets. As they broke through the clouds, three more jets moved onto position to attack and their guns began to fire, as lines of tracers arced trough the cold air.

"Dive!" Eric screamed.

Fornir dropped like a stone, back into the clouds and between two of the fighters. The rockets exploded as the guns of the fighters crossed their path with lines of bullets.

"It's a dragon" one of the pilots muttered. "And somebody's riding the thing."

"Quiet, Eagles. It's a target and we have to get it. Watch your back and make sure the unit isn't in your line of fire. Does anyone have a lock on the bogie?"

Eric's stomach slammed into his backbone as Fornir pulled out of the dive and shot back up through the clouds.

"We have to get close enough to send the signal," he said to Fornir. "If we stay close to the satellite, they won't shoot for fear of hitting it. Can you get us that close?"

"You jest, young warrior," Fornir answered. "I can keep you close enough to place your runes on the thing's surface."

"Okay. Mimir, can you patch my communicator onto their channel? Maybe I can talk them out of attacking us."

"If you can it would make the task much easier," Mimir answered. "Merely speak the name of their commander and you will be in communication with them. Tap the stud by your right ear to end communications with the pilots or start again."

"Thanks, Mimir," Eric answered. "Here goes nothing."

"We hope," Fornir answered.

Eric kicked the wyrm in response. "Eagle commander, this is Eric Johnson."

"This is a restricted channel," the commander responded. "Get off the air or you will be subject to federal prosecution."

"I'm riding that dragon you're trying to shoot down," Eric said. "You don't understand what's going on here. I'm trying to help."

"Get off the air, kid. This isn't a joke," the commander answered.

"No, it's not. The whole world is in danger and if you don't let me help we're all going to freeze."

"Kid, get off the air. I don't know where you're calling from but we're in the middle of an incident here and we need clear communications."

Eric taped the stud on his helmet. "Nuts. They don't believe me."

"Perhaps more direct action is required," Fornir suggested.

"Like what?" Eric asked.

"Like this," Fornir answered as they shot from the clouds into open space around the satellite.

The wyrm came into the clear air alongside one of the jets as it shot past. He reached out with a handful of talons and opened the wing of the plane from front to back. The plane spiraled down and Eric heard the pilot advise he was bailing out.

"Oh, crap. That's done it," Eric said. "Now they're going to shoot us for sure."

"Not if we circle their treasure," the wyrm answered. "They will not be able to shoot so long as we are nearby."

"Don't bet on it, Fornir. The Giants may want to get rid of you more than they want to save the satellite. Just keep up close for long enough to input the new information."

Eric hung on as the wyrm dipped back into the clouds then shot almost straight up and flew in tight circles around the satellite. When he felt the unit beep that it was finished he started to say something to Fornir, but was interrupted by the flight commander.

"All Eagles, check fire. The bogie is too close to the target unit." There was a change in the tone of the commander's voice. "Enemy flier. You are in United States airspace. Bring your aircraft down to the ground and surrender or we will be forced to fire."

Eric touched the stud on his helmet. "Sorry, Commander. I know I'm supposed to be polite to adults, but you really don't know what's going on here. I have to leave now." He touched the stud again. "Come on, Fornir. Let's go home, and try not to get shot in the process."

"Agreed," Fornir answered as he dropped into the clouds.

Eric's suit sensors stated the changes had been effective in the satellite and the air was already warmer by a few degrees.

"He's gone again, and no heat signature showing on any of the scans, Eagle One."

"Keep looking. We have to make sure they don't get the unit."

Chapter Nineteen

The trip from Philadelphia to the Lehigh Valley had been much too long and incredibly dangerous. The main roads were all shut down—either because of drifting snow or accidents caused by that same drifting snow—and all the back roads were treacherous and impassible most of the time. Only the size and weight of the truck and the four wheel drive capability permitted Loki to wind his way slowly north toward his goal. His companion lay slumped on the seat, the large blood stain on his tunic slowly soaking into the seat of the truck. Loki spared a few glances to his companion, but kept his attention on the road most of the time. If he could get to Mimir, he could get help for his fellow captive. If he did not reach Mimir, they were both as good as dead. Better the Aesir sleep and conserve his strength than try to help Loki find a way through the storm.

But finally, after almost ten hours of driving, they reached the access road to the observatory. The truck had oversized gas tanks, which had been full when Loki and his friend started the trip. This was a good thing since almost all the gas stations they passed were closed and dark. But as they started up the long hill to the observatory, and the gate to Mimir, the truck sputtered and the engine died.

"This vehicle can take us no further," Loki said to his companion.

The sudden jolt as the truck slid sideways into a snowbank awakened the Aesir. He looked through the windshield at the snow, a solid coating of white on the outside of the truck. He shrugged and winced.

"No matter," the wounded Aesir stated. "We must go on in any case. "Are there blankets or something in the back? These tunics will be little protection against the cold even for an Aesir."

Loki turned and rummaged through the back seat of the truck. He pulled up three blankets and a heavy parka, suitable for this winter weather.

"You must take the coat and I will wrap in blankets," Loki stated.

The wounded Aesir shook his head and sat up a bit. "Leave me two of the blankets and wear the coat with another blanket wrapped around you," he said. "I cannot walk in this weather. Go to the gate and bring back help. I will be well for as long as it takes you to climb this small hill and do what is needed."

Loki looked at his companion. The Aesir's face was drawn and white from his injuries and the pain. He knew the Aesir spoke truth—climbing this hill in his condition would possibly kill him and certainly make the journey much slower. He nodded.

"I will return as soon as I may, with a full Aesir medical team to bring you to safety," Loki stated. "You will not be long by yourself."

"I know," the Aesir said with a smile. "I trust you."

Loki squirmed into the coat in the cramped quarters of the truck. A pair of gloves tucked deep in one side pocket was a lucky find and Loki drew them on his cold hands. He turned to the back of the truck and looked through the rest of the boxes on the seat. Someone had put a small cold weather packet together, with plumber's candles and matches, dried food, water and a survival blanket with one side orange and the other silvered to reflect light and/or heat. Loki wrapped the two blankets around his companion then tucked the survival blanket on the outside, silvered side in to reflect the heat back toward the wounded man.

"There. That should keep you warm enough until I return," Loki said. "Once I have left, light one of the candles and set it in a safe place. The small warmth will keep you from freezing, even if it is not enough to keep you truly warm."

"Move swiftly, my friend," the Aesir said. "I fear we have little time to reach aid before our enemies find us again."

"I will return before the first candle has burned out," Loki promised.

"Travel safe," the Aesir said as he reached out a hand toward Loki.

"Stay well," Loki responded as he grasped his friend's wrist.

Loki zipped up the front of the parka and tied the hood almost closed across his face. Then, with the blanket grasped around him like a cloak, he opened the door of the truck and stepped into Fimbulwinter. The wind almost tore the door from his hand, and it took most of his strength to swing it closed again to protect his wounded comrade. Then Loki turned and began his trek up the hillside toward the gate to Mimir and safety.

* * *

Inside the truck, the wounded Aesir waited until he was certain Loki would not return for either something forgotten or because the storm was too difficult for travel. The thought of any storm too intense to stop an Aesir who was both angry and Controlled was not a pleasant thought. After almost half an hour, the Aesir decided it was safe enough. He threw off the blankets and touched a stud on his belt. He shimmered in the cold air of the truck and the Giant Aurnir appeared in the passenger seat. The bloodstained tunic was still the same, but Aurnir drew a small bag of red liquid out from under his belt. He dropped it to the back seat of the truck, out of the way and out from underfoot. Then he reached under the dashboard of the truck and pulled a communicator from its hiding place. He flipped it open and tapped a key.

"Aurnir here. Loki is on the way," he said into the unit.

"Excellent," Bor's voice answered. "We are all on schedule. Stay where you are in case Loki returns, but do not use any of your sensors or weapons. You are too close to Mimir and we are too close to success."

"Understood," was the only reply as he shut down the communicator and sat back in the seat.

It would be a cold wait, he thought.

* * *

Loki climbed for what seemed like days, but could not have been more than an hour, against the biting cold wind and drifting snow. The months he had been held captive by the Vanir had sapped his endurance, and he trudged upward, one foot in front of the other, with little thought for anything other than reaching the gateway All he knew was that he needed to get to the computer so he could warn Odin and Asgard of the Vanir's plans, of their movement to take over Midgard and use its resources to defeat Asgard, then return to their home dimension and defeat the Aesir forces there as well.

He pushed through snowdrift after snowdrift and almost fell many times as the fierce winds slacked off for a moment and he had nothing to push against. He wove back and forth across the roadway, feeling the edge of the hard surface drop away into gravel or grass before he could adjust his path back to the center of the road. But he was Aesir, the prime warriors of Asgard. He would reach his goal or die in the attempt, as his ancestors had done for generations.

Inside the parka, he dripped sweat and he moved forward in a haze of sensations: the wet warmth of his tunic and pants, matched by the bitter cold of the wind as if found each tiny crevice in his coat and sucked the warmth from him. His feet were little more than blocks of ice, even inside Aesir boots and he knew he would need medical care or he would lose toes at least or the foot at worst. But he kept moving forward, driven by the need to get his information to Odin and to save his Aesir companion back in the truck. And of the two goals, to save his companion drove him harder. Compassion was considered a weakness by the Vanir, but even they realized it was a strong force of the Aesir and could drive warriors to achieve goals no command or directive could accomplish. Loki knew he must save his companion and he pushed himself to near death to achieve that goal.

Loki walked along the flat top of the ridge for almost fifteen minutes before he realized he was no longer on the slope. His head came up and he moved forward with renewed energy. He was near—near to warmth, near to success, near to aid for his fellow warrior. He pushed through one last drift and saw, several hundred yards away in a freak eddy of clear air, the edge of one of the small structures atop the ridge he knew was near the gateway for Mimir. He moved forward, the force of the wind a wall he must push through with each step. But he stopped as a flash of light caught his eye, even against the blank white snow which blinded his sight for more than a few steps. The gate had activated and someone was there.

His hand automatically reached to his belt for a weapon that was not there. He carried neither sword nor ax, not rifle nor laser. All he had was his bare hands. He moved to the edge of one of the structures and peered around the corner.

The wind-driven snow blocked any line of sight more than a few yards ahead. But from what he could see, there was nothing on the ridge but snow. Loki moved forward carefully. Each step was a balance against the wind and against his search for whoever was on the ridge with him. As he neared the gate, he stopped and inched forward in what he knew was open area. As he reached the place where the gate was marked along the top of the ridge, he saw a dark figure. The dark form stood, as if he knew Loki was there and awaited his arrival. Loki moved closer until he could make out the featured of the dark form. A full hood trimmed with fur covered the figure's head. As Loki drew near, the fig-ure reached up slowly, to show what it meant to do and not alarm the

Aesir warrior. As the figure threw back the hood to show his face even in the biting cold, Loki gasped.

"Vili," Loki whispered. "But you're dead!"

"Not dead, but indeed lost for these many centuries," the Aesir answered. "And you would know this if your memories were indeed your own."

"What do you mean? I have not seen you since the final battle at the command ship." Loki looked at his uncle and stepped back a pace. "You are Vanir. You are made to look like Vili Odin's brother in form but not in truth."

Vili shook his head sadly. "No, nephew. I am what you see and I am what you remember."

"Then aid me, Uncle," Loki demanded. "One of our own lies back the road, wounded in our escape from the Vanir. Aid me in bringing him through to MMR for aid. Go and bring him here so I may go through to MMR and tell Odin what I know. The Vanir have planned the end of Midgard, and of the Aesir as well, if it be permitted."

Vili nodded. "The end of the Aesir, indeed. And they use you as their tool to accomplish this task." Vili stepped toward Loki with his hands outstretched. "Think. Do you not remember where and when you are?"

Loki stood tall and smiled at Vili. "I know indeed. I am on Midgard. I was captured by the Vanir and held these many months. I escaped and stole one of their chariots for myself and another Aesir and made our way here so I could tell Odin of our enemies plan to destroy all we hold dear."

"And who was this other Aesir?" Vili demanded. "What was his name? Are there other Aesir held captive as well? What are their names?"

Loki hesitated. "I . . . I do not remember. But the Vanir have held us both all this time together. He must be from another unit, one I do not know."

"You know all the Aesir aboard the command ship and the search ships of the squadron. And what was this chariot you rode? How did it make its way through the snow the many miles to your goal?" Vili asked.

"Why simply that the horses did break their path through the snow and force their way through the wind," Loki answered. "But you would know this as well, if you were truly my uncle."

Vili looked sad. "How long has it been since the Aesir came to this world, nephew?" he asked.

"Not so long a time," Loki answered. "We have built a home on Asgard and cross Bifrost to come to Midgard. Here the Vanir work against us but we prevail with the aid of the people of this world. They are mighty fighters in their own way. Not as great as Aesir, but good enough. And we teach them much, that they may grow in wisdom and aid our battle against the Vanir."

"Look at the clothing you wear, nephew. Could a people who dress in fur and leather craft such a coat?" Vili asked. "They would fasten it closed with bone and leather, or do you not see what you wear?"

Loki looked down at his coat and fingered the down-filled layers. "This is indeed a fine bearskin coat, and wondrously warm for all that." His fingers stroked the woven nylon.

"Focus, Nephew," Vili demanded. "Remember the warrior's sight. See what is there and not the illusion. Focus!"

Loki hesitated. His fingers rubbed the coat and he listened to the hiss of his leather gloves against the nylon. His fingers moved to push their way into the plush of the coat, as if he moved through fur. His eyes saw fur, but slowly he began to notice the differences between his senses.

Suddenly he straightened as the Vanir Control forced him to focus on his task.

"No, you try to trick me. I must get to MMR and warn Odin," Loki said. "Step aside and let me pass. I must enter the gate."

Vili shook his head. "No. You are Controlled by the Vanir. You cannot pass."

"You are not the warrior I am, Uncle," Loki warned. "I can defeat you, but at a cost. By the blood we share, let me pass lest I harm you."

"No."

"Then on your head be it," Loki said.

* * *

Without another word he threw himself at Vili. But he never reached his uncle. There was a faint buzz, lost in the howl of the wind, and Loki dropped to the ground, unconscious. Vili stepped forward and pulled the rod out of his pocket where he had fired through his coat. He touched Loki's neck to check his pulse and nodded. Then he pulled back the left sleeve of his coat and tapped his communicator.

"Loki is unconscious," he reported to Mimir and Tommy. "Better we take him to Dwarvenheim so we can find out what the Vanir planned to use to gain control of Mimir."

"Agreed, Commander," Mimir answered. "I will conform the gate for your return. I am sorry it was necessary to handle him in such a manner."

"As am I, Mimir. As am I. But at least now we can bring him back to health properly, if the damage was not too great."

Mimir was silent for a moment. "When you are ready, bring him through. The dwarves and the other Aesir are waiting."

"Thank you," Vili answered.

With great care, he lifted the body of Loki in his arms and stepped through the gate.

* * *

"No! No! No! It cannot have happened! He cannot be stopped! We planned too well! All the Aesir should be too ill to fight. How could Vili be waiting for him? He should be almost dead with the illness we sent them! The Aesir and those accursed dwarves should be as disabled at the puny humans of this world!"

In his rage, Bor picked up his desk and slammed it over onto the floor. What didn't drop and break as he turned it over smashed to pieces as the desk crashed to the hardwood floor on its top. One leg snapped off with the impact and Bor snatched it up and hurled it at the door to his office just as one of the Vanir outside rushed in to see what caused the noise. The Vanir ducked with a warrior's reflexes and the desk leg flew past him to crash into something breakable in the outer office.

"Go," Bor commanded. "Gather all our forces, all the Vanir that remain, all the humans in our control. We will attack these weaklings and wipe them from this world and be damned if the humans know we are here."

"But the attack on the cave—?" the Vanir started to ask.

"I don't care about the cave," Bor screamed as he stalked across the office and grabbed the Vanir by the throat. "I want them dead, do you hear? Dead!"

He screamed again and again at the Vanir and only when he realized he was facing the floor, his hands around the throat of the dead Giant did he stop. He stood and looked down at his hands. Then he looked up. On the other side of the outer office, two other Vanir and the human Keyes looked at their commander and down at the dead Giant on the floor.

"Go. Gather our warriors. We will finish Ragnarok!"

The two Vanir disappeared before Bor could say anything more. Keyes moved to gather the equipment from his office he knew Bor would want.

Bor went to the window and looked out on a white world and screamed his defiance and frustration into the clouds.

Chapter Twenty

Dwarvenheim resembled an anthill, Eric thought as he watched the dwarves rush across the compound from building to building in anticipation of the Vanir attack. The workshop had a high window on what would have been a fourth floor, if there were any floors below the catwalk he stood on. This end of the workshop had been designed for building large structures under controlled conditions and even had a mechanism that split away one side of the building to permit the constructs to move outside without dismantling them. Eric had climbed up to the eastern-facing window to see if he could see anything in the storm. But the blizzard of Fimbulwinter still blew snow hard enough to make vision any further away than the edge of the village an impossible task.

What Eric really wanted was a chance to slow down for a minute, to give some thought to what was coming. In the past three years, he had gone from being a normal boy going to school in Philadelphia to being a warrior from another dimension fighting monsters and demons from the stars. And now it looked like the monsters were going to win.

Eric had no doubt the few Aesir and the dwarves of the village would put up a valiant fight, but there were so few of them against so many of the Vanir. And this time the Vanir would bring all their friends to the party. The sensor array showed some movement toward the village, but the heavy snow and whipping winds made vision almost impossible and even Aesir sensors had limits when blocked by inches of ice and ten-foot snowdrifts. As near as they could tell there were humans working for the Vanir headed for the village, some of the dogs left from Fenrir's pack and however many Vanir the Aesir had yet to round up. So far it was impossible to estimate the total number of enemies headed for the village, but it was at least a two-to-one advantage for the bad guys and possibly three-to-one!

Eric felt a vibration on the catwalk and turned.

"Steph, you're all right!" he yelled as he saw his young friend.

"Just as soon as my dad gave me your magic elixir," she answered, punching him in the shoulder.

"Ow! Hey, what was that for?"

"That was for being such a dufus and getting infected in the first place," she said. She stood on the catwalk, hands on hips as she looked at him. Then she stepped forward and gave him a quick kiss on the cheek. "And that was for coming up with the answer to cure us and the dwarves and the Aesir."

"What, nothing for me?" Tommy asked as he joined the pair at the window.

Steph turned and swung to hit Tommy in the shoulder. "You were dumb enough to jump out a window and attack the biggest wolf on the planet, you bonehead!"

He dodged the blow and stepped back with a big smile on his face. "It worked, didn't it? We caught Fenrir."

"And almost got yourself chewed up in the process," Steph countered. Then she stepped up and gave him a hug. "But at least you're my bonehead."

"Um," Tommy mumbled as he looked over her shoulder at Eric.

Eric smiled and gave Tommy a thumbs-up signal.

"So Mr. Norn-Smith," Eric said in an attempt to break the mood, "what's the word on the approaching army?"

"Too many and very well armed, as far as we can tell," Tommy said as he pulled gently away from Stephanie. "Suori has the dwarves out pulling supports from a series of tunnels they've been digging around the perimeter since they took over here. It seems dwarves like to get their enemies underground to work on them. They have the advantage then, especially in tunnels they dig themselves. And the dwarves kind of figured there was a good chance the Vanir would be back to reclaim their property, since they do that kind of thing a lot."

"Smart dwarves," Eric agreed. "How much of the army do they think they can stop that way?"

Tommy shrugged. "Suori thinks they can stop any armored machines, but the ground troops can get past the ditches easy enough, unless they get caught in the collapse of a tunnel. That could still leave a lot of soldiers to handle. And if the machines stop before they get to the tunnels, they can sit and fire their guns from outside the perimeter and knock out the buildings that way."

"I guess the Aesir don't have some kind of force shield they can put over things until Odin and the other Aesir can get here?" Eric asked.

Tommy shook his head. "Mimir says they have shields for their ships in space but nothing that works on a planet. Something about the atmosphere goofs up the signal or something. But the good news is the dwarves also have a whole lot of those special crystals set up, like the ones you told me they used on Asgard when it was attacked. Dwalin's been busy with the guys here in the village these past months and they have the entire perimeter covered. If the machines and the guns get in range, all their modern weapons will be useless."

"That is good news," Eric answered. "But won't the Vanir plan for that kind of thing? I mean they've been on Earth a long time and there are a lot of other weapons they could use. Plus they know about all the crystals we're growing here on Earth already."

Tommy shook his head again. "Two things: first Mimir thinks the Vanir have been here so long they've forgotten how to fight like the Aesir. They're too used to our weapons. And none of the Vanir captured in that raid to Asgard made it back to warn them. Even the ones who were here when we rescued your aunt and Vili were using mostly human weapons."

"Okay, and second?" Eric asked.

Tommy shrugged. "We're gotten some good views of some the approaching army in the sensor units the dwarves set up. The Vanir and the humans with them are armed with human weapons and some high tech stuff the Vanir are carrying. There are some swords and spears among the Vanir, but most of the weapons are guns or something pretty much like them."

"So the good news is that they will be down to clubs and swords. The bad news is it's a lot of clubs and swords," Eric stated.

"Pretty much," Tommy agreed.

"Crap," Eric spat. "And still no word from Asgard through Mimir?"

"The time dilation problem makes it tough for Mimir to get a quick message through. He can communicate with Earth a lot better than with Asgard." Tommy shrugged. "The message is sent. We just have to hold out until the cavalry arrives."

"Why am I starting to feel like Davy Crockett at the Alamo?" Eric asked.

"Or General Custer at Little Big Horn," Tommy agreed. "But at least we know where they are. Some of the Valkyr have their mounts stabled here at Dwarvenheim so they can provide some mobile support and attack the fringes of the army with those web balls Mimir gave us. Your Uni-shield can give you and Fornir protection so you can be our aerial arm until his flame gives out. And Mimir has something like a flame thrower he thinks can be mounted for you to use when that happens. If all else fails you can always throw snowballs."

"Do the Vanir have any sort of air support with their army?" Eric asked.

Tommy shook his head. "We don't see anything on the sensors and Mimir thinks the winds have shifted too much now that the satellites are warming things for any type of Earth made aircraft to fly safely in the changing atmosphere, not that the Vanir care much about safety for their human helpers. But the winds are still pretty tough for anything smaller than a dragon. I guess they thought the satellites were worth the effort or else they couldn't convince their human allies to protect them. A village in the middle of Pennsylvania probably would not make a whole lot of sense as a terrorist camp, though."

"Which could mean they don't have any air support or they plan some other sort of surprise," Stephanie suggested.

Eric nodded. "We'll just have it play it as it comes."

* * *

Bor looked out the frosted window of the armored vehicle and smiled. He would finally have his chance to stand on the command deck of the Aesir craft and pull the information he needed from MMR. He would return to the Vanir home world a hero, with the knowledge of how to defeat the Aesir at home as well as here in Midgard. And he would bring three new realms under the control of the Vanir. Most likely, he would be left in charge of Midgard, Asgard and Jotunheim, as payment for his efforts, Bor thought. Although why he would not want to stay on this misbegotten mudball was something he would explain loudly and forcefully to any Vanir who asked.

He shifted around and looked at the box on the back seat of the vehicle next to Keyes. His secret weapon was well protected in the soft layers of foam and bubble wrap filling the container. All he needed to do was get to the village and the battle would be over. The threat held in that box would stop even the Aesir from continuing the battle once he made his threat known. None of the Aesir wanted a gateway to

193

Niflheim open in their front yard. The resulting entropy drop would suck the entire planet through to the black hole that comprised the fourth dimensional link created when the Aesir and Vanir slipped through to this dimension. Bor almost regretted how quickly the fight would be over once he reached the village. He really wanted to see how his human warriors stood up to the Aesir and those puny dwarves.

Ah, well. He could have his battle another time, once he was in control of all the worlds. But then again, he thought to himself, maybe he would just have all those warriors attack after he had control of the gateway. No sense letting a good battle go to waste, he thought with a smile.

* * *

They were as ready as they could be, given the time left to them. He stood behind Tommy as the Norn-in-training watched the sensor screens that showed the approach of the first wave of the Vanir army. Almost half the village was in the path of the dogs advancing ahead of the rest of the Vanir force.

"The people are stopping. The dogs are ahead of them," Tommy said.

"They make ready to fight," Suori said. "First they drink battle potion, then they turn to berserkers, then they come." The dwarf shook his head. "Not good to be battle-mad in this weather. Many of them die in the cold."

"Berserkers?" Eric asked. "You didn't say anything about berserkers when we were making these plans! How are we going to fight berserkers?"

Suori shrugged. "Same way we fight other warriors. Sword to ax, ax to spear. Whatever."

"We have another problem, I fear," Mimir said through his link to Earth. "There is an anomaly in one of those vehicles at the rear of the Vanir convoy. A gateway crystal is tuned and partially powered, ready to open its passage."

"A gateway to where?" Eric asked.

"According to the energy signature, to Niflheim," Mimir answered. "And if that gateway opens here, there is a good chance the entire planet will crack open and be sucked inside."

"Oh, crap," Eric said softly. He looked at Tommy and Stephanie. "Thor told me about Niflheim. It's connected to Asgard and Jotunheim, just like here to Earth, and it's a black hole. If a gate to that place opens up here it will suck in everything, including the sun."

"Can we scramble the signal?" Tommy asked Mimir.

"Not at this range. And by the time we get closer, the Vanir can activate the gate and kill anyone nearby." Mimir sighed. "I fear the Vanir have brought a Doomsday Device in truth."

"Can we get it away from them some other way?" Eric asked. "If they open the gate to Niflheim they'll be sucked in just like we will. They must want to use it as a bargaining chip."

"True. But by the time the dogs have done their damage, and the humans who follow them, there will be little left for the Vanir to fight, based on the formation they have sent toward us." Mimir lit three red points of light on the central console, equidistant across the perimeter of the village. "At this time they will come in from these points. The dogs will reach us first, followed by a human force of warriors." One of the red lights blinked. "The Vanir are here, except for those few who lead the human army. And it is here that the Niflheim crystal is located. There are dwarven tunnels throughout this area . . ." A series of blue lines became a spider web in front of the advancing red dots of Vanir vehicles. ". . . so there is likely a chance we can stop the Vanir from reaching the village, if we can obtain the crystal."

"Which means we need to get the Vanir out of the trucks first," Tommy said. "Or else they'll just start up the gate as soon as the trucks drop down."

"Boys," Stephanie said with a snort. "You always do things the hard way. Just get them to stop their trucks outside town and sucker them in with what they want. They'll come to you and you can take the gate away from them."

"And how may this be done, young Valkyr?" Freawin asked her student.

"Use some of the crystals here in the village to give the impression of the gate to Mimir and put a lot of guards around it. Make it look like we're trying to get reinforcements from Asgard and the Vanir will attack to stop us. When we sucker them in, we get the drop on them."

Eric and Tommy looked at each other and shrugged.

"Gotta admit, it sounds like it would work," Tommy said.

Freawin smiled. "You have learned your lessons well, young Valkyr. You will be a great warrior when you reach your prime."

Stephanie smiled. "I don't know. I think I'm pretty hot stuff now."

Tommy looked over at Eric. "She's definitely spending too much time with the Valkyr," he said with a smile. Then he grimaced as Stephanie punched him in the shoulder, the same one she hit before. He backed away carefully. "Definitely too much time."

"All right, we need to get moving and quickly," Eric said as Stephanie started to swing at Tommy again. "The dogs are almost in position. We need to be ready when they hit the village wall or we're up a frozen creek without a set of skis, or something like that." He looked over at Suori. "Get your guys moving to dig out from under the bomb vehicle when it gets closer and keep in touch with Mimir so he can tell you where to dig. Then get the Aesir in camp and the rest of the dwarves and set up the diversion teams. We need to be ready five minutes ago."

Suori walked close to the three children. "Children stay here and watch Vanir. Tell us what happens and where to move. But not joint in fight. Not yet grown enough to fight Vanir, especially in cold weather."

"No problem, Suori," Tommy agreed. "No way I'm going out in this weather without super-powered winter underwear."

"But I want to help," Stephanie complained. "Mist Walker will take care of me."

Freawin grasped the girl's shoulder and pulled her around eye-to eye. "And so he would care for you in battle. But would you risk his life just to prove how young you truly are, or will you follow orders, like a well-trained Valkyr should?"

Stephanie sighed. "Okay. I'll follow orders. But next time . . ."

Freawin waved a finger in front of Stephanie's nose. "If this battle goes as planned there will be no next time with the Vanir. But there will be much yet for you to learn and much work for you to do if we survive this day. Mist Walker's first rider is not here to celebrate the end of the Vanir. Would you dishonor her memory?"

Stephanie ducked her head in shame. "No, Commander. I am sorry I spoke out of turn."

Freawin patted the girl on the shoulder. "Your wish to help is good, but do not forget your lessons."

"Yes, Commander," Stephanie repeated.

"Okay, let's get moving," Eric said. "Freawin, you and the Valkyr take the right flank. Aesir and dwarves in the middle and the rest of the dwarves on the left. Go for it!"

The workshop emptied except for the three children and a curious dragon.

The dragon stuck his head into the room and laid it on the floor close to the communications array. "Is there no task you set for me, young commander?" Fornir asked Eric with a smile.

Eric smiled. "You're our secret weapon, Fornir. If the Vanir look like they're going to break through, you and I can drop some web balls on them and tie them up for a while. But we don't have enough balls, even with the supplies sent over from the command ship. We have to use them carefully."

"Well enough," Fornir agreed. "I would not care to fly in this weather without need, but to vanquish the Vanir once and for all is a need worthy of the risk."

Tommy looked up from the consolee. "Do you think we have a chance to stop them? Really?"

Eric shrugged. "All I know is that we have to try. Odin, Thor and the rest of the Aesir are all out of touch. Even Uncle Al can't get here in time to help out since he's on Asgard. Somehow we've been dropped into the command seat and we just have to do the best we can. We can't let the Vanir win, no matter what. Right?"

"Right!" Tommy and Stephanie echoed.

"Indeed," Fornir said. "But do not discount your own skills in this matter. You, Eric John's Son, have been through much in your training as an Aesir warrior, tested both by the hand of Thor Odinsson and by circumstances beyond your control, and you have triumphed each time. You, Thomas Norn-smith, have been given much training in the science of the Aesir and with only that limited training received were able to capture one of the Vanir's greatest tools- Fenrir." Fornir huffed a cloud of steam and turned toward Stephanie. "And you, Stephanie Valkyr-ca-det, have also been tested in combat far beyond your years and have also shown you are a true battle-maiden. You three are indeed more than you seem, whether by choice, by circumstance or by the will of destiny. The

Vanir believe they face a foe disorganized and unprepared. Even though they come in force, the battle ahead will not be in their favor for you three bring more to the field than the Vanir can ever know."

The three children stood for a moment and looked at each other.

"With a pep talk like that, how can we lose?" Eric asked.

"Then let's get to work," Tommy answered.

And just then an alarm went off in the workshop. Tommy spun back to the console and looked at the screens.

"The dogs have reached the perimeter. Here we go!"

Chapter Twenty-One

"Put more space between those vehicles!" Bor shouted over the communicator. "You know how those cursed, shrunken excuses for living creatures like to dig tunnels. Don't let them catch all of you in the same fall-in."

Bor watched on his monitor as the Vanir attack vehicles quickly moved further apart and staggered their lines. It had been a long time since the Vanir had truly fought a battle, especially against any sort of organized foe, and he knew his army was out of practice. But they were Vanir, the best that centuries of genetic engineering could create, and the Aesir and their poor vassals were never truly a match for a Vanir in battle. The minor skirmishes fought between Aesir and Vanir since they came to these dimensions were nothing like the true battles fought in the past between mighty enemies.

Bor looked out into the driving snow and smiled. When they came to these dimensions, the Aesir and Vanir alike had been reduced to simple sword and spear. But the Vanir had taken advantage of their situation and guided many of the developments across the globe of Midgard and those fruits were now in the armored vehicles moving toward the gateway that could lead them home. One small piece of data was all Bor needed to end the centuries of battle, to end to the hiding and deception. It was time to throw off the cloak and come forth as warriors.

"Twelve *rôst* to perimeter, Commander," the driver stated. The vehicle jerked as they ran over a frozen section of ground and Bor smiled again.

"Pass the word to stop at six *rôst*," Bor said into the communicator. "We will still be out of range of their sensors but within range of our weapons. Let us see if these puny creatures are in any shape to defend their home after our plague has decimated them. Let the beasts and those humans who serve us test the defense of the village. Send them now while we prepare." He reached around to check the case holding the crystals, making sure it was secure. Then he turned back to the communicator. "Pass the word. Prepare for battle. The Dragon's Blood will give us the power to defeat our enemies."

The cheer from the Vanir stretched out across the storm-washed ground was heard even inside the vehicle.

In each of the Vanir units, flasks of an ancient formula were being passed from warrior to warrior. As each Vanir drank deep from the container, he dropped back against the side of vehicle and locked every muscle in pain. The power of the elixir flowing through their bodies gave them the strength of ten Vanir. The cost in a shortened life span and an eventual loss of muscle tone was something the Vanir accepted willingly. When a Vanir became that weak, he died in combat. As they began to move again, each of the Vanir roared a battle cry that echoed out into the storm. By the time they reached six miles from the village, all the Vanir were ready for battle.

"Get the heavy weapons out of the vehicles and set up a perimeter," Bor ordered. "We will set a noose around the village and draw it tight to squeeze out our information. One blast of fire and they will surrender to us without a fight."

The Vanir hurried to obey Bor's order and through the snow a ring of bright lights could be seen moving from each side of the command vehicle as the Vanir activated the energy weapons they has brought with them. Unlike the weapons of Midgard, these were weapons that fired bolts of energy, even more powerful than a laser beam, able to cut through any armor less dense than Aesir battle steel. And even battle steel could not stop these beams for long. Bor knew the Aesir could not use their shields here on the planet, so any armor would be exposed to the beams and would soon be overcome. The village would have few, if any, similar Aesir weapons and Bor expected this to be a very short battle.

* * *

The dogs hit the wall of snow surrounding the village and slid back. The slight ramp made by the frozen snow was not enough to give even the claws of these great beasts purchase enough to climb over the high barrier. So the dogs moved left and right to seek a way through the wall. A howl from one of the forward scouts announced a way into the village and the dogs flowed forward in a living wave. But the dwarves had prepared their defenses well. After Fenrir's attack, the dwarves had thrown up a maze of passages at each opening above ground, to lead any attackers back and forth until they were in single file in narrow, high-walled walkways. When the last of the dogs entered the maze, the roar of an explosion echoed across the village, heard even above the whistle of the wind. The retreat had been closed off and the dogs could not leave the same way they entered. But these creatures did not have Fenrir's intelligence and did not suspect a trap. They had their orders from their Vanir handlers and they moved forward to attack.

As the dogs moved forward, the dwarves closed more and more of the passage behind them until all the dogs were single file in the narrow chutes. Then the lead dog reached the end of the passageway. A high wall of ice and snow blocked the beast from moving forward. The howls echoed back through the line of dogs as they tried to back out of their trap. But the narrow passage would not permit them to turn. Then the dwarves appeared at the top of the walls, above the dogs. The beasts tried to jump up to reach their enemies but all they could do was fall back on each other, snapping and biting in their frustration. The dwarves lifted buckets over the top of the wall and poured a liquid into the chutes that immediately expanded into a heavy fog that covered everything below. This was the Breath of the Ice Dragon, a substance long though by dwarves to be lost to the time of legends. But Mimir had the recipe in his databanks and prepared the dwarves with the information to protect their village. As the fog reached the ground below, the howls of the dogs slowed and finally stopped. In a few minutes, the fog blew away in the strong winds.

In the chutes below, all the dogs were frozen in place, safe from harm, and from harming anyone else, until the dwarves chose to free them from their ice prison.

* * *

"One down, three to go," Tommy said as he watched the dwarves check their new captives.

"That was much too easy," Eric said, looking over Tommy's shoulder at the view screen.

"Hey, take what we can get," Tommy answered. "The Vanir are coming in full force and the trick with the Dragon's Breath wouldn't stop an army of people able to think about where they were walking. At least we won't have to worry about the dogs anymore."

"Did you plan that?" Stephanie asked Tommy.

Tommy shook his head. "Suori came up with that one. Some kind of a variation on an old fish trap they used to use back on Jotunheim. The fish would swim through the maze into a small pool where they could be scooped up and they couldn't find the hole to swim back out again. Mimir came up with the freezing fog idea when he reviewed some of the old battle plans. Seems this trick was used to stop a plague of some small mouse-type creature that used to attack crops on one of the Aesir home planets."

"Kind of like army ants, I guess," Eric said.

"That's what Mimir said when I showed him some stuff about ants from the Internet." Tommy looked back at the screens and watched as the humans came closer to the village. "And now for round two."

* * *

"Wolverine unit, this is Wolverine Leader. Prepare to engage."

The team of humans, a total of two hundred brainwashed soldiers from across the United States, moved forward at the command of their Vanir masters. They were armed with some of the most effective weapons known to any armed force on the planet. But they were walking through a winter storm none of them could have imagined. Only the commands that echoed in their brains, transmitted by Vanir handlers, kept them moving forward. They reached the walls of the village and stopped. Scouts moved left and right, still in sight of their team, as they searched for an entrance through the thick ice that surrounded the village.

Finally the scouts located what looked like a gateway through the wall and the masses soldiers moved forward with explosives to open the way. One after the other, the muffled thump of explosions echoed into the storm and the soldiers rushed forward to attack the village. But what the soldiers found was a large, open hallway forty feet across and almost one hundred feet deep that led to another gateway of steel and wood. As the soldiers reached the middle of the hallway, a rumbling beneath their feet gave only a moment's warning before the floor collapsed beneath them. All the soldiers dropped into a deep pit with ice-slick sides. Most of the men managed to land without injury, but a moan here and there and the limp form of an occasional unconscious man lying on the bottom of the pit, proved the fall had not been an easy one.

The soldiers opened up with their weapons, firing at the walls of ice around them and the doorway at the end of the hall. After a minute of useless gunfire their leaders managed to get them to stop and began to organize the men into living pyramids braced against the sides of the pit so they could climb out.

Before the first soldier reached the top of the pit, a wave of water washed over the edge and all the soldiers moved back out of the way as the water turned almost instantly to ice as it washed down the walls.

"Put weapons in piles at ends of pit or water cover all of you," a dwarf voice called out from a hidden opening above the pit.

Some of the soldiers opened fire again in the direction of the voice. As the shots rang out another wave of water burst over the top of the pit, this time covering some of the men and freezing them into ice-locked statues.

"Last warning!" the dwarf voice called again as the water stopped. "Put weapons in piles or pit be full of nice statues until next Spring."

The humans might be controlled by the Vanir, but they were still intelligent beings. The commanders organized the rifles to be brought to each end of the pit and moved the men away from them.

"Small guns, little bombs on belts and all knives too," the dwarf voice called. "We find weapons on you later, you get hurt when we take them."

Slowly the soldiers went back to the piles and dropped their other weapons with their rifles, adding almost as much to the stack as was already there. Then they moved away again.

As the last soldier stepped away from the weapons, a flow of water washed over the end of the pit onto the piled weapons until a foot thick layer of ice covered everything the soldiers had put on the pile.

"Sit and relax," the dwarf told the soldiers. "Have to go talk to Vanir for a while. Be back when done. Maybe even before Spring!" Dwarf laughter echoed across the pit and the soldiers tried to find a place to sit that wouldn't freeze their posteriors.

* * *

"Two down," Tommy murmured.

"Definitely too easy." Eric echoed his earlier comment. "Can the Giants really be this dumb?"

"These are just tricks, not warriors in combat," Tommy stated. "We caught the Vanir off guard, and before they could counteract the planning the dwarves put into their village. There are still a lot of them out there and they're ready to blow this place off the map right about now. The easy part is over."

"Then we need to give them something else to think about," Eric suggested. "Mimir, start the crystal fluctuations and make it look like a gateway is opening."

"Powering up . . . locking coordinates . . . gateway linked," Mimir said. "A crystal decoy is now powered up at the east side of the village, closest to the Vanir vehicles and weapons. It's just inside the perimeter of the village and should make a tempting target."

"Let's hope they buy it," Eric said as he turned toward the view screens.

* * *

"The dwarves are opening a gateway to Asgard!" Bor shouted over the communicator. "Once we have opened the wall of the village prepare to advance and locate the gateway quickly. We cannot permit them to escape and close off our access to MMR!"

The Vanir shifted their weapons based on the commands Bor channeled through the communications link and prepared their beams to burn the village to the ground.

"Prepare to fire!" Bor commanded.

An echo of response came back down the line, confirming all the Vanir were in place and ready.

"And . . . fire!" Bor shouted.

As one, all the Vanir gunners pressed the triggers of the weapons which would destroy Dwarvenheim.

* * *

"Now!" Tommy shouted to the dwarves.

As each of the Vanir's gunners pushed the triggers, a web of energy flowed over the village from the crystals placed around the perimeter. All the Vanir weapons, unshielded here on Earth when they were removed from their place aboard the Vanir battleships, were exposed to the warping rays of the energy flow. One or two of the weapons managed a brief burst of energy and some of the buildings in the village exploded from the force of the blast. But then all the weapons began to bend and twist in the flow of the dwarven crystals and the weapons became little more than misshapen lumps of metal. One unit, to the left of Bor's position, exploded as the twisting metal caused a short circuit across the energy pack inside the weapon and several Vanir were thrown across the snow by the concussion. And the vehicles that had carried the Vanir no longer functioned as their active engines melted together into lumps of metal.

"Now, Suori! Attack" Tommy called out.

The dwarves rose up out of shallow trenches in front of the Vanir and moved through the blinding snow with ax and sword raised high. The Vanir reacted like the warriors they were bred to be and dropped the useless energy guns to draw their own weapons. But as the Vanir moved forward, gaining momentum as the energy of the Dragon's Blood flowed through them, the ground dropped away beneath their feet. Many of the Vanir dropped as much as ten feet into trenches dug by the dwarves across most of the village perimeter. The Vanir found themselves facing dwarves standing atop mounds of earth on the other side of the trenches, well above even their heads.

Bor screamed in anger. "Get the humans forward. Fill those trenches and attack. We outnumber them. We cannot lose."

The remainder of the human army under the control of the Vanir, both those humans controlled by the mind device used to brainwash humans and those humans who joined the Vanir for their own gain, pushed forward into the fight. Vanir stepped on their bodies to climb the far side and reach the dwarves, but those few who reached the top were quickly pushed back into the trench.

"Now, before they get a chance to regroup," Tommy said to one of the Aesir in the control room.

A switch was pushed and a long pipeline, planned for irrigation of the dwarves' fields next season, was diverted into the trenches. A wall of water four feet high poured down the trench around the village and made the footing even more difficult as the ground turned from frozen earth to chilling mud. When the trench was full the entire way around the village, Tommy gave another command and the energy flow from the crystals changed. The biting cold of the storm was increased even more than the Vanir had planned and all the trenches froze solid with Vanir and human alike trapped in the ice.

Behind Bor a trench opened up and swallowed the vehicle he had used to ride through the storm.

"No, the crystals," he screamed. "Keyes, get them out!"

He stepped forward to jump into the trench when a wall of water washed over the vehicle and covered it in a layer of ice too thick for even Bor's great strength to break through quickly. Through the translucent ice, Bor could see the human pounding futilely on the ice-covered doors of the vehicle. With a curse, the Vanir turned back toward the combat around him.

"Kill them, kill them all," he commanded. "And then take their village apart to find that gateway."

The Vanir not caught in the trenches moved forward with ax, spear and sword to face their enemies and a deep throated dirge echoed across the frozen ground as Vanir marched into battle on Midgard for the first time in centuries.

Back in the control room, Tommy looked at the screens and sent a message to the dwarves and Valkyr at the edge of the village.

"Here they come," the young Norn-smith announced. "And I think they're pretty ticked off right now!"

Chapter Twenty-Two

The dwarves moved back from the trenches, which were no longer a barrier for the Vanir and those humans left on the other side. The deep layer of ice actually gave the Vanir the height they needed to cross what had been an obstacle. The crystals may have destroyed their energy weapons, but sword and ax had long been a part of warfare for these people and they knew their jobs well.

Tommy looked over the battlefield, the sensors unaffected by the energy flow from the crystals. The dwarves and few Aesir left in Dwarvenheim were still outnumbered, and now all their preparations had been pushed aside. All that was left was ax against ax, sword against sword. The crash of metal against metal carried through the sounds of the storm, even into the building where the young warriors watched their friends battle for control of the Earth. He could advise Sudri and the dwarves where the Giants were attacking, and where other dwarves needed reinforcement. But as he watched, the Giants drove their opponents back as the Dragon's Blood coursed through their bodies and gave them strength to do what would have been impossible under other circumstances. Giant after Giant jumped over the trenches and attacked dwarven warriors.

One Vanir against a dozen dwarves would normally be a short fight, Eric knew, but as he watched, dwarf after dwarf was knocked aside as the Giants moved closer to the village. Sometimes the dwarf rose again and jumped back into the fight. All too often, the small bodies lay still: unconscious or dead.

At the edges of the battle, Freawin and the other Valkyr rode their snow-white stallions through the melee. To come within reach of a Giant's hands would be death for a Valkyr, so Freawin gave strict orders they were to harass the Giants only and not to come close enough to reach. Spears of Aesir metal stabbed through armor and clothing to draw blood and the path of each Valkyr was marked by a trail of red as the mounted scouts pulled a Giant's attention away from the village, even if only for a short time.

"They're getting too close," Eric said as he watched the Vanir move closer and closer to the village. "We thought that getting them all on one side of the village would be a good thing but that Dragon's Blood stuff gives them too much of an advantage."

As Eric and the others watched, the Vanir moved toward the group of guards surrounding the crystals set to imitate a gateway. There were only forty dwarves left in that group and almost as many Giants moved forward to attack what they believed was a gate.

Eric turned and sprinted for the outside room.

"Fornir. We need to get airborne! There are still too many of them for the dwarves to fight." He grabbed a prepared bag of net balls and clambered up Fornir's back as he slapped his helmet into position. He tapped the stud on his helmet and spoke to his friend as he buckled the straps to hold him in the saddle. "It will be a short takeoff, but we need to get in front of the Vanir if we can."

"And so we will, my friend," Fornir answered. He looked over at Tommy and nodded. "Open the door, young Norn-Smith, for the last of the great wyrms fights today."

Tommy hit the button and the wide doors opened into the storm sweeping through the village. Snow blew into the room and the sound of battle rose even louder than the wind. With a roar that echoed through the building, Fornir stepped out into Fimbulwinter and leaped into the air. His wings snapped down and thrust his body higher as the great dragon climbed into the blowing snow.

"Swing right, Fornir," Eric called out. "We want to come up behind them."

Fornir pumped harder and his long tail swung like a rudder to push him to the right. He continued his climb and banked around the village. The sound of metal crashing against metal and screaming Vanir echoed into the sky but the snow made sight impossible.

"Tommy, I need some directions," Eric said to his friend over his communicator.

"Your screen will now show the battle laid out beneath you," the calm voice of Mimir echoed in Eric's ear.

The screen in the helmet lit up in a representation of the village walls and the battle raging beneath—the Vanir and their allies in red and the dwarven forces and their allies in green.

"Thanks, Mimir. Any chance you can get a call in to Asgard?"

"I have been trying my friend," the computer answered. "But the nexus the Vanir brought to open a door to Niflheim is interfering with communications between the worlds. For the moment we are on our own."

"Just great," Eric said, more to himself than anyone else. "Okay, Fornir, turn a bit to your left and then drop down in a dive. Just try not to nose into the ground, okay?"

"Shall I tear their helmets from their heads, young warrior?" Fornir asked as he dived out of the sky.

Eric held on as the dragon roared out a challenge. The young warrior had one of the web balls in each hand, but almost wished he could grab the straps instead. Fornir was angry and almost as battle-mad as the Vanir. But as they neared the ground, the clouds and the snow cleared and the dragon snapped out his wings to soar close over the heads of the Vanir forces. Eric tossed a ball to each side and reached back into the pack for more. Fornir's speed made it difficult to make more than two throws in each pass, but the dragon swept back and forth across the battlefield until Eric had emptied the pack.

"All out, Fornir," Eric shouted. "How'd we do?"

"Not well, I fear," the dragon answered.

He rose up to just below the cover the storm provided for the battle so Eric could look more closely at the events below. The web balls had indeed struck Vanir and human warriors as Eric had predicted. But where a ball had trapped a Vanir, the strength given by the Dragon's Blood permitted the Giant to tear free from the webbing. Only the humans captured by the web balls were out of the fight.

"Crap. They're still moving forward." Eric looked around for any ideas for weapons Fornir could use. The great wyrm was a valiant warrior in the air, but on the ground Eric had a strong suspicion the Vanir could beat the dragon to a pulp. "Fornir, do you think you could pick up one of those vehicles in your claws?" he asked as he pointed to the abandoned vehicles behind the Giants.

"Perhaps not, but they also left weapons that are little more than chunks of metal now," the dragon stated. "Those will drop well on the heads of the Vanir."

"Let's go for it," Eric called out and they dived toward the weapons sites of the Vanir.

The energy guns were large, but not as large as a truck or car, and Fornir picked one up easily in his claws before swooping around over the battle before the walls of Dwarvenheim. The crash of metal hitting armor sounded loud even at the height they were flying and Fornir roared as he swept back around for another load.

Inside the workshop, Tommy and Stephanie watched the battle through the sensors and Tommie frowned as the Giants moved closer and closer to the walls.

"They're going to break through, and there aren't enough of our guys to keep them out. Even if Odin and the Aesir can get here, there won't be much left after the Vanir get finished." Tommy turned toward a screen showing the face of Mimir. "If the Giants break through can you stop them from getting inside you, from getting to your memory banks or whatever you call them?"

"The Vanir will not obtain any information from me, young Norn-Smith," Mimir answered. "But to stop them from my side, I would need to destroy the gateway, which will cause great damage to the village of the dwarves. And those warriors left behind would also be killed or injured in the explosion."

"Yeah, well, keep that as a last option," Tommy said. He looked at Stephanie. "You keep feeding information to the dwarves and Eric."

"And what are you going to be doing?" she asked him.

"They need reinforcements out there and we only have one thing left I can throw at them, sort of," Tommy answered. He reached out and flipped a switch that shut down the energy crystals surrounding the village.

"I'm going with you," Stephanie demanded. "You're not leaving me behind."

Tommy turned toward his friend. "Steph," he said softly, "The Giants are out to kill every human, dwarf and Aesir on the planet. And they're not being nice about it. If we don't stop them here, the entire world is gone for good. You, your parents, all of us, everyone. All gone. One small girl on a horse can only do so much and you don't even have a good weapon to use."

"And just what do you think you can do to help, Tommy Kuhns? You're not any bigger than I am." Stephanie shot him a look that would have blistered paint.

"I'm not going as Tommy Kuhns," he answered. "I'm going as the Silver Giant."

"What?" Stephanie asked. "What are you talking about?"

"The project Vili and I have been working on," Tommy answered. "The metal exoskeleton is ready to use. The weapons systems aren't powered up, but I can still use other things as weapons. Mr. Johnson has been teaching Eric and me some extra weapons training these past few months. I guess a Silver Giant and a big club will still work to try and stop the Vanir. There are enough pieces of metal in the shop that will work as a staff or club. But I need you to stay here and feed us information." He looked at his friend and put his hands on her shoulders. "Can you do that for us? For me?"

"Tommy Kuhns if you get yourself hurt, I'll beat the snot out of you," Stephanie said, throwing her arms around his neck.

"Okay, that's fair." Tommy answered. He carefully disengaged himself from her grasp. "Just keep an eye on things. I'll be able to communicate with you through the suit communicator. I'll have to wear a suit just like Eric's to keep from freezing my butt off out there."

"Just you make sure to come back," Stephanie said.

"I will," Tommy shouted over his shoulder as he raced into the workshop.

The exoskeleton lay on a table at the far side of the room, moved there when they knew Fornir would need to come inside. Tommy pulled off the metal sheet covering the framework and ran through a quick checklist, just as he and Vili had done many times. The skeleton was as ready as it was going to get and Tommy moved over to a case beside the table. Inside was another space suit, just like the one Eric was wearing. Mimir had sent three of them since their heating units would protect the young men and Stephanie if they needed to work outside the buildings in the harsh weather. He pulled on the suit with the ease of long training. Vili had insisted the young Norn-in-training be ready for any possible outcome and Tommy was glad of the extra practice. He sealed the suit and stepped up on the table and into the framework. Special cuffs fastened around his arms, legs and torso and he plugged a cable from the control unit of the suit into the framework's chest unit.

"Communications check. You online, Steph?"

"I'm here, Tommy. Are you sure I can't do anything more to help?"

"You'll do more right there than trying to fight a Giant." Tommy pushed a control and the exoskeleton powered up. With a loud snap, plates of armor extruded into position around the armor, protecting joints and the central control unit where Tommy stood. He could feel the stress against his limbs as his movements shifted the armor. "Okay, Steph. On the upper right hand corner of the console is a blue switch. Flip it up."

"Got it. There's a green light above the switch. Is that good?"

"Good, Steph." Tommy shifted a finger and triggered the communication system. "Eric, Mimir, can you hear me?"

"Tommy, what are you up to? You're coming in on a different channel," Eric answered.

"Ah, I see you have the battle armor ready for use, young warrior," Mimir said over the communications link. "Are you certain you wish to do this?"

"The dwarves can't hold them back on their own and there's only so much Eric and Fornir can do. We need everything we've got. I'm going out."

"Going out? Going out in what?" Eric asked.

"Just be careful where you drop stuff, will you!" Tommy called out as he stood up in the armor. "I'll be the big silver guy beating on Giants."

"What?" Eric said.

"Just watch for me," Tommy answered as he picked up a ten foot pole and pushed the button to open the door.

The wind whipped past the armor and Tommy was very glad the heating unit of the space suit worked well. He gave the pole a few swings to get a feel for the weight and was pleased when the reflexes of the combat armor made the pole feel just like his training staff. He switched on the built-in flood light of the armor, like the eye of a Cyclops, and ran over to the side of the village where most of the Vanir were attacking. One jump brought him to the top of the wall and he looked down at the battle below him. He shook his head as he saw the Vanir continued to push the dwarves back toward the gateway in the wall. Once the Vanir were inside the village, there would be little the dwarves could do to defend themselves.

"Here goes," Tommy said more to himself than anyone else.

He jumped from the top of the wall and out in front of the gateway. Sensors in the suit read his speed and the length of his drop, as well as how close he was to the ground. As he came closer to the ground jets shot out of the legs of the suit and cushioned his landing, flattening two Vanir at the same time. Tommy swung the staff in his hands and slammed both of the Giants in the head, to keep them out of the fight.

"Asgard!" he yelled as he began to swing the staff in huge circles.

The powerful muscles of the armor were strong enough to knock even Vanir off their feet. The Dragon's Blood that turned the Vanir into berserk warriors gave them the energy to get back up but after the third or fourth time Tommy's staff slammed a Vanir to the ground, they stayed down.

"Fenrir's Bane! Fenrir's Bane!" the dwarves shouted as they formed up behind Tommy.

The young warrior found himself at the head of a wedge of warriors forcing back the Vanir from the walls of the village. The wide swings of the staff could not hit that many Vanir at once, but the dwarves used Tommy as a way to break the movement of the Vanir, then came in at the edges of his swings to help keep those Giants knocked to the ground down and out of the battle. The huge figure eight pattern of Tommy's swings, powered by Aesir technology, was enough to make a difference in the battle.

Suddenly, to Tommy's left and behind the Vanir, a wall of flame erupted in the middle of a mass of Giants. A similar wall of flame rose to his right, as well.

"Sorry it took so long for Fornir to get warmed up," Eric called to his friend. "You take the middle and we'll try to squeeze them down both sides."

"Got it," Tommy answered. Even with the power of the armor, he was getting tired fast. If this battle lasted too much longer, he thought, they were never going to stop the Vanir.

But Tommy's powerful armor and Fornir's fire kept the Giants at bay. Tommy began to move away from the wall, between two walls of flame. With the dwarves at his back and sides, they pushed the Vanir back toward the trenches.

"That's it. We're out of fire," Eric called out. "We'll look for some more stuff to drop on their heads."

"Got it, Eric. Just be careful whose head you pick," Tommy answered.

Tommy continued his march forward, supported by the dwarves. But as he stepped in one more time to swing, the Vanir in front of him dropped down, a smoking hole in the back of his tunic.

"I thought you were out of fire?" Tommy called out to Eric.

"We are," Eric answered.

And then Tommy was hit by a shaft of pure energy. He crashed to the ground, throwing dwarves to either side as they scampered out of his way.

"Ow," he said slowly. "What was . . ." And as he started to get to his knees he saw the answer.

An opening in the Giants' battle line led straight back to Bor. The Vanir leader held a large weapon pointed straight at Tommy. When Tommy had shut off the crystals to permit the powered armor to work, Bor had found a weapon repowered and unharmed by the crystal's beams. He fired again, and Tommy slammed back down to the ground, unmoving.

"Kill them!" Bor screamed. "Kill them all."

The Vanir attacked, screaming with the fury of the Dragon's Blood.

Chapter Twenty-Three

A screaming wall of dwarves raced forward to protect Tommy. Tommy managed to get back to his feet but he was forced to drop as Bor fired his energy weapon again, clipping Tommy's left arm.

"Eric, any chance you can distract him?" Tommy called out.

"Working on it," came the answer from Eric. Bor dodged as a large chunk of metal that had been a gun mount crashed where he stood a second earlier.

The Vanir fired up into the clouds but missed the dragon as Fornir slipped into the shield of Fimbulwinter. Tommy got to his feet and picked up a chuck of metal broken off one of Fornir's "bombs." He threw it at Bor with all his augmented strength but the Vanir dodged as quickly as before and the metal slammed into the Giant following Bor. Bor fired again but this time it was Tommy who dodged. The blast passed over the heads of those dwarves behind Tommy and he quickly picked up more debris to try and keep Bor from firing his weapon.

Another chunk of metal dropped from the sky and Bor fired up at the departing dragon. Tommy saw the glare of the energy bolt absorbed by Eric's Uni-shield and knew both Eric and Fornir were safe for the moment. Tommy picked up his staff and began to move through the crowd of berserk Vanir again. He needed to reach Bor before that energy weapon did more damage to the dwarves and to the village. But the Vanir had closed in on Tommy, the only warrior in this melee who could give a Vanir a one-on-one fight. The young teen inside the combat armor was suddenly the focus of almost a hundred Vanir and only the power of the armor let him use the swings of the staff to keep angry Giants at bay.

Meanwhile, Bor fired his weapon again and again against the wall of the village, until a huge hole was formed in the barrier.

"Now, Vanir!" Bor cried out. "Attack the village and take the gateway to our prize!"

From the corner of his eye, Tommy saw another chunk of metal drop from the sky and knock the energy rifle from Bor's hand, crushing the mechanism into useless scrap. With a scream, Bor dragged a huge sword from a scabbard along his back and he rushed toward Tommy. The berserk Vanir leader pushed his own warriors aside, sometimes cutting them down if they did not move fast enough, to try and reach the teen. Tommy moved toward the hole in the village wall and planted himself in front of the breach. The staff in his hands was a blur of Aesir steel as he kept the Vanir away from the hole and dwarves moved forward to pick off Vanir concentrating on Tommy as he held the day.

Suddenly the Vanir in front of Tommy parted and he faced Bor. The Vanir leader had a froth of foam around his mouth and his eyes burned red as he attacked the Silver Giant protecting the village. Tommy parried the powerful blows of the sword with his Aesir staff and the two warriors swept the ground clear for a space of almost thirty feet as they moved back and forth in a dance of death. Tommy used all the power of the combat armor to stop the blows of Bor, but the Vanir was an experienced warrior, with over a thousand years of combat experience trained into his reflexes. Even in his berserk state, Bor was a killing machine bent on one task: killing Tommy. Finally, the Vanir managed to sweep the staff aside and slam his sword into Tommy's left leg. The combat armor protected the boy, but the force of the blow knocked him to the ground. He tried to reach his staff but Bor stood over him with his blade raised to drive into the armor and skewer Tommy. With a scream, Bor drove the blade down and Tommy closed his eyes.

There was a clang of metal on metal and Tommy heard a mighty cry of "For Asgard!" He opened his eyes and saw Bor standing above him: mouth open in astonishment, his hands empty of any weapon. Then the Vanir was swept from his feet and slammed to the ground. Bor rose quickly and turned. As Tommy looked behind the Vanir, Thor appeared from the crowd of warriors and captured his hammer Mjollnir in his right hand as it swept back through the air in a wide circle. "For Asgard!" Thor cried again and attacked Bor. The Vanir slammed to the ground again as Thor pounded the Vanir leader in the chest. Bor's breast plate dented as he hit the ground hard and did not move again.

"For Asgard!" came the battle cry again, and from behind Tommy a swarm of dwarves, led by Sudri and Dwalin poured through the hole in the village wall and attacked the Vanir. The sudden attack pushed the Giants back from the village wall. Suddenly Odin, Vili and Al Johnson were gathered around Tommy as he started to get to his feet.

"Are you okay?" Al Johnson asked the boy as he stood in the powered armor.

"I am now," Tommy answered.

"Good. Then it is time to finish this battle," Odin answered. He looked at Vili. "Come, brother. Time to fight."

Vili raised his blade and saluted Tommy. "Well done, Fenrir's Bane. Now it is our turn."

"Stay and guard the opening," Odin ordered Tommy and Al Johnson. "We will deal with these vermin."

"Yes, sir," Tommy answered as he picked up his staff.

The two Aesir turned and moved to join Thor, who stood in the middle of a wide circle of downed Vanir. Thor laughed and yelled as Mjollnir swung out at the end of his long arm or was thrown, to drop a Vanir with each swing or toss. From the greater height of his armor, Tommy saw a wide mass of warriors behind the Vanir force, fighting the Giants. The Einherjar, he realized, the warriors of Earth taken to Asgard to join in the final battle for the end of the world.

Well, this certainly qualified as a final battle, he thought to himself.

"Where's Eric?" Mr. Johnson asked. He held the Aesir blade given to him by Eric when he returned his first visit to Mimir. He also wore Aesir armor and a helmet with padding to protect him from the cold.

"He's up there, Sensei," Tommy answered with a jab at his staff to the sky. "He's been dropping stuff on the Giants' heads since he ran out of web balls and since Fornir ran out of flame."

"At least he's safe," Mr. Johnson said.

Then the two warriors moved to protect the opening in the wall from the few Vanir who made it past the dwarves and the Aesir. Tommy watched as Vili darted into the mass of Vanir surrounding Thor. The Sword of Frey was a glittering line of steel flickering around him as he sheared through Vanir weapons and dropped Giant after Giant to the ground. Odin stood his ground and waited for the Vanir to come to him, then the tip of Gungnir darted out to disarm, disable, or sometimes kill a berserk Giant. With the addition of the Aesir from Asgard, the additional dwarves with Sudri and Dwalin and the Einherjar, the Vanir were not only overpowered, but finally outnumbered. The battle was not easy, but the outcome was certain and in less than an hour, Odin, Thor and Vili returned to the opening in the village wall to speak again with Tommy. A break in the storm left the air clear, for the moment, as the small group gathered.

"You did well, today, young Norn," Odin said to Tommy. "Without your aid, the dwarves would not have held long enough to permit us to arrive. The Aesir would have arrived to find this village captured by Vanir and your world in the hands of a dark power if not destroyed."

Tommy shrugged, an interesting movement in the combat armor. "I just did what I had to do. And it wasn't just me. All the dwarves fought today and Eric and Fornir did even more than their share."

"Speaking of which, where is my nephew now?" Uncle Al asked.

"Right about there," Tommy said as he pointed over the battle.

Visibility had improved to almost half a mile, and Fornir was visible coming in toward the gateway and the breached village wall. On Fornir's neck, Eric waved a suited hand at the group and leaned down against Fornir's neck. Then Tommy saw Eric point toward the ground and heard him speak on the suit's external speakers.

"Fornir, it's Bor!"

Tommy looked as the Vanir leader climbed out from behind and beneath several Vanir bodies and moved toward him at a run. In his left hand he held a dwarven ax and his right held a huge broadsword of Vanir design. The Giant was bloody and screaming.

Thor started to swing Mjollnir but Odin laid a hand on his arm.

"Bide a moment," the commander ordered.

Bor ran closer to the group, screaming the entire way and Thor almost pulled free from his father to face his ancient foe when Fornir dropped out of the sky and landed on the Vanir with all his weight on both feet. The dragon looked down for a moment, stomped once with his right foot, then stepped forward toward the others.

"It is done," Fornir stated. "My family is avenged."

He leaned down and let Eric slide to the ground. The young warrior flipped open the faceplate of his suit and ran over to his uncle and hugged him.

"You're okay," Eric said. "And Aunt Cindy?"

"She's fine," Uncle Al answered. "She's helping the Aesir and dwarf wives treat the ones still infected. She told me to take care of you." He looked around at the battlefield. "Looks to me like you took pretty good care of yourself."

"What? You don't think Tommy and I can handle a few Giants?" Eric asked with a grin.

"I think the Giants were outnumbered from the start with you two hotheads leading the attack," Uncle Al answered.

Eric shook his head, the grin gone from his face. "No. Suori and his people planned pretty well for an attack. They knew the Giants wanted this place back and that they needed it to get to Mimir. Tommy and I helped, but most of the fighting and the credit belongs to Suori and the dwarves."

Fornir cleared his throat and looked at Eric.

The young warrior smiled. "And Fornir of course. We needed air support and he's the best there is."

"Well," the great wyrm said, "I could not let these youngsters have all the fun, could I?"

Odin looked over the battle field and watch Aesir and Einherjar gather those Vanir still able to stand in a group. The wounded of all races were also gathered and the Aesir commander nodded as a chain of carriers moved those who could be helped to Asgard.

"Do we have all the Vanir now?" Eric asked Odin.

Odin shook his head. "That is unlikely, I fear. We may have most of them, but there were some who chose not to follow Bor. They are still out there in your world."

"Nuts," Eric spat. "Then we still need to find them and after this mess they'll be hiding deeper underground than ever."

"And we still have all the Giant places to find and dismantle," Uncle Al added. "They've used our people as test subjects and robots. They would need hospitals or the equivalent to make the changes. And there are those humans left in control of government and such, too." He sighed. "The job ahead is almost worse than the one we just faced."

"Maybe the records in the Vanir labs will tell us who to look for," Tommy stated. "They had to be keeping track of their tame humans. We can use those records to find them and stop them."

Uncle Al nodded. "Agreed. But the big problem is going to be what to do with them when we do find them. Unless we have proof they did something illegal, we can't have them arrested. Can you imagine us going to the state capital, or maybe the White House, and telling people aliens have been brainwashing humans as tools?"

"Yeah, since when did the truth matter to politicians?" Eric asked. "But without the Giants to lead them, they'll be easier to stop, don't you think?"

Uncle Al looked eye to eye with Odin. "Humans have been very inventive on their own. These people can cause all kinds of trouble before we can stop them, if they think it will help them or if Bor left special instructions if he should be out of touch for a while."

"Crap," Eric spat. "More problems."

Thor laughed. "Why are you worried, young warrior?" he said as he raised Mjollnir. "We defeated them today. We will defeat them tomorrow."

"By the way," Uncle Al said to Eric and Tommy. "Where's Stephanie? I promised her father I'd keep an eye on her as well."

"I left her in the command center," Tommy stated. "Steph, you online? We got reinforcements."

There was no response to his call. He looked over at Eric. "Maybe my radio got banged up. You try to call her."

"Steph, this is Eric. Are you okay? Answer back."

Still there was no response.

"Could the Vanir have gotten past us? Or maybe some of the humans?" Tommy asked.

There was no answer as Eric, Tommy, Uncle Al, Thor and a contingent of dwarves raced through the hole in the wall toward the control center. They raced through the doors of the loading bay, opened with a signal from Tommy's exoskeleton. But the control room was empty.

"Stephanie!" Tommy called out as he climbed out of the exoskeleton, with no response.

"Look at this," Eric said as he pointed at one of the screens. "That gate crystal the Vanir brought is moving away from here. I thought we buried that vehicle."

"Apparently not deep enough," Uncle Al stated.

Freawin entered the room. "Mist Walker is not in the stable. Where is Stephanie Valkyrsdotter?"

Then the communicator crackled.

"Guys, can you hear me?"

It was Stephanie.

"Steph, where are you?" Tommy shouted. "I told you to stay here."

"That gate thing started moving and all of you were busy. I'm keeping an eye on it. Don't worry, I'm not getting close. But we need to know where it is so we can shut it off."

"What gate thing?" Uncle Al asked.

"The Giants brought a way to open a gate to Niflheim with them. That's why we had to go out after the Giants rather than just holding the wall." Eric turned to Tommy. "Where is she?"

Tommy read the screen with the speed of long practice. "About two miles out and moving away at a good clip. She's pacing the crystal." He looked again at the screen. "We're going to lose the signal pretty soon unless we recalibrate."

"Whoever has the crystal must have some sort of transportation," Eric said. "No human or Vanir could keep pace with a Valkyr stallion."

"I heard that," Stephanie said. "He's got a jeep that didn't fall into a hole and still works. There's a pretty big case in the back seat. When the signal started to move fast, I knew I needed to keep an eye on him so I got Mist Walker and followed. I didn't know how to reset the screen to follow him."

"If he gets away with that crystal, he could hold the whole planet for ransom," Tommy stated.

"Then we need to get to Stephanie and stop whoever it is she's following," Uncle Al said.

Eric just shook his head. "Here we go again."

Chapter Twenty-Four

Harrison Keyes knew a good deal when he saw one.

Working for the Vanir in Philadelphia had been relatively easy and very profitable. Bor was a difficult individual to work for, but Keyes had worked for worse. And at least working with the Vanir had provided the human with the opportunity to obtain a wide variety of toys nobody on Earth could even conceive of, much less own.

But when Bor decided to attack this compound in the middle of the country, during the worst winter Pennsylvania had ever seen, Keyes thought this might be going a bit too far. Keyes knew about the human and Vanir warriors Bor had stashed in various sites around the area, and around the country for that matter. There was no question the Vanir were better armed than anything Keyes knew of in Pennsylvania. Bringing along a bomb that was capable of destroying the entire planet was over-kill, simply too much of a good thing.

Keyes had remained in the vehicle when Bor and the other Vanir drank the Dragon's Blood. Over the years he had worked with a lot of military types, mostly those not acceptable in the formal armies of many countries. Drug use was rampant in those groups and it appeared the Vanir were no different. Keyes watched as the drugs amped up the Vanir to a killing rage. He slid down into his seat, out of sight of the Vanir gathered around their commander, and waited for them to attack the dwarven compound. Keyes was not a warrior, and made no pretense of being one. He was going to stay in the vehicle until the battle was over then he would drive the case with the bomb to his master Bor. That was as much as he planned to do today.

When the ground dropped out beneath the command vehicle, Keyes was bounced across the back seat. The case with the bomb was secure, but the corner of the case bruised ribs as Keyes slammed into it. When the vehicle was covered by water and frozen into a block of ice, Keyes pounded on the doors to open them. Pounding on the hard ice didn't work and Keyes dropped back into a seat. He was frightened, but he was thinking. He looked around inside the vehicle for options. In the rear compartment, he found a small Vanir cutting torch. Keyes used the torch to cut through the back window and the thick ice covering the vehicle in less than an hour. The rush of cold air as the block of ice on the back window slid free chilled Keyes and froze the sweat on his neck. He shut off the torch and slipped it into a pocket of his cold suit. He might need it again.

Keyes started to climb out of the vehicle, then stopped and looked down. The case with the Niflheim crystals was small enough to fit through the new escape hole. Keyes reached down and unfastened the clips that held the case. He lifted the case through the window and shoved it to the top of the trench. Then he climbed through and scrambled to the ground outside the vehicle. Keyes looked around at the assembled army formation, now empty of human or Vanir activity. All the vehicles were stalled, stopped or fallen into trenches. Many of them were covered in ice as thick as was the command car. Further away from the village were some smaller carriers, outside the trenches and not covered in ice. Keyes lifted the case and headed for one of them. The jeep was ice free and when Keyes slid in and turned the key, it started up. Whatever had stopped the other vehicles was no longer working.

Off in the distance, through the thick snow and fog, Keyes could hear the sounds of combat. If the dwarves were still fighting the Vanir, they must be better fighters than Bor planned. And if that was the case, and judging by the mass of useless hardware scattered around the jeep, Keyes considered it a fair chance the Vanir would lose the day. If that was what happened, Keyes wanted to be somewhere far away when the

Aesir came looking through their spoils of war. If Bor did win the day, then Keyes had just become extra baggage. The Niflheim crystals would give the human some bargaining power in either case. Keyes strapped the case into the back seat and turned the jeep back toward Philadelphia.

* * *

Stephanie and Mist Walker moved quickly along the ground below Eric. Fornir was high enough that he was out of sight of the jeep, barely seen through the snow and sleet falling around them. With the sensors built into the suit he was wearing, Eric could see not only the jeep but also Stephanie on Mist Walker as she paced the vehicle. The Valkyr-in-training was wearing a suit just like Eric and Tommy, the third one sent from Mimir for the teens. The jeep had managed to find a roadway, but the poorly plowed surface was treacherous and slow going.

"Steph, you have to drop back out of the way," Eric repeated. "Odin and Vili don't know what might set off that crystal matrix. We might have to blow it up to stop it from opening the hole to Niflheim."

"Are you sure you've got him?" she asked. "We can't afford to lose that signal."

"I know, and yes, I've got him. Between Fornir's dragon sight and the sensors in this suit from Mimir I won't lose him."

"All right," Stephanie said. "I'm dropping back but I'll stay close in case you need somebody on the ground to help with something."

* * *

Keyes was startled by the ping of a sensor on the jeep's dashboard. This was one of the vehicles rigged to use Vanir equipment and that equipment told him he had been targeted by Aesir sensors. Someone was following him from the village. But in this storm, unless they had him visually, he could still escape. A surge in the storm swept over him, building to a localized whiteout, and Keyes triggered the stealth equipment in the jeep. He turned off the road he was on, to one at a tight angle from his course. If the storm surge covered his tracks quickly enough, they would never find him again. And help was near, just in case they did pick up the trail.

* * *

Eric swore as the sensors in his suit lost the signal from the jeep below. "Fornir, can you see that jeep? He just dropped off the sensors."

"I regret I cannot see much of anything through this storm, my friend," the wyrm answered. "In this thick a snowfall, I can barely see the ends of my wings at this moment."

"Stephanie, any chance you have a visual on that jeep?" Eric called to his friend.

"No, and I can't see it on my sensors either. What happened?"

Eric shrugged, unseen by Stephanie. "They must have some kind of stealth gear in the jeep. It probably came in handy for dodging police in Philadelphia."

"I can still see the tracks the jeep is leaving in the snow," Stephanie answered. "I'll follow them and you follow me, okay?"

"Be very careful, Steph. These guys definitely play for keeps," Eric warned.

"I'm not getting any closer than I have to," Stephanie agreed. "But how soon can someone else get here? Like maybe Thor or Odin."

"We come, young warriors," the deep voice of Odin rolled through their suit speakers. "Watch carefully but be mindful of their weapons."

"No problem, Odin," Stephanie answered. "Mist Walker doesn't have armor and I'm not going to risk getting close."

Just then the jeep's tracks skewed off to the right and Mist Walker almost skidded off his feet as the stallion swerved to follow at Stephanie's command on the reins.

"Hey, Eric. The jeep turned off the main road and onto another, smaller one."

"I see you, Steph. Just keep following and I'll be right above you. Be very careful."

"Jeez, would you guys stop saying that," Stephanie complained. "I'm being careful, all right?"

Eric laughed. "Okay, Steph. Hang in there." Eric looked around the area where the jeep tracks led. "Hey, it looks like the jeep isn't on a road. I can't tell for sure with all the snow, but it looks like he's on a really long driveway to a farm. There's another road out the other side, but unless he already knows where it is, I'll bet he has trouble finding it from ground level."

"So we've got him trapped," Stephanie answered. "How long until Odin and the others get there?"

"Soon," Odin answered. "Watch and wait, children."

* * *

They had found his trail, Keyes knew. As he passed the gateway to the farmhouse, the red indicator blinked, indicating additional sensor readings behind him. The door to the barn opened partway, blocked by drifting snow and Keyes stopped the vehicle outside. He dragged the case with the gate crystals out of the jeep. The wind came from his left as he pushed toward the door. He slapped the door button as he went in. The door closed, but pushed a large pile of snow inside as it locked shut.

No matter, Keyes thought, he wouldn't be here long enough to worry about the puddle on the floor when the snow melted. Keyes set the case onto a low wheeled platform and moved across the open barn to the far side. A boxy column set against the wall had a large enough door in its side to permit a vehicle to enter. Keyes hit a control and the door opened to an elevator. Keyes rolled the dolly inside and pushed the button for the lowest level.

This laboratory held the rooms where the genetically engineered dogs had been grown and trained. It also held something Keyes now planned to use to get clear of the Aesir following him. The elevator opened on the lowest level and Keyes pulled his platform with the gate crystals out and down the hallway. He stopped for a moment at a control panel mounted on the wall and tapped commands into the unit. A schematic of the farm property lit up and Keyes saw three moving dots inside the perimeter of the farm. He tapped more commands and a red line glowed around the farm. Someone was close, but the farm defenses would stop anyone else from coming in. Whoever those three Aesir were, they wouldn't find him in time to stop him. Keyes had a surprise that would delay them as well.

* * *

"Eric, be advised that defense measures are now active at your location," Mimir said through the suit communications. "Perimeter defenses are up and working. Odin and his team will make contact in one minute. They will be unable to pass until those defenses are powered down."

A red line appeared on his faceplate around the farm where he and Stephanie followed the jeep. Another red dot was inside the line but it wasn't identified in Eric's display.

"Can you tell who is here with us, Mimir? I see a reading but I'm not getting any ID," Eric stated.

"Ah, that would be your friend Thomas in his combat armor," the sentient computer answered. "His communication and identification circuits were damaged in his fight with Bor. He can speak to you through the suit speakers but has no other communication ability. He made very good time and has outdistanced Odin and his team."

"Good. Maybe he can figure out how to shut off the defenses," Eric suggested.

Eric started to land with Fornir and saw Tommy in what would normally be the front yard of the farm. The Silver Giant waved a hand and stepped toward the barn to get out of Fornir's way as the wyrm landed. By the time Fornir was on the ground, Stephanie was at the barn with Mist Walker, talking to Tommy.

"He went inside," Stephanie told the Silver Giant. She held out a small sensor unit from the control room at Dwarvenheim. "And then something happened to make my sensor readings jump all over the place."

Eric ran over to the pair. He looked up at Tommy. "Good thing it's a big door," he said. Then he turned toward Stephanie. He reached up to the helmet of her suit and touched a control. "There, your suit sensors should be online now."

"Oh," Stephanie said as one hand came up to her helmet. "That's much better."

"Odin and his people are at the perimeter and attempting to pass," Mimir said to Eric and Stephanie. "Please ask Thomas to see if he can shut down those defenses as soon as possible. But please note that inside those buildings, I will be unable to maintain contact."

Eric looked up at the Silver Giant. "Mimir said there are some sort of perimeter defenses working and you might be able to shut them down and let Odin and the guys in here. I guess your radio is out after your dance with Bor. And ours will be out with Mimir once we get inside."

"Let me see what I can do," Tommy said as he stepped up to the barn. He found the door controls for the barn but when he pushed the command to open found them unresponsive. "Looks like whoever went in locked the door after himself."

Tommy looked at the door. The controls were Vanir design, but the materials used were human. Tommy selected two spots on the door, above and below the latch and rammed the augmented hands of the combat suit through the sheet metal of the door with a screech of tortured alloys. Tommy pulled and the door came free of the latch. As he pulled the door open against the drifting snow, an alarm sounded inside the room and commands in the Vanir language echoed around the building. Eric could understand them, since he had made the trip across Bifrost when Thor first took him to visit Asgard, but he knew Tommy and Stephanie could not understand.

"Look like the Vanir have defenses here too," Eric shouted over the clamor of the alarms. He turned to Fornir. "Can you stay up here and keep an eye on things. We'll be right back, I hope."

Fornir nodded. "I will wait. I fear I would be a bit cramped as you follow your prey."

Tommy was examining the control panel inside the door. He tapped a command and the sirens shut down.

"Those dumb Vanir didn't even change their security passwords," he said. "We're clear to follow whoever went in here. But we need a main console to shut down the perimeter defenses." He looked down at Stephanie. "How many were there in that jeep?"

"Only one that I saw," she answered. She looked at Mist Walker as the Aesir stallion waited patiently for his rider. "You stay here with Fornir and I'll be right back." She patted the stallion's neck.

Mist Walker snorted into Stephanie's face and looked up at Fornir.

The wyrm smiled, a frightening sight for anyone who didn't know him. "I'm certain we will be fine. It's even a bit warmer here if you are out of the wind. Now go and stop that Vanir from opening the gate to

Niflheim." Fornir moved to block the doorway with Mist Walker inside and out of the freezing wind.

"Did you get any information out of that panel about what's here?" Eric asked Tommy as they followed the combat suit toward the far side.

"Yes, this is some sort of laboratory site for the Vanir. There are four levels below with a lot of lab space as well as rooms for whatever they were working on. I get a sense that they were doing some sort of genetic experiments from the file names I reviewed."

"The dogs," Stephanie said with a gasp. "This is where they came from."

Tommy nodded. "That would be my guess too. But there's something else here as well. I couldn't tell what it was, but there's a really big room down there that has something in it. Something the Vanir were working on that was left over from a really long time ago."

"Some kind of a weapon?" Eric asked.

"I really don't know. But when we get to the lowest level, which is where this lift takes us," Tommy said as he opened the door to the elevator, "we need to be very careful. It's bigger than the dogs. I've been scanning the codes with my onboard controls in this suit and that room had a lot of security commands in the cell door code. It's still locked up and I made sure to leave it that way." He tapped the chest of his suit. "I don't know if the combat suit is up to it, but you guys better let me go first when we get down there."

"Works for me," Eric agreed.

"You can't do that," Stephanie said. "You have to be careful and we all need to stay away from whatever it is until Odin gets here."

"Steph, we need to shut down the perimeter defenses. And that means going to the command console on the lowest level, according to what I can find in the files I downloaded." Tommy looked down at her.

"I promise, no heroic stuff. Just shut off the defenses and wait for the cavalry."

"And I'll be right behind you to make sure," Stephanie said.

The lift grounded at the lowest level and the three warriors filed out. Tommy first, followed by Stephanie, with Eric bringing up the rear, putting the young girl in the safest spot. Tommy looked down at Eric and winked. They moved down the corridor, the only one leading from this elevator, toward whatever secret the Vanir were hiding.

"Just what we need, another Vanir surprise," Eric muttered.

"Shhh," Stephanie commanded.

A roar echoed down the corridor.

"That sounds like Fornir," Tommy said.

"Or more than one," Eric replied.

They reached the end of the corridor and looked through a heavy transparent shield into a huge room. The roar echoed again. The walls and floor vibrated with the power of the cry.

"Oh, crap," Eric said as he saw what was in the room.

"It's another Fornir," Stephanie said in a whisper.

"Only a lot bigger," Tommy added.

On the far side of the room, the three warriors could see a human figure working on a control panel. The wyrm inside was easily three times Fornir's size. The man was protected from the wyrm by another transparent wall and the wyrm tried very hard to tear the wall away and get at the human. Then, with a rumbling heard even over the cries of the great wyrm, the ceiling of the room opened as twenty-foot-thick doors slid aside, and the snow laden sky above was visible. The wyrm turned away from the man and looked up. It roared once more as it looked at the man behind the wall, then leaped into the air to escape.

Chapter Twenty-Five

The huge wyrm screamed as it hurled into the opening, propelled by powerful legs. As the beast cleared the boundary of the chamber, its wings snapped open and pulled it further into the sky.

"I have to get back up to Fornir," Eric said to his friends. "He can't handle that big guy on his own."

"And just what do you think you can do to help, Mr. Junior Space-man?" Stephanie snapped.

"Uni-shield," Eric shouted over his shoulder as he raced back to the elevator. "Tommy's the Norn-smith. He can handle the gate." Eric disappeared around the corner.

Tommy and Stephanie turned to face Keyes. Visible through the transparent walls, the human stood at the end of the corridor, alongside the chamber which once held the huge dragon.

"Stay back! I'll set this off," Keyes screamed. "I know what you Aesir do with prisoners. I won't be taken alive."

Tommy looked down at Stephanie and realized what was happening. In her space suit, Stephanie looked like a short Aesir. The helmet's face-plate was mirrored, the girl's features hidden. The nameplate on the suit, on the right breast like many military uniforms, read "Fonn." Tommy was still in his Silver Giant suit, his own face hidden as well.

"He thinks we're Aesir," Tommy said in a whisper. "He can't tell we're just kids."

"And this helps because . . . ?" Stephanie asked.

"I don't know," Tommy answered. "But let's see if we can play this a bit." He stepped forward to the corner of the corridor, now facing Keyes directly. "If you give us the case, we will see you are turned over to the local authorities. You will go to prison, but it will be a human prison."

Amplified by the suit speakers, Tommy's voice boomed down the hallway. Stephanie winced as the sound echoed against her suit.

"If you come any closer, I'll set this off," Keyes shouted. "It will destroy the planet. It opens a doorway to a black hole"

"If you trigger the unit, you will die," Tommy said. "Is that truly what you wish?"

"I want out of here, away from you Aesir swine and your minions. Let me go or I'll kill you all," Keyes shouted back.

"How do we know you won't just set the bomb to trigger after you leave?" Tommy demanded. "How can we trust someone who works for the Vanir by their own choice?"

"How do you know that?" Stephanie whispered. "How can you tell he's acting on his own?"

"Because if the Vanir had programmed him, he would have already set off the bomb. They wouldn't care if one of their human toys died at the same time as a group of Aesir," Tommy said loud enough for the man at the end of the corridor to hear. "Your masters are defeated. You have nowhere to run. Surrender and you will be treated honorably. You have my word."

Keyes laughed. "The word of an Aesir is worthless. You have lied to the Vanir for centuries. You even hide in the shadows while the Vanir work with the people of this world to help them."

"Either this guy is crazy or he's been programmed like some of those other people we've seen working with the Vanir," Stephanie suggested. "So now what, Fenrir's Bane?"

"Working on it," Tommy answered.

The combat suit had a full array of sensors and Tommy had been working furiously as he talked to the Vanir servant. He had the case pinpointed, but his suit weapons were offline, since Vili did not have time to complete the repairs. Tommy was running the checklist of the suit's capabilities, to see if anything else could be used as a weapon.

But as they watched, Keyes bent down and opened the case. He reached down toward the crystals and Tommy made a split-second decision. With a roar, the leg-jets of the suit ignited and Tommy literally flew down the hallway to crash into Keyes as he looked up from the case. The man had time for one scream before Tommy picked him up and, suit and all, slammed into the end of the corridor. Stephanie screamed and raced after Tommy. She stopped as she reached the case and looked at the jumble of metal and flesh in front of her.

"Tommy? Are you okay," Steph shouted.

"Ow! I'm not doing that again, even in armor," Tommy answered.

"Is he dead?" Stephanie asked.

The Silver Giant shifted slightly as Tommy read the suit sensors. "He's alive, but I squished him a bit. He'll live."

"Tommy?" Stephanie's voice quavered as she called out to her friend. "What does it mean if there's a yellow crystal blinking on this case."

"Oh, crud," Tommy answered. "He's activated the gateway!"

* * *

Fornir and Mist Walker stood just outside the huge barn looking into the sky. "Fafnir! You live! Where have you been hiding all this time?" the smaller wyrm shouted into the sky in his own language.

Eric raced across to the door. He could understand the dragon due to the effects of Bifrost, but he needed to get to Fornir before his friend took to the sky after his grandfather.

"Fornir, wait," Eric shouted. "He's been trapped by the Vanir and conditioned! He doesn't know you."

Fornir looked around at his human friend then back into the sky at his grandfather. The giant wyrm bounced off the dome of the security field around the farm. With an angry roar, he circled back toward Fornir.

Eric reached Fornir and climbed the wyrm's leg to his seat. He fastened the straps and activated his Uni-shield just as the giant wyrm dived toward the two. A lance of flame washed over the shield. The snow near the door disappeared in a cloud of steam and Eric saw the door itself melt against the hinges.

"He won't know you at all if the Vanir have been playing with his mind like they did with Vili and Loki," Eric said to Fornir. "We need to find a way to keep him under control until Tommy can get the shield down and Odin and the rest of the Aesir can help control him."

"He will be difficult to control, my young friend," Fornir stated. "And a wyrm his size is a powerful opponent."

"No kidding," Eric agreed. "And you better get in the air because he's coming back again."

Eric pointed at Fafnir as the wyrm again circled back toward the pair. Fornir tensed and leaped into the air just as another lance of flame washed across the doorway. The smaller dragon was airborne and behind his grandfather before Fafnir could react.

"Grandfather, we need not fight," Fornir shouted in wyrm-tongue. "The Vanir have clouded your mind. You must listen to me."

"Thief!" Fafnir shouted back. "You come to steal my hoard. And you bring those insect Aesir with you. Is it not enough you have the ring!"

"Ring? What ring?" Eric asked his friend as they gained altitude and circled above Fafnir.

"Did they really revive that old tale?" Fornir said as much to himself as to Eric. "It's supposed to be a ring that will permit the wearer to rule the world. It was a golden circlet that was worn around the brow and held a warrior's hair from his eyes. In truth, the circlet gave the wearer the power to speak to any living creature, a useful tool in dealing with other species, as our kind often did. What you did with that speech was of your own making, however. The story is an old tale told to young wyrms as we begin to grow. The moral of the story is that nothing or no one creature can rule the world and if you try, you usually wind up dead, along with everyone around you."

"And he thinks we want to steal this ring and some kind of hoard?" Eric asked as they slipped sideways to avoid another lance of flame from Fafnir. "So what's a hoard?"

Fafnir glanced back over his shoulder at his rider. "When this is over, I must teach you what you need to know about my kind. It is obvious much knowledge has been lost from Midgard with no wyrms here to teach you."

"Right. Lessons after the war is over," Eric said. "So what's a hoard?"

"A hoard is a wyrm's treasure," Fafnir said. "It is usually kept in a cave or some other place easy to defend from other wyrms. We are a race of creatures who covet beauty and feel we must possess it whenever possible. Our teaching tales are meant to prevent us from killing each other over trinkets. An intelligent wyrm does not covet mere gold or jewels."

"So what do you covet instead?" Eric asked.

Fornir looked back and smiled. After all their time together, Eric recognized the grimace for what it was and smiled back.

"We covet friendships," Fornir answered. "Hang on!"

Fornir spun end for end and slipped behind and above Fafnir. As he passed over the great wyrm's head, Fornir slammed his hind legs down in a mighty blow that stunned his grandfather.

Eric looked at the red line showing in his helmet display. "Come on, Tommy. Get that shield down," he said to his friend.

"We're working on it," Stephanie answered. "We're a bit busy here, so just cool your jets."

Eric had forgotten he had activated Steph's suit communicators.

"Have you got the case?" he asked. "Is the gate closed down?"

"Like I said, we're working on it," she answered.

"Well, work faster," Eric shouted as Fornir banked again out of lance of flame and pulled his nose up to circle around behind Fafnir.

"Fornir, we need to figure out a way to capture your grandfather. Any ideas?" Eric looked down at his friend, not really expecting an answer that would help.

"Actually, I have an idea," Fornir said. "If we can get Grandfather back into his cage and close the door, that should hold him until additional help arrives. After all, the cage held him for all this time quite well. So we know it has the power to keep him secure."

"Works for me," Eric agreed. "But what do we use for bait to get him back inside?"

"Give me my ring!" Fafnir shouted at the flying pair that darted around like a fly dodging a swallow. "Give me my ring and keep away from my hoard!"

"Got a one track mind over there, don't you think?" Eric commented. "Any way we can use that to help us?"

"Only if you have the Ring of the Nibelungs in your belt pouch," Fornir answered.

Eric grunted in answer and started to check his pockets on the outside of the suit as well as the suit itself. Nothing on the suit could be removed, since it was meant to protect the wearer in both space and combat. The pouches along the legs and arms held an assortment of small tools and a roll of anodized tape used for patching punctures, Eric had learned from conversations with Tommy. Eric looked at the gold colored tape and then leaned out to speak with Fornir.

I've got an idea," he shouted to his friend. "Keep out of his way for a bit and try not to throw me off, will you? I have to make something. Yell if you need the shield."

"Shield!" Fornir yelled as he dipped left.

Eric reacted with practiced skill and activated the shield, deflecting Fafnir's flames.

"Doesn't that guy ever run out of fire?" he asked.

"He has a larger reservoir," Fornir answered as the shield snapped open again to permit the two to breathe. "Be about your task and be swift. Fafnir grows most impatient."

"No kidding," the boy said. Eric unclipped a section of the straps holding him in place to give him a free length. He linked two segments together to hold him in the seat as he used the tape to wrap around the strap he freed. The sudden movements of Fornir, as he evaded the attacks of his grandfather, made the job difficult. But Eric kept one end of the strap he worked on still clipped to his harness so he wouldn't lose it. The end result was a length of strap wrapped in tape and glistening gold in the light from Fafnir's flames. Eric unsnapped the strap and used the tape to fasten the ends together. He looped the ring over his wrist to keep it safe and dropped the tape into a pocket.

"Swing up and over the farm so I can yell over to Grandpa," Eric called. "Then dive down toward the open doorway and be ready to flame if I need you. I'm going to drop the ring into the hole. Got it?"

"You have the ring?" Fornir answered. "But how…?"

"No time for questions," Eric called. He tapped the stud on his helmet. "Steph, you got your ears on?"

"Now what do you want?" she answered. "I said we're busy down here."

"Can you be ready to close the door to that big dragon's chamber when it lands? Can Tommy figure out the right button to push?"

"Hang on," she growled. "Eric wants to know if you know which button closes that big room over there," Eric heard her ask Tommy. There was a pause. "Yeah, I can do that. Tommy is working on something else."

"Great! When you see the big dragon land, close the door." Eric tapped Fornir on the shoulder. "Take us up," he said.

"What are you up to, Eric?" Stephanie asked.

"Just be ready, Steph," Eric replied.

Fornir climbed to just inside the top of the shield over the farm and swung back toward Fafnir. The larger dragon was climbing fast. Eric held up the ring in his hands and faced Fafnir. He touched a control on his helmet.

"You want this ring? Well, I don't want you to have it!" Eric called out, his voice projected by the suit's speakers. "Dive, Fornir!"

The young wyrm went into a stoop. Fornir and his rider shot past Fafnir before the larger wyrm could grab them, headed toward the open hatch of the lab where Fafnir had been held prisoner. Eric looked back over his shoulder as Fafnir sped toward them. It was obvious to him the larger wyrm could beat them to the opening. Eric whipped the ring down and into the open hatch and yelled to Fornir.

"Get clear of the opening," he yelled. "Steph, get ready!"

"No, you shall not have it!" Fafnir screamed as he dove past the two and into the hole.

The huge wyrm landed with an impact that shook dust and snow from the building. Before Eric could say anything, he saw the doors start to close with Fafnir inside.

"Now what do we do—" Stephanie started to say.

As the doors closed, the signal cut off.

"Crap! Communications are out. But he's safe now," Eric said to Fornir. "Take me back so I can go down and help Tommy and Steph."

"As you wish, my friend," Fornir agreed. "I could do with a rest for a few moments."

"Hey, you did good, Fornir! Who else could have outflown their own Grandpa and managed to catch him again?" Eric slapped his friend on the shoulder. "Here's another story for you to tell the kids."

"What kids?" Fornir asked.

"We'll work on that," Eric answered as they landed.

The door to the barn was half melted from Fafnir's flames. The metal was a congealed mess that blocked the entrance to the building.

"Any chance you could pull some of this away and get me inside?" Eric asked his friend.

"Certainly, Eric," Fornir answered as he leaned forward.

The wyrm's claws sank into the metal of the building much as Tommy's suit hands had done. With a steady pull, Fornir pulled aside enough of the wall to permit Eric to enter.

"Thanks. Keep an eye out up here and make sure Mist Walker hangs around for Stephanie. She'll be really upset if anything happens to her horse."

Mist Walker trotted from behind the barn, the safest place as flames were shooting across the barnyard.

"We will guard. You take care," Fornir said.

Eric shrugged. "By the time I get down there, Tommy will have it all figured out." He turned and started through the barn to the elevator.

"At least I hope he will," Eric said to himself as he punched the control to take him down to the basement lab.

Chapter Twenty-Six

Fafnir was still in the sky above as Tommy and Stephanie started to deal with the gateway.

"How fast is the crystal blinking, Steph?" Tommy asked. The combat suit shifted slightly as Tommy tried to move, but he stayed flat on the floor for the moment.

"About once a second," Stephanie answered. "Is that good or bad?"

"A bit of both," Tommy answered. The suit shifted again as he tried once again to rise. "Look, I'm kind of caught in this suit and can't get to the case. I need your help."

"What can I do?" she asked and moved closer to the pile at the end of the corridor that included Tommy, the Silver Giant suit, Keyes and several sections of the corridor ceiling.

Tommy shifted a hand of the suit and one of the fingers opened up at the end. "There's a cable in that finger. I need you to plug it into the case so I can get a reading on what's going on."

"Will that work for Vanir stuff?" Stephanie looked down at the case. "You won't set the bomb off if I do that, will you?"

"Actually, the case and the gate unit are Aesir models," Tommy stated. "I recognized them from some of the stuff Vili has been teaching me. And it's not a bomb. Although I've got to admit, the end result if it activates will be pretty much as destructive." He waggled the finger of the suit to show her which one he meant. "Take the cable that comes out of here and plug it in on the top of the case next to the blinking crystal."

"Okay, if you say so." Stephanie pulled the cable out of the suit's finger and stepped back to the case. She knelt down and held the end of the cable in one hand as she looked at the blinking crystal. "You're sure about this?"

"Steph, we're running out of time!" Tommy said. "Plug me in!"

Stephanie plugged in the cable and another crystal lit up. "Hey, is that supposed to happen?"

"It's okay," Tommy said with an air of distraction. "It just shows we're connected. Now…" Tommy's voice drifted off as he concentrated on the information showing on the suit's screen. "Set to activate in ten minutes. Well, eight minutes now. I guess the Giants were planning on setting this gate to open, then going through the gate at Dwarvenheim to Jotunheim before it opened. They would leave an empty world behind them, totally destroyed."

"Can you shut it down?" she asked.

"Working on it," Tommy answered.

He was silent for several minutes and Stephanie was ready to ask him another question when her suit speakers crackled.

"Come on, Tommy. Get that shield down," Eric's voice said in her ear.

"We're working on it," Stephanie answered. "We're a bit busy here, so just cool your jets."

"Have you got the case?" he asked. "Is the gate closed down?"

"Like I said, we're working on it," Stephanie answered.

"Well, work faster," Eric shouted.

"Jeez, what a grouch," Stephanie mumbled. She looked over at the suit. She knew that inside, Tommy was working hard to shut down the gate, but she couldn't see anything through the metal shell. "Tommy?" she started to ask.

"Crap! I can't shut it down," Tommy said.

"So what can we do?" Stephanie asked. "Can we get it somewhere else before it opens so it doesn't destroy Earth?"

"Not enough time," Tommy answered. "We'd have to get it to Dwarvenheim, then reset that gate to someplace safe, then go through to wherever that safe place would be. We just don't have that kind of time!"

"Well, where would be safe?" Steph countered. "Can you change the gate setting?"

"That's it!" Tommy shouted, right in Stephanie's ear.

"Steph, you got your ears on?" Eric called out.

"Now what do you want?" she answered. "I said we're busy down here."

"Can you be ready to close the door to that big dragon's chamber when it lands? Can Tommy figure out the right button to push?"

"Hang on," she growled. She turned toward Tommy. "Eric wants to know if you know which button closes that big room over there."

"See that panel on the wall behind you?" Tommy asked. "Push the third button down on the right and the top doors will close."

Stephanie nodded, forgetting Tommy couldn't see her. The she said to Eric, "Yeah, I can do that. Tommy is working on something else."

"Great! When you see the big dragon land, close the door."

"What are you up to, Eric?" Stephanie asked.

"Just be ready, Steph," Eric replied.

"What is he doing?" Tommy asked.

"I don't know," she answered.

"Get clear of the opening," Eric yelled. "Steph, get ready!"

"What?" Stephanie answered. Then she got her answer.

The huge dragon that had left the chamber just as they arrived dropped down to the floor and picked up a small ring in two of its massive claws. Stephanie pushed the button and the door at the top of the chamber started to close quickly. The huge dragon went crazy as the door closed. The walls of the corridor shook as the creature literally bounced off the walls, floor and ceiling. But the construction held, a sign the Giants knew what the chamber would need to hold secure.

"Now what do we do with it?" Stephanie asked Eric. There was no response. "Eric, are you there? Are you okay?"

"He can't hear you with that door closed. It cuts off all communications with anyone outside" Tommy stated. "Steph, I need your help with this gate. I can't get out of this suit very quickly with all the battle damage and I need to make some changes on the gate so it goes somewhere else."

"So what do you want me to do?" she asked.

"You have to be my hands. You have to make the changes in the settings," Tommy answered.

"Me? I can't do this tech stuff! Get yourself out of that suit and you do it!" Stephanie walked over to the suit and started looking for a way to open it.

"We don't have time, Steph!" Tommy said carefully. "I need you to do this. I know you can. All you have to do is follow my instructions. I can see what you're doing, I just can't get there to make the changes myself." Tommy sighed through the suit's speakers. "I trust you, Steph. You can do this."

Stephanie stood for a moment and looked down at the suit with Tommy inside. "Okay," she said, not as sure as Tommy of what she could do. "Tell me what to do."

"Kneel down in front of the case so the blinking crystal is at the top," he said.

Stephanie knelt on the floor and leaned over the case. "This helmet's in the way. I'm going to take it off." She reached for the fastening at the neck.

"Don't, Steph!" Tommy cried. "You won't know when we shut down the shields and can hear Eric again. Besides, the suit will give you some protection in case there's an accident."

"What kind of accident?" she asked as she backed away from the case.

"Don't worry about that," Tommy said with a laugh. "Just keep the suit on for now. It has some properties you don't know about and you may need to do something special for me."

"Are you getting weird on me, Tommy Kuhns?"

"More weird than before?" he asked. "Just listen. To the right of the blinking crystal are six rows of small crystals set in groups of nine. Got that?"

"I see them."

"Good," Tommy stated. "Count from the upper right, top row. Top row count in three and push down on the small crystal."

Stephanie counted carefully and pushed down on the crystal. It slid down and set in place with a click she felt through the finger of the suit. "Done. Is it supposed to click in place?"

"Good. And yes. Now, second row: count in from the right two and push down."

Stephanie counted and pushed. "Hey, another crystal started blinking! Is that supposed to happen?"

"It's okay, Steph. The case is just making suggestions on which crystal to push next, but ignore that for now." Tommy sneezed.

"Bless you," Stephanie said by reflex. "You okay in there?"

"Don't worry about me. Third row: count in five and push down."

The next crystal pushed in as easily as the other and the second blinking crystal went dark.

"Hey, it went out!" Stephanie yelled.

"Good, that blocks out the lower realms," Tommy said.

"What lower realms? Where was the gate trying to go?" she asked.

"The next obvious setting after Niflheim is Muspelheim, and we don't want to open a gate there either," Tommy said.

"Why not?"

Tommy laughed. "Well, Niflheim is a black hole, which will destroy the world if the gate opens."

"Okay?"

"And Muspelheim is a gate to a supernova erupting with the force of a sun larger than our sun. If we open that gate, the world will warm up pretty quickly, but then it will melt into a puddle," Tommy said.

"Okay, we leave that gate closed too. What's the next button?"

"Fourth row, count in six and push down," Tommy answered.

"Done," came the response after a few seconds.

"Fifth row, count in two and push."

"Done."

"Sixth row, push the first one."

"Done."

"Tommy, Stephanie? Can you hear me?"

The words echoed in Stephanie's helmet.

"Hey, Eric, you're back online. Tommy, I can hear Eric again."

"Good, that means the gate connected properly. It just sucked all the power out of the shields and opened the security field to Odin and the Aesir can get in. Nobody's been to this setting in a long time, according to Vili. We should be safe. I hope."

"So did you guys get the gate shut down?" Eric asked. "And what about that guy that had the case. Where is he now?" The doors opened at the end of the corridor and Eric came out of the elevator and waved through the walls. As he started to move around the corner, Fafnir slammed against the transparent panel right in front of him and Eric jumped back against the far wall. "Whoa! He's even bigger than he looked flying around up there."

"He can't get out," Stephanie stated. "He's been slamming against the walls all this time and there's no sign of cracks or anything."

"So what about the gate?" Eric asked as he came around the corner and got closer.

"I reset the coordinates," Tommy said from his position on the floor.

"To where? Asgard?" Eric asked as he stepped up to the case and looked down at all the crystals Stephanie had pushed blazing with white light.

"No," Tommy countered. "I didn't want to take a chance on messing something up on Asgard. I set it to go to Svartalfheim."

"Where's that?" Stephanie and Eric asked in chorus.

"Well, depending on who you ask, it's either the world of dark Aesir, or a place with even more dwarves than Asgard."

"I thought all the dwarves were on either Asgard or Jotunheim, except for the bunch we have here on Midgard?" Eric asked.

"Like I said. It depends on who you ask," Tommy answered.

"Eric. Tommy. Stephanie. Can you hear me?" The voice of Mimir sang in Eric and Stephanie's helmets.

"Loud and clear, Mimir," Eric answered his friend. "We're all okay, the gate is set to somewhere other than Niflheim and we caught the guy who had the case." Eric looked around for a moment then looked at Stephanie. "I thought you said you had him?"

Stephanie pointed to the pile of metal that was the Silver Giant and to one extra leg in blue jeans coming out from underneath. "He's under Tommy. He wanted to take a nap and we didn't want him to get cold." She looked over. "Maybe we need to get him up now."

As Odin, Thor, Uncle Al and a host of both Aesir and dwarven warriors entered the corridor, they found the three young warriors standing next to a very mad dragon, a very tired and bleeding man, and all three children laughing so loud it almost covered Fafnir's roars.

* * *

"I had Stephanie change the settings to the one for Svartalfheim and that's when the unit sucked all the power out of the building," Tommy said to Vili. "So then you guys could get through the shield and communications with Mimir opened up again."

The three young warriors were sitting in the workshop at Dwarvenheim, together with Odin, Thor, Uncle Al, Suori and Sudri and an array of other dwarves. Fornir filled the end bay of the building next to the reclining shape of the Silver Giant. The cold wind howled outside the building, but sensor readings showed the temperature was rising slowly and steadily to more normal ranges.

"Why did you choose such a setting as an alternate, young Nornsmith?" Odin asked.

Tommy shrugged. "To be honest, it was the only other setting I could remember. Vili and I talked about gate settings one day and I remembered him telling me this setting hadn't been used in a long time. He also mentioned that any time you powered up a setting for the first time in a while, the power input was a lot more than for a gate you used a lot. I guess somewhere in my head I thought if it sucked in enough power, maybe I'd get lucky and crash the system. That would kind of solve a lot of problems at the same time."

Odin frowned. "But what if the power drain fractured the crystals and there was a power flare?"

Tommy sighed. "Then I was hoping my combat armor and Stephanie's suit would protect us. It was either take the chance of an explosion or watch the world get sucked into a black hole. Not much of a choice. Besides, I had my lucky charm with me."

"And just what lucky charm is that, Mr. Nornsmith-in-training?" Stephanie demanded with a smile.

"You," Tommy answered as he reached over and took her hand.

"Jeez, guys. Cut me some slack," Eric said. He tossed a paperclip at Tommy, who deflected it with the back of his hand.

"Nice block," Uncle Al offered as he watched the interplay.

"Thank you, Sensei," Tommy said with a seated bow.

"How long do you think it will take the weather to get back to normal?" Eric asked Odin.

Odin shook his head. "Our best Nornsmiths can only guess, young warrior. The damage done by the Vanir machines and then corrected by those same machines, is still in a fragile balance. It is still the cold season in this part of the world, but the damage spread through much of this planet." He shook his head. "All we can do is attempt to repair the changes."

"And what do we tell people about what really happened?" Stephanie asked. "Between the weather and that plague the Giants started, there are a lot of people asking way too many questions. And some of them have been asking questions here at Dwarvenheim. There are a lot of military machines in the fields out there the dwarves haven't managed to clean up yet. Not counting all those tunnels they collapsed to catch the stuff. Too much happened here to keep everything quiet."

"Catch news people before they get too close," Suori stated. "Tell them big fairy tale about trying to get warm in bad storm. They go away confused, but they go away."

"That won't work forever, I'm afraid," Uncle Al said. "I'm working with Lieutenant Harris to see if we can get a meeting with some higher up politicians who might be willing to work with us. Harris knows the politics better than I do and knows some of the people at the state level. We don't want to make a general announcement, but we do need to bring some other people in on this story."

"And then what?" Eric asked. "There are still Vanir out there. We know we didn't get them all."

Odin sat straighter. "We do as we have always done when we battle with the Vanir. We deal with the damage they leave behind. We speak with the people in positions of power and warn them of what can happen. And we train our warriors to be ready for the next time they come, for there is always a next time."

"You have allies in this fight, AllFather," Fornir said from the side of the room. He raised his head and looked down at the assembled warriors. "You have an advantage no Vanir could ever imagine or believe would give you the power you possess. Not the least, you have given me back my grandfather and he will be a force to reckon with in fighting the Vanir, once he is in his right mind again." He huffed a puff of smoke from his nostrils as his emotions rose in response to the name of Vanir. "No Vanir would willingly work with anyone other than another Vanir, and only so long as that Vanir had proved he or she was stronger. No Vanir would believe someone as young as Eric Fornir's Rider, Thomas Fenrir's Bane or Stephanie Dark Star's Bane could be a threat to their plans." The young wyrm looked around the assembled group.

"Agreed, Fornir," the voice of Mimir came from a speaker set atop the control panel. "Commander, you have here the best warriors of three worlds, all met in a common cause, all prepared to fight to the death against a foe limited to a single people and a single minded course that will not change even when faced with defeat. The Vanir will fall."

Thor raised his goblet in a toast.

"To the end of the Vanir!" he shouted.

Eric looked around at the cheering Aesir, dwarves and humans. He looked over at Tommy and Stephanie as they leaned against each other. Fornir's hot breath was on his neck and he reached up to stroke the wyrm's snout.

Friends, he thought. *I have friends and a home. In fact, several homes, when you count Asgard, Dwarvenheim and Uncle Al's house in Long Swamp. They know who I am, even if I'm not certain.*

That was enough for now.

www.ingramcontent.com/pod-product-compliance
Lightning Source LLC
Chambersburg PA
CBHW060535260626
47161CB00003B/908